BOOKS BY MEARA PLATT

THE FARTHINGALE SERIES

My Fair Lily
The Duke I'm Going to Marry
Rules for Reforming a Rake
A Midsummer's Kiss
The Viscount's Rose
If You Loved Me

KINDLE WORLDS: REGENCY NOVELLAS

NOBODY'S ANGEL
KISS AN ANGEL

Cover Design by Melody Barber of Aurora Publicity
Edited by Laurel Busch

This is a work of fiction. Names, characters, places, brands, media, and incidents are either the product of the author's imagination or are used fictitiously. Any resemblance to similarly named places or to persons living or deceased is unintentional.

ISBN: 978-1-945767-08-1

THE VISCOUNT'S
Rose

The Farthingale Series
Book 5

A FREE NOVELLA

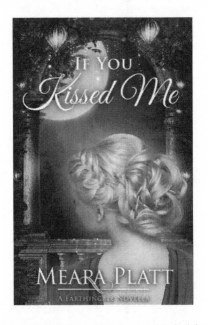

Sign up for Meara Platt's newsletter at bit.ly/ifyoukissedme
and you'll receive a free, exclusive copy
of her Farthingale novella,
If You Kissed Me.

To Samantha and Laurel, who made this happen

CHAPTER 1

Mayfair District, London
June 1813

"JULIAN, *PLEASE*. I wish you'd meet Rolf."

"Enough, Nicola! I'm not interested." Lord Julian Emory, the tenth Viscount Chatham, stifled a groan as he assisted his sister down from his carriage in front of Number 3 Chipping Way, the stately residence of her best friend, the one whose given name he couldn't recall at the moment because Nicola always referred to her as Rolf. Who would call a young lady that anyway? It was the sort of name one gave to a dog.

Nicola frowned at him. "She's wonderful, as are all the Farthingales. You'll agree once you meet them. Rolf is so much more clever than any debutante making her come-out this season. Much nicer than those supposedly elegant ladies you keep fast company with. Please come in with me, Julian."

He was about to decline, as he had every day this past week, when a small explosion suddenly rocked the quiet street. "Nicola, get back in the carriage. Now!"

"But Rolf—Ack!"

He tossed his sister inside without waiting for her to obey and ordered his coachman to drive a safe distance away before leaping over the gate, for he'd heard several high-pitched cries for help coming from the garden of the very townhouse his sister was about to visit. He ran toward the screams and noticed a small funnel of black smoke rising from a makeshift structure in the far corner of the garden.

Two young girls were being held back by two older women, but the girls were obviously struggling to break free and run toward the danger. He couldn't allow that to happen. "Is anyone in there?" he demanded to know, removing his jacket. He intended to use it as a blanket to extinguish any spreading flames, although the fire appeared to be contained and dying out on its own.

"Our sister's in there," one of the girls replied, gazing at him through tearful blue eyes.

"Her kiln exploded," the other girl said, gazing at him through identical blue eyes. Had his vision suddenly blurred? He was seeing identical faces.

No matter, he'd sort it all out once he'd rescued their sister.

Julian placed his jacket protectively over his nose and mouth, dropped to a crouch, and nudged open the door, which had almost blown off but was still hanging on one hinge. The black funnel of smoke quickly dissipated as it wafted outside, confirming the fire had burned itself out, leaving only smoke in its wake. He had only to find the sister.

Don't let her be dead or injured.

He'd engaged in enough battles on the Peninsula to understand the damage that wounds caused. The remnants were not only visible scars but invisible ones as well, the sort that pierced deep under one's flesh and festered. *Damn.* He didn't even know the young innocent's name to call out to her. "Miss? Can you hear me? Where are you?"

His eyes watered as smoke and dust enveloped him. He wasn't halfway into the small enclosure when he heard a soft moan coming from behind an overturned table. The girl was alive but in what condition? He approached and saw that her ankle was pinned under the table, so he quickly righted it and then knelt to check her for broken bones before he dared move her. The bigger risk now was a break, a bump on the head, or other unknown internal injury.

He brushed a few stray locks off her forehead and spoke gently, relieved to feel no lumps forming on her brow. "Can you move your fingers?"

"I... I th-think so." She appeared to do so without much effort. "Now raise your arms, one at a time." Again, she managed with little effort. "I'm going to touch your legs, don't be alarmed."

"Nothing will alarm me after this," she said, punctuating each word with a cough. Even so, the gentle amusement in her raspy voice sent an unexpected warmth coursing through his blood. There was a sweet, melodic quality to her voice.

"Good, because I need to make certain you have no spinal damage and then get you out of here before the roof collapses atop us." He touched her leg. "Can you feel my hand on you?" Because he sure as hell could feel her soft, shapely leg, and that warmth flowing through his blood had just turned fiery.

"Yes, I can."

He cleared his throat. "I'm going to take off your slippers and I'd like you to wiggle your toes, one foot at a time."

She was able to do as he asked but winced as she tried to move her injured ankle, which appeared to be the only damage she'd sustained. Of course, she'd inhaled some smoke. That was worrisome depending on how much she'd taken in. "Put your arms around my neck."

He lifted her into his arms while she did so and carried her out into the cool, fresh air. She coughed again as her lungs took in the cooler air and—*merciful heavens*—he felt each heave of her ample breasts against his chest.

Fiery did not begin to describe the heat now raging through his body.

Bloody nuisance.

"Who are you?" he asked. The question came out more sternly than intended, but it couldn't be helped. She was turning him inside out, and he didn't know who she was nor could he see her clearly because smoke still stung his eyes. She did not reply.

A cool, gusting breeze surrounded them now that they were outside. The bright sunshine caused his eyes to tear up worse than they had done in the shed, but he managed to set her down on the grass under a shade tree without stumbling. He wiped his eyes with his sleeve, which wasn't the cleverest idea, for his sleeves were covered in soot and now so was his face.

He knelt beside her, and the little girls with identical faces fell to their knees on the opposite side of their sister, excitedly chattering and obviously relieved she was safe and relatively unharmed. "I didn't hide my box of explosives in your kiln, Rose," one of them said. "I'd never do anything so foolish."

What?

He now knew the name of the girl he'd just carried out. But what were her young sisters going on about? Military ammunition? In elegant Mayfair, no less? He'd question the young girl later, but right now his attention was focused on the one he'd just carried out. He cleared his throat. "Your name is Rose?"

She nodded. "It is, sir. Thank you for saving me. May I ask—"

That was as much as her raspy voice managed before she erupted in a fit of coughing that alarmed the small crowd of servants who must have run out of the house when they heard the noise and saw the fire. They were now gathering around him and Rose.

A tall, older man seemed to be in charge of the worried staff and was, no doubt, the Farthingale family's head butler.

"Pruitt, she needs something to drink," one of her sisters said, wringing her small hands together in worry. "And wash cloths to clean the grime off their hands and faces. We mustn't track soot all over this lovely new house after Mama worked so hard to put it in shape."

"Right away, Miss Lily." He sent one of the maids to attend to the chore and then sent two others to the kitchen to bring out refreshments. "Will tea and cakes do for all of you? Sir, shall I send out something a little stronger for you?"

"Tea will do for me." He needed to keep his wits about him, for he had yet to regain control of his body despite the fact that he was no longer holding Rose.

Pruitt assigned several footmen the task of securing the rubble now that the fire was out, and once assured that Rose was all right, he ordered the others back into the house. Only the governesses and Rose's sisters remained beside them. "I'm Dillie," one of the girls said, smiling at him. "This is my twin, Lily."

He grinned. "I guessed as much. Identical blue eyes and dark hair. Identical faces." Same thin, gangly bodies. "Lord Julian Emory, at your service."

"Emory? As in Viscount Chatham? Lady Nicola's brother?" Rose attempted to raise herself to a sitting position, but the movement caused her to cough again.

Alarmed when the coughs suddenly mingled with wheezes, he drew her into his arms and placed a hand on her chest to feel her heart, which was beating wildly but not in a haphazard pattern that would signal something more serious than a cough. Her intake of air, despite her wheezing, appeared adequate.

After a frighteningly long moment, she calmed.

Dillie stared at him and then turned to her twin. "Why is his hand still on Rose's breast?"

"To check her lung capacity, of course." Lily frowned. "What did you think he was doing?"

"Girls, I'm right here. You can ask me... er, no. Lily just answered the question." Although it didn't explain why his hand was still on Rose's breast or why he was reluctant to draw it away. "Who is Rolf?"

Perhaps he ought to meet that sister after all. Nicola had been urging the introduction for several weeks now. Was the girl anywhere near as beautiful as Rose? Not that he'd actually taken a good look at Rose. No, his body had responded to hers in the dark. Quite another matter to study the girl by the bright light of day when her flaws would be glaringly obvious.

He finally managed to move his hand off her chest, but kept it loosely poised at her waist, easily convincing himself that she required his attendance while still unsteady and trembling from her ordeal.

He required something altogether inappropriate.

Why her? Why now? No matter, his inexplicable bout of lust for the girl would soon pass. Even if it didn't, he was never going to act upon it. Still, he was curious to study the face attached to that exquisite body. He spared her a glance... more than a glance.

Merciful heavens!

Despite the smudges of soot on Rose's cheeks and tip of her nose, there was no mistaking her beauty. She had lively blue eyes, a deep, ocean blue that glistened with mirth and intelligence. Her hair was a riotous tumble of honey-blonde curls. She had a generous, sensual mouth. "You asked about Rolf," she said, interrupting the wayward thoughts he ought not be having.

He nodded. "Is she your sister?"

Rose's full lips curled upward in a radiant smile.

Her sisters began to giggle.

Bloody nuisance.

"I'm Rolf. Didn't Nicola tell you?" Rose shook her head lightly.

Yes, his sister had told him repeatedly, only he hadn't been listening. His heart slammed into his chest. "You?"

She nodded. "Rose Olivia Lorelei Farthingale. Rolf to my friends."

"Lorelei, as in the siren who lures men with her irresistible beauty and plaintive song onto the rocks to their watery graves?" He arched an eyebrow.

She managed a soft, still raspy laugh. "At the moment I sound like a bullfrog and I've never lured any man, so I don't think your siren and I are related in any way."

"I suppose not." Clearly, Rose was far more captivating than any mythical creature ever could be. That she was modest about it only added to her allure. No! She couldn't be alluring to him. Not now. He couldn't afford the distraction.

Rose pursed her lips. "Where's Nicola? Didn't she come with you?"

He winced. "I'm afraid I tossed her rather ungently into my carriage when we heard the explosion. I ordered the driver to take her a safe distance from your home."

"Of course. That was the sensible thing to do, while you ran toward the unknown danger. Nicola's often spoken of your military service, and I see that her glowing description of your bravery is well deserved."

"I did no more than anyone else would do." In truth, he was feeling quite cowardly right now. Rose had him quaking in his boots. Nicola had spoken of her in glowing terms, and that description seemed wholly inadequate now. But he'd braved Napoleon's army, had spent the last few years on dangerous spy missions within the heart of enemy territory. Surely he could resist Rose's innocent charms until this latest mission was completed.

He had to.

Pruitt returned with wash cloths and refreshments. He handed Julian a damp cloth and another to Rose, and then set the refreshments out on a nearby table. Obviously, this is where Nicola and Rose had planned to sit during their visit, for it was quite pleasant outdoors if one overlooked the lingering wisps of smoke.

One twin grabbed slices of cake and set them out on plates for him and Rose while the other twin poured lemonade. "Rose, come sit with us."

Julian reached out to lift Rose into his arms. "Your ankle looks swollen. You had better not walk on it yet. I'll carry you to your chair."

Rose became flustered, her cheeks stained a bright pink. "Oh, I'm sure I can manage on my own. You needn't... oh, dear." She cried out softly the moment she rose and attempted to put pressure on her ankle. She fell against his chest. "Ouch! It really hurts."

He wrapped his arms about her and carried her to her seat. "Let me have a better look at that ankle." He reached out to take it very delicately under his inspection. "It could be broken." All three sisters and their two governesses gasped as he raised Rose's gown to examine it.

"I'm sure it isn't," Rose insisted and nudged the hem lower.

"And what if I'm right and it is broken?" He frowned at her, although he was more annoyed with himself for desiring to see her ankle for reasons other than medical. He wanted to see a lot more than her ankle. The pale blue muslin gown she wore did little to hide her curves. Even though his eyes still stung, he could see well enough through them to know that she was nicely shaped. "At the very least it's badly bruised and must be attended to at once. Why won't you let me do it?"

"It's most improper," she grumbled.

"He's already touched your breast," Lily pointed out. The twins were still hovering over them, curious as kittens.

"What?" Apparently, Rose had been too dazed to notice at the time. Her face was no longer pink but crimson. She gazed at him in confusion. Or was it unbridled horror? *Bloody nuisance.* Most women liked having his hands on their breasts. Why should she be any different?

"You were having trouble breathing," he explained, once again annoyed with himself for wanting her to... never mind. He shouldn't be thinking about her or her body. Done. No longer in his thoughts... well, only a little.

Perhaps more than a little.

He was about to insist on attending to her ankle when Nicola entered the garden. Julian frowned. "I thought I told you to wait in the carriage."

"I was worried about you." She started to mimic his frown, but when she saw Rose beside him her expression suddenly lightened and she couldn't stifle her knowing grin. "I see you've met Rolf."

Rose was still blushing. "In a most unusual way." She pointed to her foot. "Your brother rescued me. My work table fell on my leg."

"But I heard a blast. It couldn't have been just the table toppling. What happened? And you both have soot on your faces and all over your clothes."

Rose nodded. "Someone sabotaged my kiln."

"Oh, dear! You said this pottery business was run by scurrilous knaves. I never dreamed they'd behave so badly. Rolf, you might have been killed!"

"They only meant to destroy the kiln as a warning to me," Rose said with a stubborn set to her jaw and a passionate blaze in her eyes. "Well, they've warned me and now it is done. But they won't stop me."

Julian groaned inwardly. The girl was beautiful and strong-willed, a great combination if one were seeking a debauched night of... but never with Rolf. No, indeed. Not with his sister's best friend. "What makes you believe these knaves are done with you? Assuming this was more than a mere accident."

"I can assure you, I am always careful with my kiln. It was no accident." The swirls of blue in her eyes shone as brightly as gemstones.

Julian frowned. He was already caught up in a mission and didn't have time to protect Rose, but he wasn't about to turn his back on her if she was in any danger. "What if they try again? If what you say is true, I can't imagine your parents allowing you to continue this enterprise." He glanced at the twins. "Think of your sisters, if not yourself. They might have been standing near the kiln or by the door as it blew off its hinges."

Her mouth was drawn in a taut, thin line. "Are you through lecturing me?"

"Not nearly through." After all, he'd earned the right to speak his mind by pulling her out of the rubble, hadn't he? "What of your season? It's hardly under way and you're already hurt. I'm sure your parents put a lot of time and effort into launching you into society. They'd much rather see you married than injured... or worse."

Nicola was nodding as he spoke, a rare moment when he and his sister agreed on something. "My brother's right, Rolf. You can't put your life at risk for the sake of a dish or vase, no matter how beautiful. We're in our debut season. We promised to get through it together, so you ought to be thinking of balls and courtship and handsome eligible bachelors, like Julian, for example."

He glowered at his sister. "But not me."

Rose's eyes rounded and she blushed in obvious embarrassment. "Of course not, Lord Emory. I wouldn't presume. I'm most grateful for your assistance and promise to be more careful. You're right, of course. It galls me to have them win, but I suppose they have for the moment. My family will be relieved. As you said, they brought us to London in the hope we'd find suitable husbands." She glanced at her ankle and then looked up and cast him a wan smile. "There'll be no dancing for me for a while. In truth, I was never very good at it anyway."

Perhaps he'd been a little too stern with her. "I'm sure you're an excellent dancer. I'll claim the first waltz once you've healed." *Oh, hell.* He shouldn't have said that. Now Nicola will think her matchmaking scheme had worked when nothing was further from the truth.

Rose shook her head and laughed lightly. "Prepare to have your toes stepped on, my lord."

He arched an eyebrow and grinned. "I'll wear my thickest boots."

❧

"OUR UNCLE GEORGE is a doctor. He'll properly tend to my ankle when he returns." Rose didn't mean to appear unappreciative, but she sorely wished Lord Emory would leave before he lifted her into his arms again and insisted on carrying her into the house. She'd rather manage on her own even though her ankle was sore.

It wasn't broken, but Lord Emory had not given ground on tending it. He'd put a cold compress on it and then bound her foot and ankle with the bandages Pruitt had retrieved from her uncle's quarters. She was in as good a shape as could be expected; even Uncle George would commend him on the admirable job he'd done. "My uncle's an excellent doctor. The best in London."

Lord Emory, who was still kneeling beside her, arched an eyebrow and looked up at her, his expression a mix of cynicism, tender indulgence, and something else she didn't quite recognize. Whatever it was, it made her heart beat a little faster. "So you've told me three times already, Miss Farthingale."

"Well, he is." In truth, Lord Emory had taken excellent care of her, his medical knowledge obviously learned in the midst of battle, which only made her like him all the more for the attentive care he must have given the soldiers under his charge. He was smart and brave, and now that he'd wiped the grime off his face she could see that he was irresistibly handsome. His dark blond hair fell in thick waves almost to his shoulders, and the appealing glint in his dark green eyes made her melt a little each time he smiled.

She liked his smile.

He was muscled, too. She'd felt the sinewed tension along his arms when he'd carried her out of the shed and again when he'd insisted on carrying her to the tea table. Being a damsel in distress wasn't so bad when one's savior was as handsome as Lord Emory.

She studied his graceful movements as he rose from bended knee and took a seat beside her, noting the muscled ripple of his broad shoulders clearly outlined beneath his white lawn shirt. His jacket was ruined so he hadn't been able to put it back on. "Uncle George will properly tend to my ankle," she repeated. "You needn't wait around for him or my parents. I'll manage quite well with the help of my sisters and our staff."

He smiled at her again, his eyes crinkling at the corners. It was a miracle she hadn't melted into a complete puddle by now. Nicola had been right about her brother. He was charming, but Rose knew better than to mistake his politeness for anything more. "Are you that eager to be rid of me, Miss Farthingale?"

Lord Emory was experienced and sophisticated and knew how to go about in society. He ran with a fast crowd. Despite the unusual manner in which they'd met, she was ordinary in every respect and he probably considered her excessively boring. "Not at all, my lord. I have no wish to be rid of you. After all, you saved me and for that you shall always be welcome in the Farthingale home. But I suspect you've reached your limit of polite conversation and are eager to be on your way."

"Do I look as though I'm eager to be anywhere but here?" He was still smiling and she was still melting. *Drip, drip, drip.* Her little puddle would soon be a pond. With ducks swimming in it. And a swan or two gliding across it.

She cleared her throat. "Well, no. But you must find my conversation quite dull. You're too polite to show it."

The twins weren't nearly as polite. Having gobbled their ginger cakes, they sat fidgeting and bored until Rose took pity on them and gave them permission to return to the house. As they rose along with their governesses, Lord Emory also got to his feet. "Lily," he said with quiet authority, holding her sister back as the others walked ahead, "I'm curious about your stash of explosives. How did you come by it? May I see?"

She nodded. "I found a large pouch when we'd all gone down to see Uncle Harrison's regiment ship off for France last week. I tried to return it once I realized what it contained, but everyone was too busy to pay me any notice. So I brought it home. It's hidden under my bed."

"Under your..." Lord Emory's eyes rounded and his mouth gaped open for an instant before he seemed to recover. "I'm good friends with the regimental commander. Will you permit me to return it to him?"

If Rose could have jumped to her feet and hugged him, she would have done so. "An excellent idea, my lord. This is the perfect solution, and it can all be done quietly."

Lily frowned. "Shouldn't I tell Papa first? I've been meaning to show it to him, but he and Mama are always so busy lately I can't seem to get their attention."

"We'll figure it out afterward. Bring Lord Emory the pouch." Rose shook her head and released a groaning laugh as Lily skipped off. "Brilliantly done, Lord Emory. Thank you."

He chuckled. "And now, what were you saying about my being bored? Because I don't believe I've ever spent a more unusual afternoon."

"You're right, of course. I only meant that you don't strike me as a tea and cakes sort of gentleman."

"Is that the only reason you want me gone?" He arched an eyebrow, looking impossibly irreverent. "Or are you worried that I'll give your parents an accurate account of what happened today?"

Well, perhaps there was a little of that. "My ankle is bound, my gown is covered in soot, and the kiln is damaged. I think they'll suspect all is not as it should be. If you're worried that I'll understate the danger, rest assured the twins will not overlook a single detail. They'll probably embellish the story and have you dueling a marauding pirate or two at some point in their retelling."

He ran a hand through his hair and laughed. "I like your sisters, even though my eyes still cross whenever they stand together."

"Rolf has two more sisters," Nicola said, her own grin wide and her eyes revealing her triumphant joy in finally getting her and Lord Emory to meet. "The twins are the youngest, but there's also Laurel and Daisy. Laurel will make her debut next year and Daisy the following year."

"You all have floral names except for Dillie," he noted, nodding as Rose offered him more tea. He really was being quite attentive and polite, not at all impatient as Nicola had described him.

"Her real name is Daffodil, but she's not very fond of being called that. Yes, we're all named after flowers although our parents sometimes think they ought to have named us Nettle, or Thorn, or Bramblebush. We vex them at times."

He was smiling at her again in a charmingly seductive way that tempted her to rethink her decision to hobble into the house on her own. Why was it so important? Couldn't she pretend to be a delicate female in distress and feign endless gratitude when he lifted her into his manly arms and carried her inside?

The wind began to pick up and the white clouds suddenly turned gray, obscuring the sun. Lord Emory glanced up. The wind ruffled his blond locks, brushing them back to accentuate the strong angles of his cheekbones and firm jaw. "Looks like our run of good weather has come to an end. Miss Farthingale, let me help you into your home before the rain pours down and turns the dirt on our clothes to mud."

Pruitt must have also noticed the sudden change in the weather. He hurried out with two footmen to clear away the tea and linens. "May I help you, Miss Rose?"

Lord Emory moved possessively close. "I'll take care of her, Pruitt. See to the tables."

Rose regarded him curiously. Nicola wished for a match between them and had never been subtle in her desire, but Lord Emory's name was already linked to a recently widowed countess, a renowned beauty who traveled in his elegant circle. He reportedly was infatuated with her, if one were to believe the gossip rags, although he didn't seem to be the sort to be led about by the nose by any woman.

But what did she know about men? Or love?

Nothing, obviously. Her senses were still addled, for Lord Emory appeared to be interested in her beyond a casual concern for her injured ankle even though she knew it couldn't be so.

Shaking her head, Rose stood and carefully tested her injury by putting delicate weight on her foot. "Crumpets!" She winced as a lightning bolt of pain tore upward from her swollen toes and straight into her temples. "Very well, I'd be grateful for your help. I'll never make it into the house on my own without falling flat on my face." Her ankle was already throbbing and she had yet to take a single step.

He seemed relieved that she made no protest, but at the same time, his body tensed the moment he lifted her into his arms. Had she said or done something to displease him?

Was she too heavy?

Those ginger cakes were awfully good.

"Where should I set you down?" he asked, striding into the house with her nestled in his arms as though she were no burden at all. Apparently she was not too heavy for him and he seemed quite capable of holding her in his arms for hours.

She pretended to think about the question, for she was in no hurry to respond. She liked the solid feel of his arms and had an artist's admiration for the firm, masculine contours of his body. "The salon, I think. On one of the stools beside the fireplace."

"On a stool?" He frowned.

"Our clothes," she reminded him. "I'd hate to ruin my mother's new furniture. She took ever so long to find just the right shades of blue silks and brocades for the seat cushions and drapes."

Instead of doing as she suggested, he called to Pruitt to have one of the maids fetch an old sheet and spread it over the sofa.

"At once, m'lord," he replied without so much as batting an eyelash. Pruitt had been with the Farthingale family long enough never to be surprised by anything that happened in the household.

Rose remained in Lord Emory's arms until the task was accomplished, all the while itching to run her hands along the breadth of his chest and shoulders. She didn't think he'd understand the artistic purpose to her touch, but he also had an interesting face and well-formed limbs that merited further study.

She liked the shape of his mouth, but he would mistake her intentions if she lightly ran her finger across it.

He settled her on the sofa and then took a seat beside her because his clothes were as soot-covered as hers were and he couldn't sit anywhere else without dirtying the expensive fabrics. "Your shirt and jacket are likely beyond repair. Please allow me to pay for any damage."

His eyes widened. "No, Miss Farthingale. It isn't necessary."

"But—"

"Consider it my punishment for not coming to visit you sooner."

Her smile faltered. "Punishment? You were avoiding me? And now I've bored you to tears. Of course I have. Maybe that's your punishment."

Nicola leaped to her defense. "Rolf, you are delightful as always. Pay no attention to my beast of a brother."

He let out a soft groan that ended in a seductive growl. Despite her embarrassment, a tingle shot through her as her body responded to that very male, very animal sound.

"I didn't mean..." He ran a hand through his hair again. "I had a perfectly acceptable time with you, Miss Farthingale. The visit is not a punishment at all. Indeed, I plan to call on you tomorrow if you will allow it."

Nicola's eyes rounded in surprise and Rose could see that her friend was almost squealing with joy. She would have been excited too, but his meaning was obvious. He took no pleasure in seeing her. He only meant to stop by to ensure that his medical attention had done the trick and perhaps to report that the pouch Lily had just brought down was now safely returned to the regimental headquarters. "Lord Emory, you and your sister are always welcome here. But it isn't necessary. As I mentioned, my uncle is one of the most capable doctors in London. I'll receive the best care possible."

He nodded. "Then that settles it."

Rose nibbled her lower lip to stem her disappointment. *Fool! He offered to visit and you rebuffed him!*

What was wrong with her? She'd enjoyed his company and now he would never call on her again. Perhaps it was for the best. She liked him.

Probably more than was wise.

She felt the graze of his fingers against her forehead as he brushed back several locks that had fallen out of place. "I'll see you tomorrow, Miss Farthingale."

She glanced up, confused. "You will?"

He nodded. "There's a saboteur on the loose. I'll be staying close to you until we find him."

CHAPTER 2

"THERE HE IS," Rose whispered excitedly the moment she noticed Lord Emory enter the Farthingale parlor and make his way toward her with a casual ease. She tried not to fuss with the lilac ribbon wound through her hair or her new gown of delicate lilac silk, but it was hard to appear calm when her heart was pounding through her chest.

"Crumpets! Is that Nicola's brother?" Laurel asked, craning her head to steal a better look at him while he stopped to pay his respects to their parents and the other elegant visitors who'd stopped by today. Although the Farthingale family was new to Mayfair, her father and uncles had extensive connections among London society so there had been a constant flow of friends and family through the townhouse since their arrival a few months ago.

Daisy grinned at her. "The twins weren't exaggerating. He's very handsome. Quite the Corinthian."

Rose shook her head and sighed. "He's also taken, if Nicola is to be believed. Apparently Lord Emory is often in the company of Countess Valentina Deschanel, and I hear she's sophisticated and stunningly beautiful. Even her name sounds beautiful. Valentina." Hers was just plain Rose, or worse, her friends insisted on calling her Rolf, which wasn't even a proper girl's name, but one better fitting for a dog.

"Nicola disapproves of her," Laurel pointed out with a look of determination that caused Rose to chuckle. She loved her sisters and was particularly close to Laurel since they'd shared a bedchamber for all of their lives. For this reason, she understood Laurel well. If

Laurel were a knight, she'd already be tossing down her gauntlet and challenging the countess on her behalf.

Still grinning, Rose shook her head again. "It signifies nothing. He won't listen to his sister and he'll probably offer for the countess before the season is over."

"All the more reason to do something about it before it's too late," Laurel insisted.

"No. It's none of our business." Her grin slipped a little. "I know you mean well, but I can fight my own battles. Lord Emory is exceptionally handsome, I will admit. But he isn't the only bachelor in town."

Daisy gave her a pitying look and placed a hand on her shoulder. "I'm sorry, Rose. I can see that you like him."

"Nonsense, I don't even know him." But the sudden heat to her cheeks probably gave her away.

"Ooh, he's coming our way!" Daisy jumped up and grabbed Laurel's arm. "Quick, let's go help Mama. I'm sure she needs us for something important."

Her sisters giggled and darted away just as Lord Emory reached her side. Could they be more obvious? He took a step back to avoid being run over and then arched his eyebrow and cast her a knowing grin.

She winced. "I apologize for my sisters, Lord Emory. They seem to have developed a shocking lack of manners."

"I have sisters, too. Two besides Nicola." He shook his head and laughed, a deep, resonant rumble that felt like a caress against her skin. "As well as two younger brothers who have made it their life's ambition to irritate me whenever possible." But he spoke the last with such affection she knew he loved his siblings.

He shifted closer. "How is your ankle?"

"Still swollen and not a pretty sight at the moment, but Uncle George assures me the yellowish-purple bruising is a sign that it is on the mend."

He nodded. "Well, the rest of you looks passable... more than passable." He leaned close enough for her to catch the scent of lather and sandalwood along his jaw, a subtle male scent that caused her already pounding heart to beat even faster. "Are those violet flecks in your eyes?"

"What?" Goodness, why was he looking at her eyes? "No, they're just blue."

"Violet, too," he insisted. "Indeed, most unusual. And there... a hint of silver gray, as well."

"Are you an artist? No one's ever commented on the color of my eyes before, but you seem to notice everything."

The corners of his eyes crinkled and in the next moment, he smiled. "Not an artist's eye, but a soldier's eye. One is trained to remain alert when surrounded by enemies and cannonballs are flying all around you."

Rose inhaled lightly. "Forgive me, I get so caught up in my own world of colors and textures that I forget the very real dangers that exist before us. How stupid of me—"

"Not at all," he said, his smile fading as he leaned toward her, his nearness making her tingle. "Like your father, I do my best to protect my family from the ills of the world. Joy and innocence are what keep us from descending into despair, especially after one sees the senseless destruction that war brings. Never underestimate the importance of goodness or gentleness."

"Thank you, Lord Emory." She wanted to reach out and put her arms around him in that moment, but couldn't in the crowded parlor. Even if no one were around, it wasn't the sort of thing one did with a stranger. Even if one ached to do so. "And now I shall make it my life's ambition to be gentle, because I'm not sure I can promise to be good. My sisters and I do try to be on our best behavior, but something unexpected always seems to happen."

"Like yesterday's incident?"

She nodded. "I've given it considerable thought, and I'm sure I know who's behind that nasty bit of work." She curled her hands into fists. "And if that weasel thinks he'll get away with it or that I'll back down, he has a surprise coming to him."

"Rose...er, Miss Farthingale." Lord Emory shifted uncomfortably as he frowned at her. "You can't take on a dangerous scoundrel like that all by yourself. Who is this man anyway? I'll have a talk with him and—"

"You? How is it any of your concern?" Her eyes rounded in

surprise when he tossed her a stubborn look similar to the one Laurel had tossed her moments ago. In truth, he had the look of a handsome knight in shining armor and she felt a thousand butterflies fluttering in her belly at the thought that he might throw down his gauntlet to defend her.

"I rescued you. That means I'm now responsible for you." He shifted even closer as though to emphasize his point.

A young lady with less sense might grow giddy at the notion.

Not her.

No indeed.

However, the parlor suddenly felt too warm. She began to fidget with the delicate silk of her gown, smoothing it and then picking at a nonexistent speck of dust. "Nonsense, I'm the one who's indebted to you, my lord."

He gave her a charming smile. "Julian."

"What?" She placed a hand on her stomach to stem her flutters.

"Call me Julian. And I shall call you Rose."

"But—"

He arched a golden eyebrow. "Must I insist? Or point out that we've reached a certain intimacy in the few hours of our acquaintance—"

"We have not." Rose gritted her teeth. She wasn't one of his fast lady friends, and by the subtle glances he was casting at her bosom, she understood the intimacy of which he spoke. "Tending to me as I had trouble breathing is not at all the same as… as…" She frowned as he smirked at her. Had she truly thought him charming a moment ago? "As being intimate with the likes of you."

"Rose," he said quietly, but with unmistakable authority, "you mistake my meaning. I've expressed myself badly, but rest assured that I am not making untoward advances."

"You're not?" She schooled her features so as not to reveal her disappointment.

"But I fully intend to stay close to you until this villain is apprehended. If you wish to be rid of me," he said, frowning lightly, "as you clearly appear to be, then tell me all you know about him."

She nibbled her lip in consternation, uncertain whether or not to encourage him. She liked the notion of spending more time with

Nicola's brother, but feared it would only serve to break her heart. Oh, she hardly knew him, but he was handsome and poised and utterly overwhelming. "Lord Emory, I can deal with him myself."

"The name's Julian, and I will not allow you to confront this man on your own." He puffed out his chest and stuck out his chin in a stubbornly protective gesture that melted her heart more than a little.

She cleared her throat. "I have plenty of male relations who can help me out."

"They're not trained in such matters. Would you have them hurt?"

Her eyes widened in horror. "Of course not. But—"

He slapped his hands on his thighs and stood. "Then it's settled. I'll take care of it. What's his name?"

She hesitated, for this truly wasn't his problem.

"His name, Rose, or I shall be forced to send out an army of Bow Street runners to round up everyone remotely connected to the business of pottery and—"

"Very well, I'll give you his name before you cause a riot in the London streets. Sir Milton Aubrey. But you aren't to hurt him." She tried to rise along with him, but her blasted foot would not cooperate and she sank back in her seat with a wince. "Promise me."

"I'll do no such thing. He'll get what he deserves. That explosion might have killed you and he knew it. The man deserves no mercy."

She was shocked by the iciness in his expression. "I won't have you in trouble because of me."

He arched an eyebrow. "I can take care of myself. I—"

The twins bounded in just then, putting an end to their conversation as they hurried toward Lord Emory with welcoming smiles. Lily was carrying a smaller version of the pouch of explosives she had handed to him yesterday. She was holding it delicately as she moved across the room toward them.

"Oh, no," Rose and Lord Emory muttered at the same time, for Lily looked quite contrite.

Rose winced. "I ought to have thought of this yesterday, but I was distracted by my swollen ankle. She held back some of those explosives, no doubt to experiment with them."

"Good heavens," he muttered.

"But Dillie must have prevailed on her to give it back." She sighed and shook her head. "Lily's the smartest of us all. I'm sure she'll save the world someday with one of her brilliant discoveries, but Dillie is the sensible one. She looks out for her twin and is often the only one who can convince Lily that what she is about to do is dangerous and nonsensical."

Lord Emory appeared to be listening attentively. "I understand. Lily is book smart, but Dillie is... heart smart. That is, she understands people and knows how to gently guide them to do the right thing."

"Yes, that's very well said. I'm impressed, my lord. Seems you're quite perceptive as well as wise."

He shook his head and laughed. "It doesn't take a great mind to know that Lily will clear your salon in a trice if your other guests find out what she has in her grasp."

An appealing thought, Rose decided, for she was not quite recovered from yesterday's incident. Though she refused to admit it to Lord Emory, she had a throbbing headache as well as a throbbing pain in her twisted ankle. She dearly wished to return upstairs and spend the afternoon in bed with her foot comfortably raised, but couldn't yet. "Oh, no! I thought Lily was coming toward you, but she's going to tell Father first. That's not good."

They watched as Lily paused to tug on John Farthingale's arm and drag him toward the private corner where she and Lord Emory were seated. "What's going on?" her father asked, acknowledging Lord Emory and then tossing a questioning glance at her and Lily.

"Perhaps I can explain," Lord Emory said, holding out his hand to accept the small pouch from Lily.

At the same time, Rose tried to make light of the matter. "Ha, ha. Funny you should ask, Father."

"Oh, blast." He groaned. "What now?"

Lily pointed to the pouch now in Lord Emory's steady grasp. "Lord Emory has promised to return the... er... um... to the regimental headquarters for me."

Rose was certain her father gained a new gray hair amid his thick, dark mane. "What's in the pouch? Lord Emory, may I see it?"

He held out his palm and waited for him to hand it over.

Lord Emory sighed. "I suppose you ought to be told."

He held it out, sparing a mere glance at Rose while her father peered inside. "Merciful heavens," he said with a groan, his face now red and his expression apoplectic. Rose thought it was a bit of an overreaction. After all, they'd been vexing him for years and he ought to be used to it by now.

He peered into the pouch again as though its contents might miraculously turn into something as unassuming as licorice sticks. Of course, no such miracle occurred. He shook his head and turned to Lord Emory. "You knew about this?"

Rose scrambled out of her chair and hopped on her good foot to defend Nicola's brother. "We all did. Lord Emory was merely trying to help us out by returning it to its proper place. You ought to be very proud of Lily for telling you about it instead of—" She paused to clear her throat, for she was about to admit that she and Dillie had wanted to conceal the truth from him.

Honestly, the less the elders knew about some of their adventures, the better. "She tried for days to gain your attention, but you and Mother were too busy with all our visiting relatives to pay her any notice. So we were quite grateful when Lord Emory stepped forward to take up the slack."

Her father ran a hand across the nape of his neck. "One daughter has her workshop blown to bits and the other is determined to demolish our new townhouse." He turned accusingly toward Dillie. "And what are you up to?"

She cast him an innocent look, her big, blue eyes as round as saucers. "Nothing, Father. I'd never—"

"Spare me," he said with a sigh. "Lily, you're to remain confined to your bedchamber for the rest of the week. You ought to know better than to bring something so dangerous into the house."

Lily tipped her head. "That's my punishment? Not to leave my room for a week?"

Rose struggled to stifle her grin. Lily dreamed of being left alone to read her scientific tomes, so this confinement would be utter joy for her.

She spared Lord Emory a glance.

He winked at her.

Her heart melted a little more at this shared intimacy. Why did he have to be so appealing?

He tucked the pouch safely into one of his pockets and bowed to her and her father. "I had best return it to the headquarters now. Miss Farthingale, will you tell my sister that I'll be back in an hour or so to escort her home?"

She nodded. "Certainly. Thank you, my lord."

The salon seemed to dim the moment he departed, and Rose wished she could disappear upstairs as Lily just had. Their father had meant for Lily's punishment to commence after this round of afternoon visits, but Lily couldn't wait to start serving her sentence. She'd been working on a research paper for the Royal Society and was eager to finish it in time for the society's annual competition.

Rose didn't have the heart to tell Lily that she'd never be accepted into that male bastion. But who was she to cut short her sister's dreams when she had artistic dreams of her own and understood the difficulties of a woman being accepted into a man's domain? It hadn't stopped her from trying, nor should it stop her sister.

However, she wasn't stupid. This latest incident with the kiln was an unexpectedly dangerous escalation in Sir Aubrey's threats. She'd admit defeat for the moment, for her attention had to be on her debut season anyway. But she wasn't going to let go of her dream. Quite the opposite, she would resume pursuit of it as soon as Nicola's brother had properly trounced the villain.

Her mother approached, distracting her from her thoughts. "Rose, you shouldn't be standing. Sit down at once, my dear."

She dutifully complied.

"Your father told me what's been going on." She nibbled her lip in concern and drew a cushioned stool beside Rose's chair, gently settling Rose's foot to rest on it. "It's a wonder you weren't more seriously injured. How do you feel?"

Her head and foot were still throbbing, but she wasn't going to worry her mother about little aches and pains that would soon pass. "I'm in the pink, truly. You needn't fret about me."

"You're my daughter. You girls are my very heart and breath." Sophie Farthingale shook her head and sighed in resignation. Rose noticed a few gray hairs on her mother's dark mane as well and felt bad that she and her sisters must have put them there.

"I'm glad you're taking it so well. Father was incensed." She eyed her mother curiously. "Why aren't you?"

"With you temporarily incapacitated," she said with a gentle grin, glancing at Rose's raised ankle, "and Lily confined to her quarters, that puts the odds in my favor, doesn't it? Only three daughters left to run amok. Since Daisy can always be relied upon to behave, that leaves only Laurel and Dillie. I think I can manage two daughters on the loose."

No, she couldn't. But Rose didn't have the heart to tell her so.

Rose spent the next hour chatting amiably with their callers, several of whom were eligible bachelors who were paying her particular attention. She ought to have been flattered, but they all paled in contrast to Lord Emory, and by the way their eyes lit up as they glanced at the shiny objects decorating the parlor, she knew they were only attracted to her trust fund anyway.

Nicola joined her in the corner, and as most of the guests began to leave, she and Nicola finally had a moment to compare notes. "What do you think of those bachelors, Rose? Any good prospects?"

She sighed. "None of them were in the least appealing to me. What about you? I noticed several following you about the room. Lord Bennington Simmons appeared quite attentive to you."

Nicola shrugged and pursed her lips in distaste. "His friends call him Bunny. How can I take such a man seriously? Ugh! Bunny?"

"He's quite decent looking and heir to an earldom."

"Rose, you of all people should not be lecturing me on this topic. You know that my views on marriage are similar to yours. I'll only marry for love. You had better hold to your principles as well."

"Of course I will. All Farthingales marry for love and I'm not about to break with that proud family tradition. What did you think of the other eligible gentlemen?"

Nicola's shoulders slumped. "Some of them were so refined and elegant that I felt like a rustic despite the years of lessons in preparation for my debut." She patted her auburn locks as though worried her fashionable curls were coming undone. "They had prettier hair than mine. Can you imagine? No, I will not consider a man who spends more time looking at himself in the mirror than I do when fixing my own hair. The rest of those bachelors were so unbearably arrogant I wanted to poke them in their imperial, aquiline noses."

That's why she liked Nicola—there was no artifice about her. She was honest and direct, and they always had a good time together. "The right gentleman will come along for you, Nicola. You're far too pretty and clever to be overlooked. He's out there somewhere. We just have to find him."

"That's the problem. I don't think I'm going to find him among the balls, assemblies, and musicales going on in London, but Julian insists on my partaking in these affairs and he's been such a wonderful brother to me I hate to disappoint him." Her sober expression suddenly turned quite impish. "So, have you fallen in love with him yet?"

"With your brother?" Rose rolled her eyes. "No, and I won't be doing so anytime soon."

Her friend looked crushed. "Why not?"

"Nicola, he's sophisticated, intelligent, and handsome as sin. Yes, he's handsome. I readily admit it," she said, feeling the heat of a blush steal into her cheeks. "But he's a viscount and I'm the daughter of a merchant. He can aim far higher in search of a wife. Even if he weren't inclined to do so, what do I have to offer him? I know so little of the world, unlike his elegant countess."

Nicola frowned. "But that's just it. On the surface Julian may appear to be elegant and sophisticated, but on the inside he's a family man who loves staying close to home and hearth. Until recently, he hated these *ton* affairs. He never liked going about in society and thought those *mushrumps* who drank too much or lost heavily at the gaming hells were not the sort of men he'd ever consider friends. But he's changed for the worse ever since meeting the horrid Countess Deschanel."

Rose patted her friend's hand to calm her as she was becoming noticeably distressed. "Nicola, my father has an expression that he often quotes. He says that people don't change. If your brother is a kind and caring man—"

"He is."

Rose nodded. "Then that's who he is at heart, and the wicked countess won't succeed in leading him astray."

Nicola's lips began to quiver and her eyes watered. "I wish I could believe you, but you haven't seen him when he's around her. He's like another man, a complete stranger to me."

Rose reached out and hugged her dear friend, wishing there was something she could do to ease her desperation. "That's why you're so eager to make a match between him and me. I understand your motives, but it won't work. You can't force him to love me. He'll either feel it or he won't. If his feelings for the countess are sincere, then there's nothing we can do about it."

Nicola wiped away the stray tear now rolling down her cheek. "I wish my parents were alive. They'd know how to keep Julian in line, but he's the viscount now and there's no one to offer him proper guidance."

"Not even your uncle?" she said, referring to the Earl of Darnley. Nicola's brother was next in line to the title since the present earl and countess had no children. Nicola was staying with them during her season, for she couldn't very well reside with her bachelor brother. Earl Darnley and his countess were lovely people and Rose liked them very much. She'd been invited to their home several times since Nicola arrived in town and looked forward to more visits during the season.

"You know my uncle would like nothing better than to hide out in his library all day, but my aunt won't let him. He was an outrageous scoundrel in his younger days, but he's a scholarly sort now and not one to impose his will on Julian. Oh, what's the use? My siblings and I will just have to accept the fact that we're about to lose our beloved brother to that witch."

Rose was about to offer more words of comfort when she heard Lord Emory's voice in the entry hall. It seemed odd that she should be so aware of him when she hardly knew him, but there was something about the quiet assurance and authority in his manner that set her body tingling the moment she sensed his presence. "Hush, Nicola. We'll speak of your problem later. Your brother has returned to pick you up."

"Rose," she said in an anguished whisper. "I'm desperate. Please think of something to keep him from that woman's talons."

Rose tried to feign disinterest, but found herself smoothing her gown and sitting up a little straighter. She couldn't resist patting her curls to make certain they were all in place.

Nicola noticed the subtle change in her demeanor and inhaled lightly. "You *are* falling in love with him. I knew it!"

"Don't be a goose."

Her friend remained persistent. "Please, Rose. Do fall in love with him or my entire family is doomed. He'll marry that harpy and then she'll force him to disown us and we'll all be cast out into the streets and miserable for the rest of our lives. You're my family's only hope."

Rose sighed as she stared at Nicola's brother, who still stood in the entry hall having a few words with her father, no doubt about Sir Aubrey and his band of pottery ruffians now that the rest of Lily's explosives had been safely returned to the regimental headquarters. "And just how do I go about luring him away from Countess Deschanel? I'm no temptress. I wouldn't know how to go about seducing him. In any event, he sees me only as your best friend."

"You can't abandon me!"

She hated the despair in Nicola's voice. "I won't, but are you certain she's as bad as you claim?"

Nicola collapsed back in her chair, placed one hand over her brow, and clutched her heart with her other in a display of dramatic arts to rival the best-known actresses on the theatrical stage. "She's ever so much worse."

"Very well, I'll offer my help in stealing him from the clutches of the evil countess." Still, it seemed odd that a man who appeared so intelligent in every other way should be such an idiot in matters of love. Then again, the expression "besotted fool" had to spring from somewhere.

Nicola's eyes lit up with joy. "Thank you. My entire family is eternally grateful to you. Now, how shall we go about saving him?"

Rose shook her head and sighed. "You'll have to trust me unquestioningly."

Nicola crossed her heart. "I promise. My brothers and sisters will do the same. My aunt and uncle, too."

"Good, because we're about to wage war on your brother and his countess." She smoothed her gown again. "Quick and devastating surprise attacks. Shh, not another word. He mustn't suspect." She smiled sweetly at Lord Emory as he joined them.

Nicola was utterly beaming.

Rose maintained her smile but was in silent panic. She hadn't a clue what to do and had only acted as though she had a plan in order to soothe her friend. Fortunately, she had clever sisters, and if ever a situation called for a meeting with Laurel, Daisy, and the twins, this was it. She'd confide in them tonight. But for now, she needed to appear serene and assured for Nicola's sake. "Is the pouch safely returned, Lord Emory?"

She blinked at him coquettishly.

He folded his arms across his chest and nodded slowly. "All safe." He studied her for an uncomfortably long moment before groaning lightly. "What have you two been plotting in my absence?"

Oh, dear! Was this her first tactical mistake? Weren't men supposed to like a mild flirtation? Perhaps she had blinked too hard. Or not hard enough. Though her gaze was trained on him and not Nicola, she felt a sudden quiet by her side, as though all breath had been sucked out of Nicola. Honestly, did the girl have no guile in her at all? "Nothing, Julian. *Oh, ha, ha, ha.* What could we possibly have to plot about?"

He was still frowning and his arms were still crossed over his broad chest as he ignored his sister's fidgets and giggles and continued to stare at Rose as though certain she was the nefarious mastermind. So what if she was? It wasn't very nice of him to think the worst of her. "Indeed, Lord Emory, what possible plot?"

His gorgeous green eyes darkened with concern. "That's what I'd like to know."

CHAPTER 3

JULIAN KNEW HIS sister well enough to realize immediately that she and Rose were up to no good. But what were they planning to do? Confront Sir Aubrey on their own? *Good heavens!* They couldn't possibly be thinking to blow up his kiln in retaliation, could they? No, Nicola was never that bloodthirsty. But he didn't know Rose very well. Would she behave so foolishly?

"*Oh, ha, ha, ha.*" Nicola was still tittering inanely and protesting their innocence too vehemently for his liking.

Rose was spirited and a bit eccentric, but Nicola wouldn't adore her if she were malicious. In any event, Rose was still hobbled by her sprained ankle and couldn't move stealthily if her life depended on it.

He cleared his throat, continued to train his gaze on Rose, and spoke in imitation of one of his haughty Oxford professors, his tone sarcastic and imposing. "Since my sister is going on like a demented cockatoo, perhaps you'd like to confess your misguided scheme."

That imposing professorial tone often worked to instill fear in the more timid schoolboys in his classes, but he'd never been a particularly timid lad and that haughty condescension had never worked on him.

Apparently, it didn't work on Rose either.

He stifled a laugh when the girl stopped feverishly blinking at him and now stared at him with eyes wide and innocent. Her lush lips were slightly parted and rounded in a kissable *O* that revealed her consternation. Although her middle name was Lorelei, she obviously had none of the seductive talents one would associate with that name.

Surprisingly, it made him hunger for her all the more.

Really hunger for her.

Bloody nuisance.

"I don't know what you're talking about, my lord," she said, her smile achingly sweet as she slid her hand into Nicola's to subtly calm his sister.

Did she think he wouldn't notice the gesture?

He arched an eyebrow and shot her a stern glower, although inside he was struggling to restrain his hearty laughter. Rose was not to be underestimated. She had a nimble brain and a soft heart, as evidenced by her affection for Nicola. Unlike Nicola, she had a fighting spirit, for any other young lady would have been in tears and still trembling over yesterday's incident.

But not Rose.

She ran her thumb comfortingly over his sister's hand and was subtly signaling to his sister to keep quiet. They were definitely plotting something. "You aren't thinking of dealing with Sir Aubrey on your own, are you? I've already spoken to your father about him and will take care of the matter this very afternoon."

She puckered her lips in concern. "Do be careful, Lord Emory. He's a blackguard and quite dangerous. The competition is cutthroat in this business, and he's still enraged that I won the Runyon Pottery Mill contract away from him." She tipped her nose into the air and gave a little sniff. "But my cobalt blue glazes are so much finer than his. So are my burnished copper glazes and gold leaf—"

"Fascinating, Rose." Obviously, she'd decided to leave the matter of Sir Aubrey to him. So who was their doomed target? Poor chap!

"And even if Sir Aubrey got the colors right, which he never will," Rose continued, her pert nose still pointed upward in disdain, "he has no sense of artistry. He doesn't understand the magic in every creation, the enchantment in just the right tilt of a swan's wing in the design of a soup tureen or the drape of a leaf or petal in the floral design of a teacup. The man is an oaf. I very much appreciate your assistance in dealing with him, but if he ever attempts to blow up my kiln again, I'll—"

"You had better not take matters into your own hands," he said with a growl. "Not ever. I forbid it."

She opened her mouth to protest but must have thought better of contradicting him, for she snapped it shut again. Or so he thought. In the next moment, she furrowed her brow and glowered at him. "Lord Emory, you are in no position to forbid me to do anything. You're not my father and you're certainly not my husband."

"The name's Julian. I do wish you'd stop scowling at me." He rolled his eyes and sighed. "I have the distinct impression that you'd never obey your husband anyway."

A light pink blush stained her lovely cheeks. "I'd try my best to honor his wishes... when they made sense."

He considered Sir Aubrey fortunate that he, and not Rose, intended to confront him. Indeed, he was glad that he and Rose were allied. She would make a formidable opponent were they ever to find themselves on opposite sides of a battle.

He unfolded his arms and set his hands on either side of her chair. Leaning close, he took another moment to study her expression. Lord, the girl took his breath away. "You're staying home these next few days, right?"

Her eyes were once again wide and innocent. "Yes, my lord."

"And you're not going after Sir Aubrey, right? You're leaving him to me. I want your promise."

She nodded. "You have it. I promise."

Rose spoke the last with such genuine sincerity that he took it for the truth. In any event, Nicola was no fool and she couldn't abide liars. His sister and Rose would never be friends if his sister couldn't trust her.

But they were definitely plotting something. What in blazes was it? No matter, he'd get it out of Nicola on the carriage ride home. He had his own important mission to accomplish and didn't need to be worrying about these girls.

He took another moment to discuss the matter of Sir Aubrey with John Farthingale and then left with Nicola.

After helping his sister into the carriage, he settled opposite her against the soft, black leather bench. "Start talking," he said, noting the way she stared out the window of his sleek conveyance and purposely avoided his gaze as they rolled down Chipping Way.

"I don't know what you mean, Julian." His sister was now staring up at the ceiling. He continued to question her, but to his surprise, she didn't break and spill all their plans. Not that he tried very hard to intimidate her. No, not at all. Ever since the sudden deaths of their parents in a boating accident, he'd taken special care to be gentle and supportive of his younger siblings. Two brothers and three sisters.

He'd been at a loss as to how to properly raise them and was greatly relieved when his uncle had come to his rescue. He couldn't have managed Nicola's introduction into society without the assistance of the Earl of Darnley and his countess. That all his siblings now resided with them was also a great burden off his shoulders, for he'd been in the middle of an investigation for the Crown when his parents' accident happened and it was still ongoing. In truth, it was so close to the end he couldn't risk letting anything interfere with it now.

He dropped Nicola off with his aunt and uncle, spent a few moments catching up with his other siblings, then took himself off to his bachelor residence to prepare for the Duke of Wrexham's ball. Later, he would make the rounds of the gaming hells with Valentina and her dissolute companions. He'd been cultivating their friendships for the past year, particularly playing the besotted fool for Valentina.

Convincing Valentina of his infatuation hadn't been difficult. The countess thought quite highly of herself and naturally expected men to yearn for her. That she'd chosen him above all others had been the break he and his fellow agents in the Prince Regent's elite circle of royal spies had been hoping for. The woman's wealth did not come from the generosity of her dearly departed husband, but from Napoleon himself in regular monthly payments, to be precise.

Julian had quietly nurtured their affair, taking almost six months to earn her trust and another six months to work up the pyramid of her English connections to discover the identity of most of the traitors working in her organization. None had been taken into custody yet, for it was to England's advantage to feed them misleading bits of information to send off to Napoleon.

These traitors were mere minnows in a vast ocean and could be caught in the royal net at any time. But the Prince Regent needed the name of the powerful nobleman who stood at the tip of that pyramid—someone within the highest echelons—and relayed England's most sensitive war plans to Napoleon through the countess.

Julian was so close to finding him now.

"Don't wait up for me, Buckley. I may not come home tonight," he muttered to his valet as the man fussed with his formal evening wear, adjusting the bow on his silk tie and brushing lint off his stiff black jacket.

"Very good, my lord."

Although Buckley was careful not to show his displeasure, he'd been with the Emory family for almost thirty years, attending to Julian for the past ten years, so Julian understood the subtle nuances of his valet's expression. "You disapprove."

Buckley stepped back and gave a curt nod. "It isn't my place to judge, my lord."

"Good, because the lady may be my viscountess some day." The hell she would, but it was important for Valentina to think he was considering marriage. This was the bait needed to gain her complete confidence and get the name of her contact within the Prince Regent's closest circle of friends.

He called for his carriage and picked up Valentina on his way to Wrexham's ball, playing his part as the devoted and attentive suitor throughout the evening. After the ball, he ought to have played his part as her ardent lover, but the image of Rose kept coming into his mind at the most inconvenient times and he knew that an entire year's work would be ruined if he mistakenly called out the girl's name while he was supposedly in the throes of ecstasy with Valentina.

"I've had this damned, blistering headache all day. Can't seem to shake it," he muttered when the ball ended and he and Valentina were once more in his carriage on their way to meet her friends at one of the more elegant gaming hells.

She ran her gloved hand along his cheek and leaned in close so that he felt her breasts against his arm. "My poor darling. Come upstairs into one of the private rooms with me and I'll make it all better." She slid her hand downward and rested it on the bulge between his thighs. "I want you tonight."

"I always want you, my love. But I can't this evening. I'll make it up to you tomorrow, and the day after that... and perhaps..." He purposely paused, allowing the hint of a permanent commitment to linger heavily in the air. "Let me go home, Valentina. Now my stomach's acting up."

She pursed her lips in a practiced pout. "Very well, but I'm staying here. I wish to gamble. Lord Braswell will take me home. He's madly in love with me, you know. Are you jealous?"

"Desperately so. You are ever in my thoughts, my love. I'll call Brassy out if he dares to touch you."

She shook her head and laughed. "He's merely a boy and you're a man. You needn't worry about him."

"It isn't only him." He feigned a worried look. "Promise me there's no one but me who holds your heart. Promise me, my love. You know I would do anything for you."

The coachman stepped down to open the carriage door at that moment, interrupting Valentina's response, which would have been insincere anyway. She smirked and took the man's offered hand. "Julian," she said, turning to face him as he walked her to the door of the gaming hell, "do regain your strength."

He smiled and this time feigned a cough that had her drawing away before he could kiss her. "Good night, Valentina. Dream of me." He coughed again for good measure and continued to play his part until she finally joined her friends inside.

He climbed back into his carriage and eased his frame against the leather squabs. "Edred, get me out of here." He'd done enough work for the night, dropping hints among their friends about his intention to propose to the dark-haired, gray-eyed diamond of the first water.

But he had a big problem.

His thoughts were on Rose, the stubborn and irritating chit who was the true diamond among the *faux* gems paraded before him each season.

Bloody nuisance.

Why couldn't he stop thinking of Nicola's best friend?

"I'LL SIT BESIDE you at Lady Winthrop's musicale tomorrow evening," Nicola said, bounding into the Farthingale parlor two days later and dropping into the seat beside Rose while Pruitt rolled in the tea cart laden with cakes and an appealing assortment of scones. The Farthingale parlor was crowded today with more family and friends stopping by to pay a visit.

Rose's mother and her spinster aunt Hortensia were busy dashing in and out to greet their guests. Aunt Julia had also joined them, although she was rather subdued now that her husband had gone off to battle Napoleon. In truth, all the family elders were subdued now that Harrison had gone to fight.

Rose worried about him as well, for he was the youngest of her uncles and the most adventurous. Her father, John, was the eldest, then came Rupert, then George, and finally Harrison. Hortensia was actually their aunt, but not much older than her nephews so they treated her as more of a sister than a family elder. "Oh, dear! Will you go?" Nicola asked, interrupting her thoughts.

"To the musicale?" Rose smiled at Pruitt as he set down the teapot and sugar cone beside her. "I don't know." She poured a cup for Nicola, trying not to be distracted by the teacup and pot, for they were of the finest bone china from a lovely set of Staffordshire floral design that her mother had recently purchased. The colors were magnificent and the graceful cascading sweep of—

"Ugh! Rose, stop counting the flowers on your teacup and talk to me. Will you come with me to Lady Winthrop's?"

Her sprained ankle chose that moment to twinge. "I think not. I had better stay off the foot for a few more days."

Nicola's mouth curved downward in a pout. "No, no, no. You can't leave me alone to face that horrid Valentina on my own. She'll be there with Julian, brazenly clinging to his arm. What am I to do? The rumors are rampant that he intends to propose to her by the end of this month."

Rose patted her hand. "That gives us a fortnight to come up with a plan."

Nicola's shoulders sagged. "Come up with one? Do you mean to say you haven't got one yet? Oh, Rolf! I was counting on you to save us! My family is doomed unless you think of something. You must!

And you can't abandon me to face that witch alone. We'll be seated most of the time anyway, forced to endure Lady Winthrop's daughters singing and playing their harps, both abysmally. The only one worse at the harp is your sister Lily and I'm sure she does it on purpose because she's brilliant in every other respect. Surely she can master the workings of a few strings if she sets her mind to it."

Nicola paused only long enough to take a deep breath before continuing. "But enough about Lily. Why isn't your ankle healed yet? Isn't your Uncle George the best doctor in all of England?"

"Of course he is. But he isn't a magician." She rolled her eyes in exasperation. "Do calm down. It isn't as if you're facing Napoleon's army. The countess is just one woman."

"But an evil one!" Nicola said in an emphatic whisper.

Rose rolled her eyes again. Fortunately the din in the parlor drowned out their conversation so that no one could overhear them. "You think she's evil because you don't like her, but your brother must see something special in this woman to take her into his heart."

Nicola's eyes began to water. "Believe me, I've searched and searched for a reason, but I can't find one. She's hateful. What can I do, Rolf? I must stop their wedding or she will ruin his life."

"Very well." Rose sighed, wishing the countess would conveniently disappear. However, she was not about to condone her murder. "My sisters and I discussed the possibilities and finally settled on a solution. I fear it's an imperfect one, but here's the plan."

"You do have one, after all!" Nicola let out a squeal. "Why didn't you tell me sooner? You know I'm in agony over my brother's idiotic choice. We actually have a plan? Thank heavens!"

Rose had never seen her friend so exuberant. In truth, it pained her, for her plan wasn't very good and not likely to work. "It will require the cooperation of your aunt and uncle. They—"

"They're in. Whatever it is, they'll agree to it." Nicola's eyes were now glowing with excitement. She popped a piece of lemon cake into her mouth and eased back, her relief evident. "What must we do?"

Rose took a sip of her tea to calm her nerves. "You're going to abduct him."

Nicola, who had also just taken a sip of her tea to wash down the lemon cake, gasped. The tea went down the wrong pipe and she fell into a fit of coughing. Too late, Rose realized she ought to have slowly eased her friend into the plan. In her own defense, she was uncertain about it and knew that she had to blurt it out before she turned coward and didn't propose it at all.

Well, it was out there now, hanging in midair like a cannonball on a dangerous trajectory. Nicola finally calmed enough to respond. "I must have misheard. What did you just say? Abduct my own brother?"

"You asked for a plan and I've come up with one. If you don't like it, we don't have to go through with it. After all, there's so much involved in its proper execution. Anything can go wrong at any time. Forget I said anything. It's too absurd to contemplate. I'm sorry I even suggested it. Can you ever forgive me?"

Nicola wiped her lips with her napkin and set it back on her lap. "Rose, you misunderstand. I *love* the idea. I think it's brilliant."

"You do?" The contents of Rose's stomach began to churn and she felt herself grow pale, unlike Nicola, who had now stopped coughing and wore a broad grin on her face that accentuated her dimples.

"Yes, and so will my aunt and uncle think it is the best idea ever." She edged closer and smiled conspiratorially. "What must we do to put this plan into effect?"

"Leave London. Your uncle has a lovely estate in the Cotswolds, near Chipping Camden, doesn't he?"

Nicola frowned. "Near Birdslip to be precise, but why must we go there when my brother is here in London?"

Rose glanced about for help from her sisters, but they were busy talking to their neighbor, Lady Eloise Dayne. They'd known the kindly older woman only a few months, but she was quickly becoming as dear as a grandmother to Rose and her sisters. "Oh, Nicola, remind me to introduce you to Lady Eloise. She's simply wonderful. We all adore her."

Nicola nodded. "I know her already. She's great friends with my aunt, Lady Darnley. I'll greet her in a moment, but do go on. I'm on the edge of my seat with excitement. My brother is in London and we're to go to Darnley Cottage, my uncle's charming home in the

Cotswolds. Why?"

"The plan is to lure him out there." She cleared her throat. "As Lily explained it to me, the object is to separate one deer from the herd, to lure him away from the other deer who might protect him. This is what predators such as lions and tigers do when they hunt on the vast plains of Africa."

Nicola simply stared at her. "What are you saying? Are we to put him on a packet ship to Africa?"

Rose sighed. "No, you miss my point. He's to remain in England. We're all to stay in England. But you say that he's a home and hearth sort of man, only he seems to have forgotten himself while in London. So you'll take him away for a week in the country. Your uncle will ask him to escort you all to his cottage."

"And?"

"That's where you'll remind him of the simple pleasures that he truly loves and how the countess would be completely out of place in the peaceful countryside, and if he is still too dense to realize it, then... then... you'll just have to keep him there until he comes to his senses."

Nicola shook her head in disappointment. "It isn't a very good plan, you know."

Rose nodded. "I know. But do you have a better one? Short of doing away with Lady Deschanel?"

"No," she admitted. "Will you come to the Cotswolds with us? You must, Rose. You've taken the lead in this delicate mission, so you might as well see it through to the end. Besides, you like Julian, so why can't we make him like you? It can work. Once we separate him from his disreputable herd, he's bound to notice you. He's the stag and you're the sweet doe he's destined to love." She frowned lightly. "Or wait, are you the predator who separates him from his herd? No, my family will be the predators because you need to be the sweet doe."

Rose shook her head and sighed. "Stop, Nicola. The more you go on, the clearer it becomes to me that this scheme will never work."

Nicola now had a stubborn set to her jaw. "It's excellent and it will work once Julian has the chance to know you. I'll ask my uncle to write a note to your parents today and invite you to the cottage.

We must have you as bait for Julian."

"Bait?" She didn't wish to be compared to a wriggling worm or pieces of raw, skinned meat.

Nicola nodded. "You're the reminder Julian needs or he'll never break off his affair with that witch."

"I'd rather not. Truly, I'm not necessary to this plan."

Nicola took her hand. "Rose, I beg to differ. You're vital. You're the only one who can work this miracle. Good. It's settled. You're coming with us."

"Oh, this is a mistake." Rose shook her head and groaned. "I'm not a predator."

"Heavens, whoever said you were? No, your role is the temptress. After all, your middle name is Lorelei so it must be significant. Close your eyes and think seductive thoughts."

"I will not."

"Especially about my brother. I'm sure he wouldn't mind being seduced by you."

Rose gasped, the thought of herself and Nicola's brother with their arms wrapped around each other and their bodies arched in a passionate embrace, posed like those scandalous Greek statues on display in the halls of the various royal societies and museums around London, too shocking to contemplate. "No."

"Please, Rolf."

"Stop it, Nicola. I'm no temptress."

"You are. You're the Lorelei."

"In name only, not in any special knowledge of the seductive arts. I wouldn't know how to get your brother to kiss me. This is ridiculous."

A deep, male chuckle came from behind her. "If you wish me to kiss you, all you have to do is ask."

Rose leaped out of her chair, spilled tea all over her gown, and landed on her sore ankle, which promptly collapsed under her weight. She let out a yowl and lost her balance, certain she was about to fall to the floor and land in an unladylike sprawl. But Lord Emory caught her in time to prevent her humiliation. That he'd heard their discussion was humiliating enough.

"Are you hurt?" he asked, drawing her firmly against him and seeming to be genuinely concerned. "I didn't mean to startle you." She felt the quiet rumble of his chest as he spoke, for her back remained pinned against his hard body. His arms were securely around her, the heat of his body so intense she melted into him. Or was it her heat? Her blood was on fire and her limbs were quivering.

She had no chance to respond, for everyone was now gathered around them and fussing over her and her ruined gown. She was so roiled with unfamiliar sensations that she couldn't have responded to Lord Emory even if she'd known what to say.

"You've strained your ankle again," her aunt Hortensia chided, her tone muffled for Rose's heart had flown upward into her throat and was now pounding through her ears. "How will you ever recover if you insist on walking about on it? Too soon, my dear. You must rest."

"Indeed, Miss Farthingale. You must do as your aunt suggests." Lord Emory turned her slightly to face him as he spoke. He had an odd expression on his face, a mix of puzzlement, concern, and hilarity. She was not mistaken. The bounder was struggling to hold back a roar of laughter. She would have been more offended if it weren't for the fact that even she considered her predicament hilarious.

Nicola added her thoughts before Rose had time to apologize to her brother for staining his clothes as she leaned against him. And why shouldn't Nicola speak up since everyone else seemed to have an opinion on her condition? "I heartily agree, Hortensia. Isn't that what I was just telling you, Rolf? You need plenty of rest and good country air, so you must come to Darnley Cottage with me this week."

Lord Emory released her and turned to his sister. "You're going to the country house? When was this decided?"

"Just last night. Yes, all of us are going and I want Rolf to come too." She turned to Rose's parents, who had rushed forward and were now standing beside her. "Please say you'll let her go with us. My aunt and uncle will take excellent care of her, and my brothers and sisters adore her. She can't attend any balls yet, so where's the harm?"

Rose cast her parents a pleading gaze although she wasn't certain whether she was pleading for them to consent or refuse. Lord Emory was still standing too close to her, his hand now on her elbow to brace her while she struggled to balance on her good foot.

She couldn't think clearly while he remained so close. She'd spilled tea all over herself and ruined her new gown. Her ankle was heavily bound, and everyone in the room was now staring at her in horror. But all she could think about was Lord Emory. Had he meant his words? That she had only to ask and he would kiss her?

She glanced up to him, wondering how it would feel to have his lips on hers. Warm. Nice. Magical, she supposed. "Miss Farthingale, you're shaking. Do sit down before you fall again."

Heat shot into her cheeks. Indeed, everyone in the parlor was watching her, and all she could think of still were how good his lips would taste. Like coffee, perhaps. A hint of whiskey and mint. Maybe a little salt like an ocean spray.

Her mother took her into her arms and began to guide her from the parlor. "You're right, Nicola. Perhaps a few days in the countryside is just what my daughter needs, especially after that nasty business with her kiln. Rose, I've never seen you look so foggy. This isn't like you at all. You must have bumped your head."

"No, Mama. Truly, it's been an unsettled few days but otherwise I'm fine."

Her mother patted her arm and then turned to Nicola and her brother, both of whom had followed her out of the parlor. "Lord Emory, we're truly in your debt for saving Rose's life the other day. What a frightening incident. I know my husband has extended his warmest gratitude, but it doesn't seem enough. We are entirely indebted to you. Will you remain in the country with your family?"

His brow furrowed as he glanced at her and then Nicola. Sighing, he ran a hand roughly across the back of his neck. "I'll have to escort them because no one else will dare ride with my unruly younger brothers. But as for remaining the entire week, I doubt it. A few days at most. I will however return at the end of the week to escort them back to London."

Her mother nodded. "I'd be more comforted if you stayed the week, but at least you'll be traveling with them. Although you've brought Sir Aubrey to task, who knows what other pottery ruffians may be lurking about? I wouldn't want them to harm my daughter."

Why was her mother going on as though she were a delicate fribble? Admittedly, she was still injured but the ankle was practically healed. "I'm not afraid of those scoundrels."

Her mother frowned. "And that's what worries me most. You ought to be, Rose."

"But I—"

Lord Emory emitted a soft groan. "I'll protect her, Mrs. Farthingale. I give you my word of honor."

Rose's eyes rounded in astonishment. What? Their ridiculous plan was falling into place? It couldn't be. But what if it was? More important, would Lord Emory truly kiss her if she asked him?

If she were truly a fribble, she would now fall into a swoon.

But she was sensible.

She didn't swoon.

That her limbs were tingling and her legs still as soft as melted butter was of no moment. That her heart was pounding like a war drum was a mere coincidence.

Tingles and heart pounding did not count.

Nor did the butterflies madly fluttering in her belly.

Did Lord Emory realize it would be her first kiss ever?

Would he mind?

CHAPTER 4

"THANK GOODNESS YOU'RE here!" Nicola accosted Rose as soon as she and the rest of her family made their way into Lord and Lady Winthrop's elegant townhouse the following evening. Rose's ankle was feeling better so she had decided to attend the musicale after all. Her improving ankle and the dozen desperate notes from Nicola begging her to attend had swayed her.

"You look so pretty, Nicola." Her friend wore a lovely mint green gown that brought out the cool green of her eyes and the lush auburn of her hair. She looked as refreshingly sweet as the lime ices one would find in the best confectionery shops.

Nicola blushed lightly. "So do you. But you always do."

"Nonsense, I feel so uncomfortable. I'm afraid to breathe for worry that I'll damage the delicate fabric." Her own gown was of the palest blue silk, almost a white-blue that shimmered in the glow of candlelight. "I'm not good at feigning elegance, but I have practiced walking around with my nose in the air. However, I shall be careful not become too full of myself. I'll keep my feet firmly planted on the ground and my eyes clearly focused on where I'm walking."

To emphasize her point, she gave a little wave of the decorative white cane she sported that almost matched the color of her gown. She'd borrowed it from Hortensia. Not that she really needed the cane, but it was her first full evening of keeping pressure on her ankle and she didn't wish to make a fool of herself if it gave out.

They both giggled and continued to chatter as they made their way outdoors into Lady Winthrop's garden. The walk they chose was lit with pretty lanterns hanging off lush tree branches. In the distance, fancier torches lit the lesser traveled walks.

Rose took a deep breath. "Isn't it a lovely night? I'm so glad Lady Winthrop decided to hold the recital out here. Can you imagine the crush of hot, perspiring bodies crammed inside their music room?" She inhaled the light scent of roses, so much more pleasant than the heavy perfumes the older ladies and gentlemen seemed to adore.

The rain earlier in the day had ended so the Winthrop garden had managed to dry out in time. The summer sun had warmed the roses, and their petals were draped in full bloom across the arched trellises, their fragrant lemon and rose scent filling the air. "Is your brother here yet?"

Nicola gave a curt nod. "He and his countess are in the card room. Julian," she said with a wrinkle to her nose to mark her displeasure, "is involved in a high stakes game of whist."

Rose arched an eyebrow. "Whist? It's a popular game. Doesn't sound quite so alarming as you make it out to be."

"It isn't the game so much as the people involved and their wagers." She quickly surveyed their little piece of the garden to make certain no one could overhear them. "They're betting items of clothing."

Rose shook her head in confusion. "That's ridiculous. The loser has to purchase clothes for the winner? The haberdashers and modistes ought to be pleased."

"No, silly. They're not betting on articles of clothing to put *on*. They're betting on what's to be taken *off*. As in, the loser strips off a tie or a glove or a shirt. Or a gown if the loser is a female. But they won't enforce their bets here. They'll go to their private gaming club later and take a private room to watch the losers strip off—"

"That's appalling!" Rose didn't require further detail. "How did you learn of this? And why didn't you tell me all the gloriously sordid details sooner?" She gasped. "Will your brother partake in this... in..."

"The orgy?"

"Nicola! He wouldn't! Would he?" The mere thought of Lord Emory stripping out of his clothing to bare his hard, muscled body sent so much heat shooting into her cheeks that she knew they had to be a dark and fiery cherry red by now. "Oh, my heavens! Do you mean to say he'd strip naked?"

Nicola nodded. "Ew! The thought of my brother, ugh!"

Not quite the same response that Rose was having, for the thought of Julian Emory's hard, golden body was quite the opposite of "ew." Her own body was intensely hot and throbbing from the tip of her nose to the tips of her toes, and if she didn't soon calm down, her usually pale skin would permanently remain that horrifying shade of cherry red.

"There you girls are," came a familiar voice from behind them. Lord Emory, of course. Did his timing always have to be so inconvenient? Her skin was still so flushed that she resembled a fruit—namely, said cherry—instead of the delicate, alabaster-skinned debutante she was supposed to be.

She didn't want to look at him, but he came around to stand in front of them, planting his large frame in front of her so that she couldn't ignore him. She felt the heat of his gaze on her and heard him clear his throat as though hinting that she ought to acknowledge his presence. *Crumpets.* She couldn't snub him. "Good evening, Lord Em—"

The words caught in her throat the moment she glanced up. Standing beside him, indeed clinging to his arm, was the beautiful Countess Deschanel.

Crumpets again!

The woman was more beautiful than Rose had imagined. She radiated beauty in even the harshest angles of fading evening light. The pink, violet, and orange rays of sunlight seemed to shimmer around her as the sun set, each hue bringing out the pink blush of her porcelain cheeks and the violet black of her glistening dark hair. Even the orange tones, a difficult color for any woman to sport whether young or old, seemed to give her skin a magical golden glow.

For that reason alone Rose wished to dislike her.

Well, not really.

But she understood Nicola's distress. How could Lord Emory not be enraptured by this woman? In comparison, she was entirely lacking. Her honey-gold hair never behaved, and she was always fighting back a loose curl springing up here or a stray curl pointing up there. Even when freshly washed and left down, her hair never draped like silk over her shoulders but cascaded in a wild tumble down her back.

Rose stifled a groan. While Countess Deschanel's eyes were a perfect dove gray, her own eyes were an imperfect blue muddled with flecks of gray and violet as though they didn't know what they ought to be, so they were a mix of everything. As for her skin? It was still flushed that hideous cherry red.

Nicola's brother introduced her to his goddess. "A pleasure," Rose said, offering a short curtsy and smiling warmly in response, because it wasn't the woman's fault that she was perfect in every way and that men—even intelligent ones—fell in love with her at first sight.

The countess smiled icily in response. "The music is starting soon, Chatham. Your sister and her odd little friend are obviously capable of looking after themselves. No need to worry about them."

Odd friend? Rose definitely felt the air turn glacial in this woman's presence. Indeed, Lord Emory's goddess appeared quite adept at sucking all warmth from a room and even from the expansive outdoors in which they stood. Quite a feat, for the evening air was slightly damp and still held the heat of the long summer's day.

Surprisingly, Nicola's brother held back when she attempted to draw him away. "Miss Farthingale, may I help you to a chair? You appear to be struggling on your feet."

Obviously, he'd mistaken her embarrassment in imagining him naked for difficulty in walking about with a sprained ankle. Only her ankle had healed just fine and although she carried the cane, she wasn't limping or feeling particularly uncomfortable in the area of her foot. No, the discomfort lay squarely in her heart. "You needn't concern yourself with me, my lord. I'll *waddle* over to the concert seats on my own."

The countess sniffed to mark her displeasure.

Nicola's brother shot her a grin and masked his chuckle by bringing one of his fisted hands to his mouth and coughing. "Stay within sight of Lord and Lady Darnley or the Farthingales. I don't wish to be worrying about the pair of you." He glanced at his goddess and his smile turned wicked. "I have better things to occupy my time this evening."

He strolled away with the countess still clinging to his arm, never once looking back. Rose stared in his direction even after he'd disappeared from view. "We're doomed, Nicola. I knew she was beautiful, but I never thought it possible for anyone to be so exquisite. Not even I would choose me over her."

"Hah! You're much prettier than she is and it's obvious that Julian thinks so, too." Nicola wrapped her arm in Rose's as they walked together toward the concert area, where seats had been set out and flower garlands and silk bows decorated the prettily fashioned bowers.

Rose sat beside her parents and tried her best not to fidget during the interminable concert. Nicola's brother and his goddess sat in the same row but across the center aisle from them so that Rose had a clear view of his profile as he stared straight ahead at the Winthrop daughters standing on the raised dais.

Having been admonished twice already by her mother to stop fidgeting, she withdrew her small pencil and dance card from her silk reticule. There was to be dancing after the concert but Rose had no intention of participating yet, nor would anyone be signing her card. She began to aimlessly sketch on it.

Nicola's brother happened to be the perfect subject, for he was not only handsome but artistically appealing. He had the sort of features that would make for a spectacular portrait—a rugged, manly face with enough smooth lines and angles to appear refined and yet enough raw, male features to remind one of a medieval warrior. Battle hardened but not coarse. After all, Lord Emory had served many years battling Napoleon on the Peninsula.

"What are you doing?" her mother whispered, leaning over to have a peek.

Rose tried to draw the card away, but saw by her mother's expression that she was too late. "You told me not to fidget. So I'm drawing instead."

"My dear," her mother said gently, "you've captured him perfectly." She paused a moment to let out a long breath.

Rose understood the meaning of her mother's forlorn sigh. "I know, Mama. I do find him fascinating, but he's in love with someone else. I won't allow my heart to be engaged."

Her mother patted her hand. "I'm afraid you lost your heart to him that very first day. That's how it happens with Farthingales. One look and they know. But all hope is not lost. Despite appearances, I think he may be beguiled by you as well."

Rose couldn't help letting out an oinkish snort in response to her mother's comment. Of course, the sound drifted across the center aisle to reach Lord Emory's ears. He turned to stare at her, and then his expression softened and she saw the crinkle at the corners of his eyes just before he gave her a rakish smile.

Her mother gave her hand a gentle squeeze. "Most interesting."

The man may have smiled at her, but he was going to undress for his countess tonight and propose to her by the end of the month unless she, Nicola, and the entire Emory family succeeded in changing his mind. *Crumpets, what a coil!* Would he still like her after she abducted him?

THE DISCORDANT SOUNDS of Melissa Winthrop's harp filtered through Julian's ears with as much charm as metal grinding on metal. Was everyone else struggling not to wince? Or was he the only one who considered the sound offensive to his ears?

Usually, he slipped away during these tedious recitals. But not this evening. He'd taken the first seat in a center aisle so that he could stretch his long legs, but his position also offered him a clear view of Rose and that was a problem.

He couldn't keep his eyes off the girl.

He studied her through hooded lids. Discreetly, of course. Too much was at stake to do otherwise. He had to feign disinterest until he found that man at the top of Napoleon's ring of English traitors, the one who could bring down the Prince Regent and his family and deliver England into the little Corsican's hands.

Valentina had her usual death grip on his arm, for she considered him one of her possessions and no one would share him until she was ready to move on to other amusements. He would then be thrown into her refuse pile along with the other men whose hearts she had broken. He longed for the day to arrive. This assignment had long ago grown tedious.

He stopped staring at Rose and forced himself to keep his thoughts off the girl and her soft blue eyes.

When the recital ended, the guests drifted off to various entertainments. Those who sought to dine found the supper tables groaning under the weight of the abundant cold meats, salted fish, and succulent sweets on display. Card tables were set up in the card room, and the Winthrops had engaged an orchestra that appeared to be ready to open with a waltz in the ballroom. Julian thought of his promise to Rose about her first waltz, a promise he desired to keep, but he dared not claim it here.

He glanced around and saw that Rose and Nicola were now seated among the wallflowers, chattering between themselves and making it clear to all the young bucks in attendance that neither girl was interested in dancing. He understood Rose's hesitation, for she had not quite recovered from her sprained ankle, but Nicola had no such impediment. Why wasn't his blasted headstrong sister making herself available for a dance?

"You seem far away, Chatham," Valentina said, attempting to follow his gaze. Fortunately, the ballroom was packed and she wasn't tall enough to make out what had distracted him across the room.

"No, my love. Right here. Just making certain Braswell isn't eyeing my sister." That rankled Valentina. Braswell was her toady for the moment and she wasn't about to share him with anyone. "Ah, no. I see he's moved past her and is gulping down a cup of ratafia. No doubt he's spiked it. The drink is vile. Not even I can stomach it plain."

He took Valentina into his arms as her frown eased, and he danced the waltz and then a quadrille with her. He gave silent thanks when Lord Braswell approached Valentina to claim the two sets he'd marked on her dance card.

With Valentina occupied for another hour at a minimum, Julian took the opportunity to approach his sister and Rose. They saw him coming and scampered outside, Rose moving with surprising grace as they both hurried down the terrace steps to the privacy of the garden. Were they purposely trying to avoid him?

Bloody nuisance.

He followed after them, telling himself that it was only to protect the girls from the unscrupulous bachelors lying in wait for the first young innocent of ample fortune to walk down the darkened path and fall into one of their traps.

Wasn't he honor bound to protect them? After all, Nicola was his sister and Rose was his sort of responsibility ever since he'd pulled her out from her sabotaged pottery shed. In any event, he'd promised her mother that he'd look after her. It mattered little that they were talking about the upcoming trip to Darnley Cottage and not this musicale.

A promise is a promise and I mean to keep it.

If Valentina noticed, he'd simply tell her the truth. She'd believe that he'd been chasing after his sister to keep the irritating sibling out of harm's way. No need to make mention of Rose. Indeed, the less said about her, the better.

He strode down a darkened bend and almost barreled over the two girls, catching them up in his arms in time to prevent them from falling into a heap at his feet. "Nicola, why aren't you on the dance floor?" He steadied both girls and then released them, nodding toward the crowded ballroom. His body still tingled in the spots where Rose had fallen against him, and his hand still shook from the ache of wanting to touch of her soft, warm body again.

"No one asked me." Nicola shot back a glower, obviously not in the least distressed to be considered a wallflower.

He frowned. Any dutiful brother would be concerned to find his younger sister ignored by the reputable young bucks on the hunt for a suitable wife. "Let me see your card."

"No." She tucked it into her bosom.

Julian rolled his eyes. "And you, Rose? Has no one approached you either?"

Hoping he didn't ask to see her dance card and discover his likeness on it, she glanced down at her ankle as though to point out the obvious. "I can't possibly accept anyone until you claim the first dance. Do you recall your—"

He groaned inwardly. "Yes."

But Valentina would run him through with her sharpest blade if he dared to dance with another young lady. He'd been foolish to suggest it and would now have to disappoint Rose. Either that or claim that first dance in the privacy of this isolated moonlit garden. He'd still have to wait for Valentina and her cohorts to be reliably distracted before he'd ever dare attempt it.

Lord, he was mad to even consider such a thing.

A year's work tossed away for a pair of beautiful blue eyes. "Rose, you'll get your first dance once we're out in the country." He turned away from her before she could accept or issue protest.

Now in ill humor, he trained his annoyance on his sister. "Nicola, I had better see you dance at least once this evening with a proper suitor or I'm going to take it upon myself to find you a husband. So, unless you wish to be forced into a marriage with someone of my choosing by the end of this season, you had better get out there and find yourself a duke or earl or some other pimple-arsed nitwit who'll find you tolerable."

She scowled. "You're bluffing. You'd never saddle me with an unwanted match."

He folded his arms across his chest. "Wouldn't I?"

As Nicola folded her arms to mimic his pose, Rose attempted to intercede. "She finds your friend the Duke of Edgeware interesting. Perhaps you might encourage—"

"Stop protecting my sister, Rose." He shook his head and sighed. "Everyone knows the duke has no intention of ever marrying. You've craftily mentioned the only bachelor in London who will never be conquered. It won't buy Nicola a reprieve. I know she has no interest in him."

"You do?" Rose tipped her head in confusion. "How can you possibly be so certain?"

"Nicola is terrible at hiding her thoughts. So are you, by the way." A slow grin stretched across his face. "I know exactly what you're thinking."

"Crumpets!" she muttered, her eyes rounding in alarm. "If you're so clever, then tell me what I'm thinking right now."

"Easy." He arched a devilish eyebrow. "You're wondering whether I'm bluffing about Nicola. I'm not. And wondering whether

I'm on to the scheme you and she have contrived and were most busily whispering about in your own little corner of the Winthrop ballroom. I am." She gasped and her eyes once more rounded in alarm. *Bloody nuisance.* His guess had been squarely on the mark. They were indeed still scheming, but about what?

As the girl recovered from her surprise, she met his gaze in challenge. "An obvious guess. If you're truly that perceptive, then what am I thinking about now?"

His grin broadened and turned rakish. "You're wondering whether I would truly kiss you if you asked me."

She inhaled lightly. "Nicola, let's go inside. The gnats are rather a nuisance this evening and so is your brother."

Julian watched Rose skitter back into the townhouse with his sister following closely at her heels. Only once she was out of sight did he release the breath he'd been holding. "Bloody nuisance," he muttered again, desperately wishing she wasn't quite so beautiful.

"Indeed," the Duke of Edgeware said, stepping out of the shadows. "Chatham, should I be heartbroken that your sister doesn't desire me?"

"Oh, bollocks. Ian, I didn't know you were out here." He'd been working with Ian Markham, Duke of Edgeware, another agent for the Crown, for many years and had long since stopped calling his friend "your grace" or Edgeware.

"I often sneak away," Ian said with a nod, "sometimes for an assignation, but mostly to avoid those aggressive, marriage-minded mamas and their drippy-nosed daughters. I'd never slip away with a good sort like your sister, so you needn't worry about her."

"They're not all horrid. Some of these young ladies are quite tolerable."

Ian nodded toward the townhouse. "Like Rose Farthingale? I've heard about those Farthingale girls. Supposedly they're all beautiful, even the youngest ones. Lady Dayne is already dropping hints that one of them might suit me." He shook his head and gave a mock shudder. "I'm depraved in many ways, but I never rob from the cradle."

Julian threw his head back and laughed. "They're unusual and far more interesting than your ordinary assortment of English flowers. You ought not rule them out."

Ian cast him one of those dismissive looks that seem to come naturally to all dukes. "Only trysts and tawdry liaisons for me, old man," he said, even though Julian didn't know anyone else as brave and hard working as Ian. The duke lowered his voice to a whisper. "I return to France within the week. It's my turn to follow Napoleon's messenger and see where else the man will lead me. Perhaps I'll return to find you married. I pray that it won't be to that black widow spider, Valentina. Not even the salvation of England would be reason enough for me to make that sacrifice."

Julian sighed. "Let's hope it doesn't come to that. I've made a solemn promise to Prinny and intend to hold to it. So I really need to discover the name of the traitor inside the royal inner circle before the month is out or I'll be forced to take that next step and offer for said black widow spider. I won't go through with the wedding, but she needs to think I will. She needs to trust me implicitly."

"Good luck." Ian glanced toward the terrace, where ladies and gentlemen were beginning to crowd since the ballroom had no doubt grown too warm. "I had better go back inside. You ought to do the same before your spider comes hunting for you."

"Damn. I know."

Ian patted him on the back. "I'll keep an eye on your sister and claim a dance if she truly intends to declare herself a wallflower. After one dance with me, the other young bucks will be clamoring for a turn."

"I'd be grateful for it." He cleared his throat. "But just one dance."

Ian held up his hands in mock surrender again, but his expression was somber. "You needn't worry. One is all I'll claim. Nicola's a decent sort and one of the few debutantes who actually intend to marry for love. I admire that. Don't be too hard on her. She knows what she wants, and it isn't her fault there are so few worthy specimens to be found."

Julian snorted. "When did you grow to be so clever?"

"I've always been brilliant," he replied with a grin. "I'm shocked you haven't noticed it sooner."

They walked inside as the set was ending and the men were

escorting their partners off the dance floor. Julian crossed the crowded room toward Valentina and Braswell to lay claim on her and act the part of jealous suitor. "I believe the next dance is mine, my love." He cast Braswell a glower. "You may take yourself off now, old boy. You've had all the turn you're going to have this evening."

Valentina let out a throaty chuckle. "Chatham, don't be cruel. Lord Braswell only means to be kind to me."

"A little too kind for my liking." He frowned at Braswell, wondering what this man's interest was in Valentina. Was he truly enthralled by her? Or did he believe she was a rich widow and he could to get his hands on her wealth? The latter, he supposed, for the man struck him as a disreputable sort. Julian knew for a fact that Braswell often lost at the gaming tables and his viscount father had severely cut back his allowance.

The dissolute was not particularly good-looking either, and even less so now that he was sweating from the heat of the ballroom. He reeked of whiskey and had likely shown up at the Winthrop townhouse already in his cups. If Valentina tolerated him, it was because she thought she could recruit him to work for Napoleon.

He shook himself back to attention. The music had started up and he resumed his role as besotted lover, placing his hand at the small of Valentina's back to whirl her around the floor in time to the waltz. She closed her eyes and began to sway seductively against him. He went through the motions of subtly responding to her overtures, but his gaze was directed to the wallflower corner and the honey blonde seated beside Nicola.

He had to stop thinking of Rose Farthingale.

But how could he when her smile was as beautiful as a sunrise over a tropical ocean and her eyes were an incandescent blue?

The girl was to join the Emory clan at Darnley Cottage for the upcoming week. He'd promised her mother he'd watch over her.

That wasn't the problem.

He'd watch her all right.

And think of her in the early hours before dawn as he lay achingly alone in his bed.

And dream of holding her warm, naked body in his arms as she lay curled beside him. That was the prim and proper version of his fantasy. The real fantasy involved him exploring and teasing her glorious body until she was wild and writhing and screaming his name while he brought her to ecstasy.

How was he to keep his mind—and hands—off her next week?

CHAPTER 5

ON THE FRIDAY after the Winthrop musicale, three carriages clattered out of London in the early morning hours on their way to Darnley Cottage. Rose rode in the first carriage with Nicola, the jovial Earl Darnley, and his delightful wife, Lady Bess. Nicola's sisters and their governesses were in the second, while Lord Emory rode in the third with the two "little savages" also known as his brothers.

Rose tried not to make more of her upcoming week in the country than was warranted, but the thought of spending all that time in Lord Emory's presence had her heart hopelessly aflutter. She chided herself for thinking of him and turned her attention to the scenery.

The roads were dry and not particularly crowded, so they made good progress. The charming inn they stopped at in late morning to rest and water the horses was not crowded either, although she knew from travels with her family that it would begin to fill up soon as the mealtime hour was approaching. They had stopped early, around eleven o'clock. "Just in time for elevenses," the earl said, chortling as he lumbered down from his carriage and rubbed his rotund stomach.

Lord Emory purchased ale for the men, lemonade for the children, and tea for the ladies. He then requested the staff deliver these libations and the simple fare he'd also ordered to the outdoor tables that were set up under one of the shade trees in the inn's expansive garden.

Rose drew up alongside him as she and the Emory family strolled along the grassy path toward the tables. "An excellent idea to dine outdoors, my lord."

He smiled his usual gorgeous smile and slowed his pace so that they fell back from the others. "It's merely a matter of self-preservation on my part. I shudder to think what my brothers would do to me and my shiny new carriage were I to force them to sit still any longer. How are you managing, Rose?"

"Very well." She closed her eyes momentarily and tipped her head upward, allowing the sun to warm her cheeks. She breathed in the scent of grass and lilac that carried on the breeze and mingled with Lord Emory's clean lather and spice scent. She opened her eyes and returned his smile, wanting to nestle in his arms and just breathe him in, but it was a ridiculous notion and she dismissed it immediately. "I love the countryside. In truth, I feel much more at home out here than in London."

His gaze turned thoughtful. "Do you not like town or the entertainments of the season?"

"Alas, I do not." She shrugged as they ambled down the garden walk, trying not to sigh or quiver with delight each time her shoulder grazed his arm, for the walk was narrow and his shoulders were quite broad. "The town is splendid, I will admit. I love the museums and shops and all the structures of historical importance, but the townspeople are the problem."

His brow was now furrowed, as though he was listening with interest and her feelings mattered. "How so?"

"Everyone's so worried about impressing the 'right sort' that they forget who they really are on the inside." She pointed to her heart. "And yet I try not to judge others, for I've been blessed with a wonderful family and have never lacked for anything. I don't know what sort of person I'd be if my circumstances were dire and my family impoverished. I'd fight for them, but I don't know to what lengths I'd go. My courage has never been tested like yours has."

"Rose, I beg to differ."

She hadn't meant to engage him in a more serious conversation, but he didn't appear to mind. Indeed, he seemed to quite enjoy it. While the children ran around the grounds, celebrating their freedom from confinement in the carriages, she and Lord Emory continued to walk around the grounds and chat. Nicola was playing with the children, squealing and giggling along with the noisy brood, and the Earl of Darnley and his wife had taken seats in the shade.

"Your courage has been tested and you've shown your bravery." He watched his younger siblings chase each other around a circle of raised flowerbeds.

She shook her head, confused. "When?"

"From the moment you acted upon your dreams to pursue your art knowing the odds were against you in competing against men. In your determination not to be stopped by Sir Aubrey's ruffian tactics. You never once wilted or cowered in fear." He arched an eyebrow and laughed. "However, do not take my comment as permission to go after him on your own. I've dealt with him and he won't be bothering you again unless he's an utter idiot with a death wish."

"He is one." She pursed her lips in mild displeasure at the thought of her pottery rival. "It's only a question as to the degree of his idiocy."

Their conversation was interrupted by Lord Emory's eight- and ten-year-old sisters, Emily and Kendra. They squealed and leaped into his arms when he bent down to tickle them.

Rose sighed. Was there ever a more heartwarming sight?

Robert and Callum, the younger boys, then joined them, demanding equal time with the older brother they obviously adored. Robert was twelve and Callum fourteen. To Rose's surprise, Lord Emory allowed his siblings to drag him into their games and he was soon chasing the boys and giving the girls piggyback rides.

Rose and Nicola joined in too, but in the less frantic sports, for Rose knew that her ankle was still delicate and had no desire to risk twisting it again. The countryside would be a perfect place for walking. She wanted to take full advantage, not be hobbled again and forced to remain indoors while everyone else was out in the sunshine having fun.

To include her in one of their games, Lord Emory contrived a silly race in which they were all to walk fast instead of running around the perimeter of the garden. "You, too?" The thought of him wriggling and waddling speedily along the path brought a giggle out of her.

"Heavens, no." He cast her a look of mock horror and stood with his arms outstretched and his chin elegantly tipped upward. "I shall act as the imposing finish line."

Callum won the silly walking contest while Nicola and Robert elbowed each other all the way to the end for second place. Lord Emory wisely declared it a draw. "Upon my honor," he declared, "not even a whisker separated the pair of you. You crossed at the exact same moment."

Kendra came next. "Does that mean I'm in third place?"

"No," Robert grumbled. "You're fourth. I should have been second all on my own, but Julian's distracted by—"

"Have you learned nothing about good sportsmanship?" Lord Emory intoned, cutting off whatever his brother intended to say.

Rose ought to have come in alongside Nicola and Robert, but she had taken pity on little Emily, who had tripped and fallen. She remained behind to soothe the girl and brush blades of grass off her gown and the palms of her little hands. Once Emily was no longer crying, Rose encouraged her to finish the race even though only the two of them remained.

Rose finished last, of course. She wasn't about to allow little Emily's pride to be crushed even further by having her lose the race. Lord Emory met them at the finish line and bent down to hug his little sister, who had wiped away her tears by then and was once more in good humor.

As the others took off to join the Earl of Darnley and his wife by the tables, Lord Emory held Rose back a moment. "What you did just now for my sister," he said in a husky murmur, "thank you. You were splendid."

She regarded him mirthfully. "I have younger sisters, too. I know this game is a little thing to us, but it means so much to the younger ones. Emily was crushed that she couldn't keep up." She sighed and shook her head. "Her sorrow simply tugged at my heart. I'd gladly lose to her any time if it would help to bolster her spirits."

He said nothing, just stared at her for the longest moment.

She had the oddest feeling that he wanted to kiss her.

THE CARRIAGES DREW up to Darnley Cottage in the evening while the sun was still shining, although Rose knew that within the hour it would emit its last gasping glow. But at this moment, she was enchanted by the vibrant play of light upon the cottage and beautiful front garden, for the dazzling sun had blanketed them in warm shades of russet, gold, and amber.

She peered out the carriage window, eager to descend and begin to put the idyllic scene down on paper, glad she'd thought to bring along her sketchbook and coloring pencils for just such an occasion. The cottage and its surroundings were so beautiful she expected to be drawing madly every day, catching the sunrise over the pond or watching cardinals frolic in the birdbath in the center of the garden.

Nicola and her sisters had purchased new straw bonnets just last week. Rose imagined them sporting those bonnets while picnicking under a shady elm or chestnut tree in the distant meadow and couldn't wait to capture that scene as well in her sketchbook.

She also looked forward to drawing portraits of the entire Emory clan as a gift to the earl and his wife in appreciation for allowing her to join them. Lord Emory's siblings would be easy to bring to life in her sketches for they were all so vibrant and expressive. The littlest ones had bright pixie green eyes, copper hair, and freckles. She would have so much fun depicting them as sprites or woodlands faeries.

Lost in her thoughts, her gaze was on her surroundings and not on that tricky first step as she climbed down from the carriage. "Crumpets!" She suddenly realized her foot had hit air instead of that solid first step and she felt herself begin to tumble forward. In that same moment, the family's plans to abduct Lord Emory flashed before her eyes and she despaired of ever keeping him out of the clutches of the predatory countess, their well-planned trap ruined because she was hobbled by her clumsiness.

Would Nicola ever forgive her?

She pitched forward with arms flailing, but was surprised to find Lord Emory standing beside the door in time to catch her. "Rose, look out!"

She landed bosom first in his waiting arms. In the next moment, he groaned lightly as her breasts squashed against his hard chest and her hands grasped his solidly muscled shoulders. He made certain she was unharmed and then laughed lightly, surprising her by wrapping his arms more securely about her unsteady body. "You're a clumsy little thing, aren't you?"

She blushed and began to sputter. "I... y-you see... not usually, I assure you." She was never clumsy or distracted except around him.

That she was close enough to breathe in his glorious scent of spice and lather added to her distress. How did he manage to smell so good after a long day's travel and those midday games? It took great effort to refrain from resting her head against his shoulder and impolitely sniffing him.

He took pity on her when she became obviously flustered. "Are you certain you're all right, Rose?"

She nodded, sincerely grateful for his timely presence. He must have leaped out of his own conveyance before the wheels had stopped rolling, eager to escape from the little savages he called brothers. It was fortunate for her; otherwise she would have landed face first on the ground, giving herself a broken nose and knocking out a good number of teeth. "I'm so sorry. You must think me an utter ninny."

"Hardly that," he said in the soft, husky voice that always sent tingles through her body in surging waves. He continued to study her in bemusement.

Rose scampered back a step, but he must have believed her to still be too unsteady to be trusted on her own. He held out his hand. Unthinkingly, she wrapped her small hand in his firm, larger one as though it was the most natural thing to do.

Neither of them wore gloves.

She loved the rough warmth of his palm against her skin.

After a moment, she realized what she'd just done and tried to draw it away, but he maintained a gentle hold and wouldn't allow her fingers to slip from his. She didn't quite know how to extricate them without appearing rude, so she ignored the obvious fact that her fingers were entwined in his and began a casual conversation to distract him from the fact that she'd almost taken a plunge off the carriage step or that he was holding onto her as though she were a toddler in desperate need of guidance. "I see you've survived the journey in one piece, Lord Emory. But can the same be said for your brothers?"

His eyes crinkled and he grinned. "I barely survived. They were little monsters the entire ride, but I exercised my noble restraint and did them no lasting harm. In truth, I didn't scold them even once. How could I, for I was much worse as a lad?"

He gazed at her legs and then wordlessly scooped her into his arms to carry her a few steps down the pebble walk. "Wait right here until the others have all descended from the carriages. I'll escort you inside."

"You needn't bother. Despite appearances, I can walk on my own." She felt the heat of another blush creep up her cheeks. Goodness, his every touch affected her. The less he touched her, the better.

He frowned. "Are you certain you're fully mended? No aches or twinges to the ankle?"

"No, all healed. Just clumsy." Fearing to lose herself in the green depths of his eyes, she stared at the wrinkles noticeable on her frost blue gown which was just a shade paler than robin's egg blue, or so Madame de Bressard had pronounced as edict when she and her mother had gone to the fashionable modiste to purchase this new traveling gown. "My mind wandered, that's all. I was thinking of the landscape and how I might capture it on paper when I ought to have been thinking of the carriage steps and how one's legs are often stiff and ungainly after a long journey."

He ran his gaze up and down her body once more, his expression one of appreciation more than concern. "There are many lovely walks on the cottage grounds. It would be a shame for you to miss them because of another twisted ankle."

She nodded. "I'll be careful. I promise."

"Good. Nicola and my other siblings are eager to show you around. There's a particularly lovely walk to the nearby village and our pond is stocked with fish. Do you fish, Rose?"

She nodded again. "All the time in Coniston. That's where my sisters and I were raised. It's a charming town, not very far from

Windermere. Do you know it? The district is quite beautiful. A bit more rugged than the Cotswolds, but we quite enjoy it."

"I know the area well. Good fishing, too. Since you appear to be expert at it, I'll rely on you to teach my younger siblings. They might listen to you. They never listen to me."

Although he appeared to be jesting, Rose nibbled her lip in consternation. Did his teasing remark mean that he wasn't staying? Not even for the day? "Will you not join us?" She held her breath, wishing she hadn't asked. He'd think her forward and was probably silently groaning and thinking up excuses why he had to tear away.

Did he sense that she was foolishly infatuated with him?

Even so, that's all it was.

She would never give her heart to one who did not love her in return.

"No, I doubt I can. Too much work to attend to while I'm here." He cleared his throat. "A couple of days at most and then I'll be off for London, probably by the day after tomorrow."

Rose once again lost herself in his sober green gaze. Why did he seem so troubled? No matter, she was also troubled and already missing him even though they'd just arrived and she had two whole days to spend with him, assuming he didn't bury himself in the cottage's study all day long.

"Julian, will you never let go of my friend's hand so that I may take her inside? Come along, Rolf. I'll show you to our quarters and once you're settled I'll give you a tour of the house." Nicola wriggled her way between the two of them. Goodness, Rose hadn't noticed that they were still holding hands. Had he realized it?

His thumb blazed a trail of heat across her palm as he casually released her.

Heart not engaged.

She silently repeated the thought several times to make certain she'd remember, but there was no avoiding his presence in the beautiful cottage, which was as grand as any manor house she'd ever seen. It contained no less than a dozen elegantly appointed guest rooms, a music room, a breakfast parlor, a large entry hall, an even larger dining hall, a smaller dining room, a study, a library, a cozy ladies' parlor, and much more. "Cottage, indeed," she muttered under her breath, quite taken by the magnificence of this country home.

"We'll have to work hard to keep him here all week," Nicola said the moment they'd finished touring the house and were alone in the guest quarters they were to share for the week. Their bags had been brought up and they had been requested to change out of their dusty clothes, wash up, and return downstairs for a light meal. It was late, and after being trapped in their carriages all day, no one other than the boys had much of an appetite.

Rose followed Nicola's lead and changed into an informal tea gown, a pale pink confection. Tomorrow's supper would require a more formal attire, but tonight was a simple family affair. The children were to dine with them this evening, but otherwise only she, Nicola, and Lord Emory would join the earl and countess at the supper table.

Rose quickly understood why. The boys gobbled down their meals as though they were wolves coming out of hibernation. They inhaled the generous servings of cold duck, seeming to suck the meat down their throats without so much as chewing on it, not even once.

Lord Emory grimaced.

The earl and countess harrumphed to mark their displeasure, but it fell on deaf little ears.

Emily began to cry.

Since Rose was seated next to her, she naturally took on the role of tending to her. "What's the matter, sweetling?"

"I don't like duck."

Callum dropped his fork onto his plate with a clatter. "Well, I'm sure the duck doesn't like you much either. Here, give me your plate. I'll eat it."

Emily began to cry harder.

The girl was little and slender, so Rose simply plucked Emily off her chair and set her on her lap. "Sometimes my stomach is delicate. Nothing looks appetizing to me at those times either. I usually settle for some hot bread fresh out of the oven and I slather it with marmalade. That holds me over until my stomach settles. How does that sound to you, Emily? Would you like me to scoop some onto a slice of warm bread for you?"

The girl whimpered a yes and nodded.

Rose gave her a hug of encouragement. "Would you like to stay on my lap as you eat it?"

She nodded again.

Lord Emory leaned back in his chair and gave her a soft smile. "Thank you," he silently mouthed.

Heart not engaged.

But she knew it was. Every time he looked at her, she felt a stirring in her blood. A tingling sensation in her limbs. A flutter in her belly.

An ache in her heart.

She smiled in response, but couldn't wait for the meal to end. Lord Emory was looking at her as though she was filling his heart, and she knew it couldn't be true. His heart belonged to Countess Deschanel.

Perhaps Robert was as eager to be done with it as she was, because he startled them all by spilling his water glass on the table linens.

Lord Emory growled softly and pushed back his chair as he rose and attempted to sop up the spreading flood with his own napkin. "All right, boys. Upstairs before I mount your heads over the mantel beside that of the wild boar."

Nicola and the governesses took the children upstairs while the earl ordered port wine and glasses to be brought out onto the terrace. The task was promptly attended to, as though the staff had anticipated their desires. Rose realized this must be a nightly ritual for them. "Care to join us, Julian?"

He nodded with a boyish grin. "Just promise me you won't spill that splendid port, Uncle."

The earl chortled. "Don't be too hard on your brother. He was excited to be dining with us and managed to behave throughout most of the meal. If memory serves me correctly, you never lasted through the soup course before wreaking havoc."

Lord Emory laughed heartily. "I'm sure you have me confused with someone else. I was the perfect child."

The earl turned to Rose. "He was a terror. I remember it well!"

He nodded toward the glass doors leading onto the terrace. "My wife and I enjoy a fine port before retiring for the evening. Care to join us as well?"

"I've never had port," Rose admitted.

"Then we must ply you with some," Lord Emory teased.

"Pay no attention to my wicked nephew. You shall not be corrupted while under my care. I'll order lemonade for you," Lady Darnley kindly assured her.

Rose politely declined and commented that she would retire to bed. She didn't trust herself in her nephew's daunting presence and certainly didn't trust herself while drunk. She kissed the earl and his countess goodnight and watched as they sauntered outdoors arm in arm. The older couple, so obviously in love with each other, picked up their wine glasses and leaned against the balustrade while enjoying each other's company in the warm night breeze.

"I'll join you in a moment, Uncle," Lord Emory called out and circled the table to intercept Rose as she was about to leave. "Don't go yet."

"All right." She shrugged her shoulders and waited for him to explain his request. They were now alone in the dining room, the candlelight casting shadows of them along the wall. The shadows blended as Lord Emory leaned a muscular shoulder against the door frame very close to where she stood.

He studied her, saying nothing, so she spoke up to fill the silence. "I hope you didn't mind that I took Emily onto my lap. She isn't an infant, but is still a sensitive girl and—"

"I didn't mind. She misses our mother and needs a good cuddle every once in a while." He shifted closer, so close that she could feel his warm breath teasing her ear. Her limbs began to tingle again. "Rose, aren't you going to ask me?"

She swallowed hard, for he was standing divinely close and she felt as though they were the only two people who existed at this moment. He overwhelmed her with his mere presence and she had to lean against the wall for support. His eyes were expressively steamy. She'd never had a man look at her with such fire and heat in eyes before. She swallowed hard again. "Ask you what?"

"Ask me to kiss you," he said in a husky rumble.

Heart not engaged.

Heart not engaged!

Her eyes widened in surprise. "Would you—"

That's as far as she got before he groaned out a yes and lowered his lips to hers with glorious urgency. She'd only meant to ask if he truly meant it or was merely teasing her, but he captured her mouth before she managed to utter another word. *Heavens!* His lips were warm and gentle and probing, his body hard and straining as he gathered her into his exquisite arms—they were indeed exquisite—and without breaking contact, drew her up against him in one smooth, sweeping motion so that there was no mistaking what he was doing.

He was kissing her!

Kissing her!

She circled her arms around his neck and leaned into him, loving the feel of his body against hers. Loving the heat of his mouth on hers as he deepened the kiss and slid his tongue between her slightly parted lips. Then his tongue gently invaded and sweetly plundered, moving in and out in slow, languid thrusts.

His arms tightened about her waist to hold her securely against his body, as though fearing she might draw away.

"Julian," she said in a breathless whisper, clinging to him and hoping he would never let her go.

He chuckled against her mouth. "Finally. I like the sound of my name on your lips."

She felt the beat of his heart thrumming against her chest, for he was holding her off the ground and she was still pressed against him so that their hearts were aligned. Even though he stood a foot taller than she, at this moment they were eye to eye and shoulder to shoulder. Her heart was wildly pounding in rhythm to his, and she felt every hungry throb of both hearts.

Her eyes fluttered closed when their lips met again, the better to experience each fiery sensation, to feel his straining muscles, to taste the hint of wine on his breath and revel in the heat of his body aching for hers. "I'll never forget you," she whispered, knowing he wasn't hers to keep beyond this intoxicating moment.

He groaned again and set her down gently so that her back rested against the wall she desperately needed for support. Her hands splayed against it to hold herself up so she wouldn't simply melt into a puddle of wanton desires. Of course, she was already deeply aching for him, but she dared not let on. She knew he was a handsome rogue who only meant to steal a kiss.

She was the only one in danger of turning it into something more. Her thoughts were so muddled she couldn't put two words together, much less use her two feet to walk out. "Hell and damnation, Rose," he said with a groan that seemed to tear from the depths of his soul. "This isn't what it seems."

She opened her eyes to study him. What was he talking about? "This wasn't a kiss? My first kiss. It certainly felt like one."

He ran a hand raggedly through his hair. "Your first? Your very first? Have you never been kissed by any man before?"

She didn't understand why he suddenly seemed irritated with her. "No. Not a one. Should I have been?"

"Hell, no. Of course not. It isn't your fault. That's how my luck has been running lately." He muttered something under his breath, but she couldn't make it out. However, it couldn't have been too awful, for his gaze grew tender and he tipped a finger under her chin to nudge her face upward slightly. "Yes, it was a kiss. One hell of a great kiss."

She couldn't help but nod in agreement because she was still reveling in its afterglow.

However, he wasn't quite so cheerful now. "But you must be wondering why I chose to kiss you."

In truth, he'd rendered her senseless and she wasn't thinking at all. She managed to smile up at him. "No, not at all. I was too busy taking in all these new sensations and liking them very much."

He ran a hand through his hair again. "Bloody nuisance. When I'm... this isn't supposed to happen... you're... and I'm... damn it, I'm a blasted fool."

"We both got carried away. You needn't worry that I'll expect more, much as I do hope for more. As I said, I rather enjoyed it."

"No, Rose. You can't. And I can't."

She put a hand to his cheek, his earlier tenderness toward her emboldening her. "But we just did."

He groaned once more and leaned his forehead lightly against hers. "I know. My apologies, but this can't be happening. Not now."

"You needn't worry that you've led me on or hurt me." She ignored the ache to her heart. Although she knew little about men, she'd been warned about their carnal needs. Did a hungry kiss count as carnal? His lips hadn't felt base or dirty or insincere. Quite the opposite, it felt as though he'd put more of his heart into this kiss than she had. Of course, this was her first time and she didn't know what she was doing. But he knew.

He wasn't happy about what he'd done, but didn't seem regretful.

In truth, he appeared to be at war with himself. If she didn't know better, she'd think he wanted to kiss her again. But that was impossible. He'd appeased his curiosity and would now return to Countess Deschanel, the true Lorelei, for that sophisticated beauty was experienced in the art of seducing a man and keeping him under her spell.

So why was Lord Emory still standing so close to her?

And why was his gaze on her still smoldering?

CHAPTER 6

JULIAN FORCED HIMSELF to turn away from the golden-haired innocent with lush, kissable lips and the biggest blue eyes. He needed to regain hold of his senses, which always seemed to career out of control the moment Rose was near. He knew he had to stay away from her, but it was more easily said than done. "I'm sorry I detained you, Rose. You may go."

"You didn't merely detain me," she said with a soft laugh that trickled over him like warm sunshine. She ought to have been shocked, remorseful, and certainly offended, for he'd not only overstepped the proper bounds, he'd trampled them.

She merely sounded amused.

She set her hand gently on his arm to draw his attention back to her. *Hah!* If only she knew how completely she had him rapt! Not even turning away from her had helped, for his gaze was now on his aunt and uncle sharing a port wine on the balcony, every movement of their aged bodies as they leaned toward each other an indication of the loving devotion each held for the other. "Lord Emory—"

"Julian," he insisted with a quiet growl, another impulsive mistake on his part. He ought to be drawing away from the girl, not insisting on more intimacy.

She sighed. "Very well… Julian. Isn't it beautiful the way the earl and his wife get along? They're so obviously in love with each other. That's what I wish for myself. I know it is something that you're not willing to give me, so I'm quite satisfied to treasure the memory of my first kiss and leave it at that. I'm glad it was with you, a man with a good, caring heart toward his family and perhaps a little fondness for me. I'm most flattered, although quite surprised, that I managed to pique your interest in any way."

He shook his head and sighed. "Rose, do you have any notion how beautiful you are? Not only outwardly, but deep inside where it counts most?"

"You're flattering me again. I must warn you that I'm quite susceptible to it, especially from you. Perhaps I had better retire before I say something I'll truly regret." Her hand slid off his arm. "Good night, Julian."

He nodded. "I may not see you tomorrow. I'll probably ride out early."

She stopped in mid step. "Ride out?

He nodded again. "Yes, back to London."

"Back to London?" Her eyes rounded in surprise, and other feelings that he couldn't quite make out seemed to be roiling within her all at once. "You can't! Not now!"

"Why not?"

"Because... er..." The poor girl suddenly appeared bereft and he began to understand why. Her facade of calm had been just that. No doubt he'd stirred her innocent passion and she didn't understand the heat and turmoil now bubbling within her. "Er... what about sharing breakfast with your siblings? You can't disappoint them. It would be cruel."

What had he done? And how was he to undo the damage?

"They'll be heartbroken," she continued, seeming to be desperately groping for reasons to hold him here. In truth, he wanted to stay, but it wasn't safe to remain so close to her when he hadn't mastered control over his own feelings yet. "And... and... weren't you supposed to stay for at least another day? You can't change your mind now. The little ones will think you broke a promise to them. They might never forgive you."

He frowned lightly. "My aunt and uncle will explain my absence to them. Nicola and Callum will certainly understand. You needn't fret. I'll see you all when you return to London next week."

Her blue-violet irises were in a turbulent swirl. "Next week will be too late."

"For what?" He rubbed the nape of his neck, now worried that he'd overstepped quite badly and overset Rose far more than expected. It was all his fault, of course. Damn it, he shouldn't have kissed her. "I'm quite certain my brothers had enough of me on the carriage ride here. And Emily has you as her new best friend so she won't miss me in the least. Kendra might, but Nicola will entertain her."

She still appeared to be groping for reasons to keep him here. Was she in love with him? Deeply and helplessly so? He liked Rose well enough. Indeed, as soon as Valentina gave up that last important name, he and the others of Prinny's agents would sweep down on that spy ring and toss them all in prison. Perhaps it would all take place this week and he'd be free to court Rose by the time she returned to London.

Merciful heavens! Had he just considered courting Rose?

All the more reason to leave as soon as possible.

He needed to sort out his feelings for her. *Bloody nuisance.* She was his sister's best friend. Once he began to court her, assuming he decided to do so, there would be no turning back. It would have to end in marriage, not only because she was Nicola's best friend but because he knew that once he wooed her in earnest, there was no way he'd keep his hands off the luscious girl.

Or his lips.

Or his tongue.

He cleared his throat. "I hope to have news of importance to convey to you by next week. Rose, I—"

"Oh!" She shoved away from him and ran upstairs, her shapely derriere wiggling delightfully as she hastened up the steps. "No, no, no. Oh, dear!"

He scratched his head as he watched her run off like a scared rabbit. Women considered him handsome and often praised his seductive prowess, but he'd dismissed their claims as silly sexual flirtation.

Had he been wrong all this time?

Was his kiss so sexually potent that it had driven Rose wild and wanton, stirred the chasms of her untapped passion?

If so, it was a delayed reaction. She had seemed perfectly fine after their kiss, but it must have taken time for this new experience to work its way through her delicate system. He'd have to use gentle care when dealing with her the next time they met.

But he puffed out his chest with pride.

He had no idea he was so devastatingly appealing to women.

"YOUR BROTHER IS a complete and utter idiot," Rose insisted, bursting into the bedchamber she shared with Nicola and quickly shutting the door behind her.

"Rolf, what's wrong? What did he do to you?" Nicola put down the night clothes her maid had earlier set out on the counterpane and regarded her with concern. "You're breathing heavily and your face is flushed. Calm down and tell me what just happened."

"Disaster, that's what happened. First he has the gall to kiss me and then he decides to scurry back to London so that he can propose to the wicked witch. Well, if that's the news of importance he wishes to convey to me next week, I'll clamp my hands over my ears and refuse to listen."

"He kissed—"

"The idiot!" she said again and began to pace across their bedchamber. "What else can the news be but that he's going to marry that dreadful woman? Obviously, we have to come up with another plan to keep him here all week."

"But—"

"I know! Your uncle will have to feign a bout of... of... something hideous, I just don't know what, but it has to be something serious enough to keep your brother here and yet not serious enough to have him maintain a constant vigil at your uncle's bedside or he'll soon realize your uncle was faking." She continued to pace across the room. "But what sort of disease? Gout? Dyspepsia? Or some unspecified inflammation that will keep him indisposed for several days."

Nicola intercepted her and clamped her hands on Rose's shoulders. "My brother kissed you? When did this momentous event occur?"

Rose nodded. "Just now, but it doesn't matter when it happened or even that it happened. Haven't you been listening to me? He's going to run off and marry Valentina. We have to stop him tonight. But how? I can't go downstairs and talk to your uncle because Julian will see me and suspect something is amiss. He already suspects us of plotting mischief."

Nicola eased her grip on Rose's shoulders. "I'll knock at their door as soon as I hear them come upstairs. They usually retire after they're done with their glass of port so it won't be long now. But you must go downstairs again and keep Julian distracted while we come up with another plan and put it into motion. There's no way we can allow him to leave tomorrow morning." She pursed her lips, now also lost in thoughts of their scheme. "Drugging my brother's wine should be no problem, but how will we do it now?"

"Drugging him? That sounds awful. I don't know. Think of something else, Nicola."

"I'm trying my best. Stop pacing, Rolf. You're distracting me."

Rose sank onto her bed with a fretful sigh and then snapped her fingers. "I have it! He wouldn't leave if there was a sudden report of poachers."

"Brilliant! That's how we'll delay him until tomorrow. The footmen will prepare the abandoned hunting lodge right after daybreak to make it look as though these villains are using it as their meeting place, but we'll definitely need more time. That tumbling wreck is an hour's hard ride away, longer by carriage, and I doubt the staff can have it cleaned, er... I mean, set up to look like poachers reside there and have all in place before tomorrow afternoon or early evening."

"But he'll be gone by then." Rose tried not to sound as alarmed as she felt. Now that Julian had stormed into her life, she didn't want him storming out of it, especially not now that he'd kissed her in that magical and perfect way.

Nicola reached over and held up Rose's nightgown that had been set out on Rose's bed. It was a sheer, white linen material that clung gently to her curves because she had filled out a little more in her chest and hips in the last few months. "This might work."

Rose had acquired new bed clothes along with all the new ball gowns, day gowns, and tea gowns that had been designed to her more womanly proportions. Frankly, she hadn't wanted them, for she was appalled by how much her parents were spending on her debut. Few girls thought of financial matters, but she was determined to start her own decorative pottery and glassware business and was acutely aware of costs. Every pence saved could be applied toward her other four sisters who would make their come-outs over the next few years, and she had no wish to beggar her parents before any of them had their turn. "What might work? I don't like the way your eyes are gleaming. I won't do it, whatever it is you're thinking to have me do."

"You must or Julian will be lost to us forever. Do you want that to happen?" She didn't wait for Rose's response before continuing. "Put this on and get back downstairs. Let one sleeve casually slip over your shoulder while you speak to him."

Rose rolled her eyes. "You've gone mad. I will not go downstairs dressed like that, or rather, undressed like that. And even if I did, what would I say to Julian?"

Nicola patted her on the shoulder. "It is obvious that you are rarely around virile young men or you would never ask such a question. If you approach him dressed like that, he won't be listening to a thing you say. He'll be too busy wondering what your body looks like under this flimsy gown and how fast he'll descend into hell if he attempts to slip it off you to find out." She shot Rose a smug smile. "The point is, he'll stay another day or two—"

"Your brother is too honorable. He'll flee immediately rather than stay and risk ruining my reputation."

Nicola rolled her eyes. "Men are so predictable in that regard. My brother is no exception. He won't leave. You must trust me on this, Rolf. He kissed you. That is of earth-shaking significance. Please, you can't let that horrid countess win."

Rose put her hands to her cheeks as they began to flame. "It can't possibly work."

Nicola was now smirking at her. "You'll never know unless you try... Lorelei."

"This is madness." But she snatched the nightgown out of Nicola's hands with a groan and then turned to face away from her. He had kissed her. Did that mean he would kiss her again? "Help me out of my clothes. And stop calling me Lorelei."

She knew this latest scheme could only end in disaster for her. What if Julian laughed at her? Or was revolted by her? Or found her woefully lacking? "I shall never forgive you for talking me into this... this... enormous mistake."

Nicola helped her out of her gown. "You'll love me forever and finally admit that I'm as brilliant as your bluestocking sister. Well, almost as brilliant as Lily."

Once undressed, Rose slipped the flimsy sheath over her head and then took a deep breath. She was about to admit defeat and beg out when Nicola began to pull the pins out of her hair. She attempted to resist, but to no avail. "Nicola! What are you doing?"

"You can't leave your hair in a prim bun—it will ruin the effect. You must look like a siren, and everyone knows they have long, flowing tresses. You won't intrigue anyone, certainly not my brother, with your hair coiled tight and your lips pursed in that sour expression. Stop scowling at me and shake your head so that your hair looks tousled as it cascades down your back."

"I will not." She turned to the mirror and began to braid her hair.

Nicola stopped her. "Don't you dare. Leave it alone and get down to the business of seducing my brother. We're crafting a moment here. You as an artist ought to understand the nuances of setting a mood, conveying a story. Your story is that you were preparing for bed and developed a sudden thirst for milk. You only meant to sneak downstairs to fetch a glass for yourself. Got it?"

Rose nodded halfheartedly, silently kicking herself for even considering this ridiculous scheme. But if she didn't do it, then Julian would leave and forever be trapped by the awful countess. "What if he's ensconced himself in your uncle's library with the door closed?"

"Are you being purposely dense, Rolf?" She sighed. "Then your story changes. You'll steal into the library to retrieve a book to read in bed and be startled to find my brother there. Give me a believable look of surprise."

Rose shot her another scowl.

"Excellent. You care for him, don't you? I know that you do. Now get to work and do what you must to keep my brother here another day."

"It isn't work so much as folly," she muttered and hurried downstairs before she lost her courage. In truth, she wasn't a coward, but their ploy was doomed to failure. Julian was still outside on the terrace with his aunt and uncle. Pretending to go to the kitchen to fetch a glass of milk for herself would not work. He couldn't see her tiptoeing down the hall unless he had the ability to see through brick walls.

"The library it is," she muttered, although chances were slim he'd notice her in there either unless he happened to turn at just the right moment and catch a glimpse of the flimsy white fabric against the bookshelves. Even so, he'd have to be curious enough to leave the terrace and come into the library to investigate. The odds were against that happening.

In truth, she was relieved. Deceiving him felt terribly wrong. She and Nicola would simply have to catch him in the early morning and tell him the earl wasn't feeling well. That was a much better plan. Still terribly wrong and deceptive, but it didn't feel quite as bad because it was the earl who was pretending to be ill and not her. Failing that, they could use that made-up story about poachers.

However, she entered the library and decided to select a book for herself before she skittered off to bed. A lone sliver of moonlight shone in from the window so she used it as her light to read the spines of the books that were faintly illuminated by the moon's glow. She dared not use a candle, for it would gleam too brightly and attract Julian's attention. Despite Nicola's entreaty, she was sorry she'd listened and come downstairs in her bedclothes. It was improper and ridiculous.

Having finally come to her senses and determined to retreat upstairs before anyone noticed her, she withdrew a large volume with an ornate, embossed red cover. "Oh, this looks interesting. Florentine art."

"My favorite," someone said with a throaty chuckle from behind her.

Julian. But how?

She licked her lips and willed her heart to stop leaping about like a startled frog. "Yes... er... the Italians are masters of the arts. Florentines, Venetians, Romans. Their paintings and statues are quite magnificent. I'm intrigued by their ability to create the most vivid colors that survived centuries of sunlight and wear. The Egyptians are also masters of color. Did you know…"

Her voice trailed off as he unfolded his crossed arms and moved toward her with purposeful grace, his strides long and slow, his approach like a lion who'd cornered his prey and was now merely savoring the game. Little did he realize that he was the prey being cut off from his herd and she was the bait to lure him away. *Crumpets!* His gaze never left hers as he held her in his thrall.

She felt trapped, but in a magical, transporting way, as though he were a powerful wizard who'd cast a spell on her. She licked her lips again, and finally tore her gaze away to awkwardly open the book and begin to fumble through it. Actually reading it was impossible for there wasn't enough light and even if there were, her thoughts were in too much of a muddle to make sense of the words.

Whatever had possessed her to choose such a big, ungainly book? The dratted thing was as heavy as an anvil, but she wasn't about to set it down. How could she when it served as the only barrier between her and Julian? "Haven't you ever… um, wondered how those colors remain true… er, even after thousands of years? I've… um, learned that they mixed their paints with egg and—"

His hand gently fell on hers to stop her prattling. "You shouldn't be down here dressed like that."

"Well… heh, heh… oh, ha, ha…" She tried to give him a sultry look, but by his unchanging expression she knew she'd failed. "I didn't think anyone would notice." Her stomach began to churn. "Warm night. Hoped for a quick dash into the library and quicker hop back upstairs."

"Where's your dressing gown?"

She swallowed hard and tried to tear her gaze from his devastatingly appealing green eyes. "Oh, ha, ha… funny thing. I, er… um,… couldn't, well. I don't have it on."

He arched an eyebrow. "I noticed."

"You did?" She stifled the *eep* threatening the leap from her throat. Seduction wasn't as easy as Nicola had led her to believe. "I couldn't find it." Not quite a lie, although she couldn't find her dressing gown because she hadn't bothered to look for it. And why should she? She knew exactly where it was. "And you may ask, why didn't I simply borrow Nicola's?"

He stood silent, his eyebrow still arched.

"Well, I didn't think it was necessary. You were on the terrace with your aunt and uncle, and who knew you had the finely tuned senses of a bat? How did you know I was in here? Are you following me?" She pretended to take offense. "If it's another kiss you're after," she said with a sniff, tipping her chin upward in feigned indignation, "you won't get it." Yes, toss him the challenge. What else could she do? Her seductive glances weren't working.

Quite the opposite, he looked as though he wanted to explode with laughter each time she tossed him a come-hither look. She had no idea being sultry was so difficult.

"A kiss?" He edged closer, their lips achingly close because she'd made the tactical blunder of looking up at him. "It hadn't crossed my mind."

Of course not. Why would he want to kiss her again? He'd tried her out and found her lacking. She found him magnificent in every way and still couldn't take her gaze off him. "As I was saying... oh, ha, ha... fascinating discovery... the ancients mixed egg and—"

He reached out to brush a stray curl off her forehead, the gesture stopping her heart as well as her tongue. "Your hair's longer than I realized, and a deep gold, even in the moonlight."

Her hair was the bane of her existence, long and quite unruly because of the thick curls that fell in a springy riot to her hips. "I ought to have braided it, I know. I shall when I return to my bedchamber." She held the book tightly against her chest for protection, not against him but against her wayward heart. Thankfully, it was beating again, but rampantly and haphazardly. "Which I ought to do right now."

But she couldn't move. She was still rapt in the spell he didn't realize he held over her. His expression hadn't changed, but she felt a delicious danger in the way he continued to look at her. As for herself, she'd gone through possibly a thousand changes in her expression during this long, uncomfortable moment. Drat, he had a molten way of looking at her that set off little explosions of heat throughout her body.

She took a deep breath to calm herself.

And another... and another.

As she did so, one sleeve slipped off her shoulder leaving it bare. *Eep!* She shifted the heavy book into one hand and grabbed her sleeve with the other, but Julian let out a low, hungry growl and reached out at the same time to slip the errant fabric back over her shoulder. Their hands met, fingers entwining.

She quickly drew hers away. His remained resting lightly on her bare shoulder. "Rose," he said in an agonized whisper, making no move to draw away.

He stroked his thumb along her bare skin.

She closed her eyes and took another deep breath to still her thunderously pounding heart. Was this really happening? She wanted to remember everything about this moment — the coolness of the night air, the sweet fragrance of medieval roses drifting in on the light breeze, the scent of books and polished bookshelves. The clean, rugged scent of Julian and the taste of port on his lips as he lowered his mouth to hers and kissed her with a hot intensity she'd treasure always.

He eased the book she was desperately clutching out of her grasp. "No barriers between us, Rose. Not ever." She heard a soft thud and felt a small vibration when the ungainly thing landed on the carpet beside them.

"No barriers," she repeated in a squeaky whisper as his fingers slid under the delicate fabric, slipping it lower to cup her breast. *Hot crumpets with clotted cream and strawberries piled high!*

His palm felt warm and perfect against her flesh.

He drew her closer, one arm now around her waist and the other gently kneading the exposed mound. Then his mouth was no longer on hers but moving lower, his lips and tongue working magic on her throat, and nipping lightly at her shoulder, and... *ooh, oh... oh!* His lips closed over her nipple and he began to suckle and tease it into a hard bud with his tongue. Was she seducing him? Because it felt quite the other way around. She was ready to surrender everything to him.

A fiery heat built up within her and every part of her body began to throb with excitement. She wanted to touch him in the same way and wanted him to ease the pressure building up inside of her. "Julian." She called his name in breathless wonder, winding her hands in his hair and arching her back to take in every hot sensation.

She wanted it all, but didn't know what it was she wanted.

He knew and she suddenly felt cool air against her legs as he slid her nightgown upward to expose her legs to his touch.

She gasped and clutched his shoulders, her senses heightened and body eager to be consumed by his touch.

His hand immediately stilled between her legs. He lifted his mouth off her breast. "Hell, Rose." He sounded tortured and in deep agony. "I'm... this is why I have to leave. I can't resist you, but I must. I'll only hurt you."

"You'd never hurt me. You were gentle with me. Wonderful."

He moaned as though she'd cut him with a knife. "This can't be. Not now, at this worst possible moment." He slipped the bodice back into place to cover her breast and smoothed the rest of the fabric down over her legs, trying in vain to put her back in order. But there was nothing orderly about her desire for this man. "I had better leave tonight. Right now."

"No!" This wasn't a ploy. She truly despaired of losing him, and she would lose him forever if she let him go now. This idiotic seduction scheme was having an unintended effect, making him want to run as fast as he could from her instead of keeping him here longer. She had to tell him how she felt. Enough of those silly feminine wiles that she didn't understand how to use in the first place.

"Please, Julian." Her breath was now ragged and she sounded desperate to her own ears. "Please give us one more day together. Just one. If this is all I'm to have of you, then grant me this one request." She felt tears well in her eyes and she blinked to fight them back. Her heart was breaking but she didn't want him to know it, for she didn't quite understand this intensity of feeling she held for the man.

Tears began to slide down her cheeks. Perfect, now he was sure to run as fast as he could from here... from her.

She started to turn away, but he took her gently by the shoulders and held her in a way that forced her to face him. "I'm so sorry,

Rose." He drew her into his arms. "I never meant to hurt you. I hope you know that."

She nodded against his chest and sniffled. "I know."

He sighed. "But I did hurt you badly. You're crying."

She nodded again. "I'm trying not to. It isn't your fault that I like you and don't want you to leave. Everything feels right when I'm with you, but you must have that effect on all young ladies because you're so handsome and smart, but most of all you're kind and decent."

"I'm not. I've taken unpardonable advantage of you."

"And I've encouraged you."

"You're innocent and trusting, which makes what I just did to you all the more despicable." She felt his knuckles graze against her cheek in a caress and then he began to stroke her hair, winding his fingers in her long strands.

"Please stay, Julian. All I ask is for one more day."

He shook his head and groaned. She thought he was about to pull away, but he must have changed his mind, for he drew her more firmly against his chest and held her in his arms for a long and splendid moment. "This is a mistake, but... very well. No one's expecting me back in London yet."

"You'll stay?"

He kissed her lightly on the forehead. "Lord help us both. I'll stay."

Chapter 7

JULIAN SLEPT FITFULLY into the wee hours of the morning, tossing and turning and lying awake for hours at a time staring at the full moon glistening outside his window until it began to fade against the early morning light. He ought to have left for London when he had the chance, but he desperately wanted more time with Rose.

An epic tactical mistake on his part.

He knew it was, and yet he remained eager to charge into the fray, said fray being Rose's outrageously sensual body. But it was much more than mere physical desire on his part, for as much as he felt right for her—or so Rose had claimed—she also felt undeniably right for him. The sight of her standing alone in the library, clad in a thin night rail that hid nothing of her slender body, her golden locks curling about her hips, had stopped him dead in his tracks.

The last of his control had fled the moment the sleeve had slipped off her cream-white shoulder. She'd looked delicate and frail, and he ought to have acted the gentleman and left right then and there. Instead, every beastly urge ignited within him.

His desire inflamed, he'd become an unthinking brute, needing to claim her, possess her, wanting to make her his own.

He'd never lost control like this before, never felt the ravenous urges Rose aroused in him. He'd hungrily kissed and tasted and stroked her beautiful body and he was still starved for her.

He flung off the covers and rose naked from his bed, yawning and stretching, and praying for the strength not to make a fool of himself today. One more day and then he'd be gone. Of course, the passing hours in her company would be nothing but torment and torture for him. This was his cursed fate, to be tempted beyond resistance by the one thing he could not have... not yet.

He drew aside the curtains and winced as the now bright sun shone into his eyes. "Bloody nuisance."

After hastily washing and dressing, he made his way downstairs to the dining room. It was still early. Hopefully no one else was awake yet and he could quietly sip his coffee and muster his defenses against the girl.

"There you are, Julian," his uncle joyfully chortled as he entered. "We were beginning to think you'd abandoned us all and slipped off to London in the middle of the night."

Eight faces around the dining table were all gaping at him—his five irritating siblings and the wonderful aunt and uncle who'd shown him nothing but support and kindness. But the face that captured his attention was that of Rose. She looked so incredibly vulnerable, like a doe caught in a hunter's trap, that he ached for what he had done to her last night.

But that didn't stop his beastly urges from surging to the fore, making him want to do the very same thing to her again, only this time he'd properly finish the job he'd started and rouse this expressively passionate girl to...

He groaned inwardly.

Hell, did Rose have any notion what she was doing to him?

"Don't just stand there, Julian. Take a seat," his uncle commanded with another chortle. "I forbid you to leave us until you've sampled the fare set out before you. I'm sure you'll find a tempting morsel. You have only to open your eyes and look."

Did the old rogue suspect his feelings for Rose? *Bloody nuisance.* He hoped he wasn't that obvious.

Rose fidgeted, regaining his attention. In truth, she'd never lost it. He couldn't look away or think of anyone else but her.

"No, I'm here for the entire day. I'll leave for London tomorrow morning." He settled into the only empty seat at the table, which happened to be beside Rose, no doubt purposely contrived by his meddlesome family. If only they realized just how aware he already was of the girl.

His siblings cast him the warmest smiles.

"Can we go on a picnic today?" Emily asked, her big eyes wide with excitement. She was seated on the other side of Rose so she had to lean her little body forward to be seen by him. "By the pond?"

He couldn't disappoint her. Lord, he loved the little nuisance. "Of course." He leaned forward as well and reached out to tweak her nose, ever aware of Rose seated between them and looking lovelier than any young lady of marriageable age had a right to look. A light blush stained her cheeks as he leaned closer. "Sounds perfect, Em. And as your reward for coming up with such a clever idea, I'll carry you on my shoulders all the way to pond."

The little urchin squealed with delight.

Rose smiled at him.

He wanted to kiss her.

He cleared his throat instead. "I'll have Cook make up a basket for us. The footmen can bring chairs for you," he said, turning to his aunt and uncle.

"No, Julian." His aunt glanced at her husband. "We'll forego the pleasure this time. Your uncle isn't feeling quite himself this morning."

Julian frowned. "Nothing wrong, I hope."

"No, no. Just a little inflammation, but you go have fun with the children. They miss you so much when you're not around. I wouldn't dream of spoiling their pleasure."

He nodded, but remained worried. "Uncle, let me know if you start to feel worse. I'll pack us up and take you all back to London this very—"

"No!" Everyone cried out at once, sounding like a chorus of frantic hens.

He held up his hands in surrender. "What's the matter with all of you? I get it. You needn't render me deaf. Nobody wants to return to London."

"We hate London," Emily said with a vehement pout.

Julian frowned again. Had something happened to his family that he was not aware of? Had someone tried to harm them? Anger burned inside him, not only at the possibility but at himself for being so immersed in protecting king and country that he'd neglected his own precious siblings. "Why don't you like it, Emily?"

"Because Nicola said that something dreadful will happen if we—"

Rose sneezed. And sneezed again. "Forgive me. Something's tickling my nose. Emily, is it you?" She tickled Emily, who giggled and squealed and forgot the rest of what she was about to tell him.

He wanted to press his sister on the topic, but she chose that moment to forego her pout. Instead, her smile was suddenly as brilliant as sunshine. She clambered onto Rose's lap and gave her an emphatic hug. "I love you, Rose."

"Oh, Emily. Sweetheart, I love you too. I have a wonderful idea. What if I take you outside and draw a portrait of you among the flowers."

Kendra's eyes lit up. "Oh, me too!"

Rose had a devastatingly gentle smile for his sisters. "Of course."

Robert and Callum scrambled to their feet. "Will you draw me as a pirate?" Callum asked.

Robert wasn't about to be outdone. "Me too!"

Rose laughed and shook her head. "Come along, all of you. Meet me in the rear garden. I'll run upstairs and fetch my sketching book and pencils."

Julian set down his coffee cup and lifted Emily out of Rose's arms and held her. "Shall Rose draw you as a tulip? Or a bluebell? Or a bright red poppy?"

"A red poppy! I want everyone to notice me, especially you, Julian. Will you carry the picture of me with you wherever you go? I don't want you to forget me."

He tried not to sound too serious, but her words had affected him. "Em, silly. I would never forget you. Don't you know that I carry you in my heart always? When Rose is done with your portrait I'll hang it in my entry hall so that everyone sees your bright red poppy face when they walk in."

"When my sisters were younger," Rose said, smiling at him as she drew back her chair and stood, "I drew them as the flowers after which they were named. Laurel, Daisy, Lily, and Daffodil. My parents had the drawings framed and placed them in our entry hall at Coniston."

Kendra appeared distraught. "But what about you, Rose? Do they not have one of you?"

She rolled her eyes and emitted a mirthful laugh. "Yes, I drew one of myself. But I had to look at myself in the mirror to do it, so it wasn't quite perfect. My eyes came out like this." She mimicked a cross-eyed expression that looked silly and adorable.

"I'm sure it was lovely," Julian's aunt said and his entire family quickly agreed.

His brothers and sisters ran into the garden while Rose and Nicola went upstairs to fetch her sketchbook and pencils.

Julian was left alone with his aunt and uncle. "She's quite something," his aunt said quietly, but the words struck him hard. Of course, Rose was wonderful. A man would have to be a monumental fool not to notice. In truth, he was surprised that a legion of eager young bucks hadn't followed her to Darnley Cottage armed with flowers and poems of unrequited love.

They might still come.

He shifted uncomfortably. "I'll sit out on the terrace and watch her work."

He felt their eyes on him as he strode out and settled in one of the wrought iron chairs that overlooked the cottage garden. He distracted himself from thoughts of Rose by watching the children run along the garden paths. They now appeared joyful and carefree. So what was this nonsense about not wishing to return to London?

Was it simply that they enjoyed the country? Or was there a more sinister reason?

Nicola and Rose soon joined them, interrupting his thoughts. They both had put on floppy straw hats to shade their faces from the summer sun. He studied Rose. All he could see were her big blue eyes and her heartwarming smile. She wore a pale lavender gown that managed, despite its demure simplicity, to draw his attention straight to her breasts. Perhaps it was merely his beastly instincts flaring again.

He couldn't be around the girl without his body catching fire.

It wasn't his fault that she had a perfect body.

Bloody nuisance. He was in serious trouble. *I need to leave tonight.* He'd still have an hour or two of daylight left if he rode out after supper.

Rose, thankfully unaware of his turmoil, turned away from him and began to issue instructions to the children. They gathered around her like bees to a hive as she settled under a shady chestnut tree, opened her tin box of pencils, and turned to an empty page in her sketchbook.

He couldn't hear what she was saying as she spoke softly, but she must have been instructing his sisters, for they nodded and began to pose. All three of them, even independent and headstrong Nicola, appeared quite earnest and eager to please. They obeyed her without the slightest protest, something he found quite extraordinary since they rarely obeyed him and never unquestioningly.

Rose worked the same magic on his brothers, having them strike poses and hold them at length, which he thought quite a remarkable feat on her part because these boys were bodies of perpetual motion and no one, until this very moment, had ever succeeded in holding them still.

Julian sat forward, intrigued by the power Rose held over him and his entire family. Finally, he stood up and strolled to the chestnut tree. "Mind if I watch while you draw?"

She peeked up from under the brim of her hat and blushed as he knelt beside her. He liked that little touch of pink on her cheeks, a telltale sign that he affected her. "These are just rough sketches, mind you. Nothing fancy. Just some ideas I thought the children might like."

She appeared reluctant to show him what she'd done, but he leaned closer and plucked the sketchbook from her slender fingers.

He glanced at the top portraits and inhaled sharply. "Rose, these are incredible." She'd drawn his brothers in various poses as pirates, capturing their youthful enthusiasm even as she fashioned those imps into rough and tumble blackguards with swords and eye patches.

Her blush deepened.

He turned the pages and laughed heartily. "You're amazing. They're beautiful." She'd drawn his sisters not simply beside the flower beds, but as little flowers themselves, capturing the innocent radiance of their faces, even Nicola, who was far too knowledgeable about matters no young innocent ought to know about. Fortunately, her knowledge had been gleaned from books and not actual firsthand experience or he would have been forced to badly maim any young buck caught circling around her. That he'd behaved worse toward Rose was of no moment. His intentions were honorable, even if his thoughts were not. "I'm engaging you for the earl's portrait."

"And yours," Nicola interjected. "You ought to be painted while you're young and handsome, not when you're old, fat, and bald."

He shook his head and laughed. "Ah, Nicola. Ever my champion."

His sister poked him. "Can you draw him, Rose? Now, in this garden."

Rose's smile faltered. "Perhaps another time. I see the servants carrying out our picnic basket. Shall we walk to the pond?"

"An excellent idea." He grabbed Emily and hoisted her onto his shoulders, wincing only slightly as she gleefully shrieked into his ear. Kendra bounced along beside him, while the boys ran ahead, pushing and shoving each other because merely walking side by side was a concept that was foreign to them.

Nicola and Rose followed behind him and when he looked back, he noticed that Rose had brought along her sketchbook and pencils, no doubt to capture his siblings at play beside the pond and in the Cotswolds countryside.

He tried not to think of the girl or how truly talented she was. No wonder those pottery ruffians were quaking in their boots. She wasn't merely talented, but a rare treasure. It would take a special sort of man to encourage her dreams and not stifle them. He refused to consider that he might be that man.

But he sure as hell wasn't letting anyone else assume that role.

His thoughts lingered on Rose during their walk until he was distracted by his idiot brothers, who thought it would be great fun to jump into the pond fully clothed, without even bothering to take off their boots. In the next moment, Callum was out of the water and holding a fish in his palms, chasing after Kendra and trying to drop it on her head.

"For the love of—" He set Emily down on the grass next to Rose and ran after a shrieking Kendra and a soaking wet Callum, who was fiendishly dangling the fish from his fingers. "Give me that, you mushrump."

Kendra was still shrieking and running in circles around Nicola and Rose. Callum tore straight for them and would have run Rose down if Julian hadn't caught the little wretch in time and hauled him over his shoulder. "Julian, put me down!"

"With pleasure." He tossed his brother back into the pond and grinned when the little pest landed with a yelp and a loud splash. Rose picked up the fish his brother had dropped and tossed it back into the water. "The poor little thing was flailing on the ground. I couldn't let it die."

He was still staring at her as she stood beside him when Callum began to splash him with a vengeance, soaking them both.

Rose gasped, but instead of scolding Callum, she laughingly kicked off her slippers and hiked her muslin gown up to her knees, revealing long, slender legs. "You'll get yours, you dastardly pirate," she teased and began to wade into the water after the boy.

Julian stood ready to intercede if his brother forgot she was a girl and played too rough, but it wasn't necessary now. In any event, he liked Rose's unaffected playfulness and wasn't keen on reminding her that debutantes were not supposed to do this sort of thing. As he stood watching, his other siblings, including Nicola, followed Rose into the pond and did a commendable job of dousing Callum.

"Come in, Julian," Robert called to him. "The water's delightful."

"I'm quite comfortable where I am." But he took a step back from the shore as the menacing young horde began to approach. They'd grown bored with dunking Callum and obviously intended to turn their aim on him.

He was up for the challenge. After quickly removing his boots, jacket, and cravat, he waded in with a roar that quickly had all his siblings hooting and shrieking. He dunked his brothers, but took extra care to be gentle with his sisters, especially Emily. She wanted so badly to participate, but she was little and delicate and would get hurt if he and the boys played too rough.

He needn't have worried. Rose purposely stayed close enough to lift Emily into her arms and hold her protectively whenever they came too close.

Lord, did the girl have a fault?

If so, he had yet to find it.

As the children grew hungry, they all piled out of the water. The boys took off their shirts and set them in a sunny spot on the grass to dry. The younger girls took off their dresses and remained in their undergarments. However, that possibility was not available to Nicola or Rose, so they merely wrung out their wet hems and stood in the sun, hoping their gowns would dry while on their bodies.

He tried not to gawk at Rose, but she looked spectacular and he couldn't help himself. Her hair had taken a good soaking and now tumbled wet and wild down her back. Her gown clung to her every outrageous curve. She still had it raised to her knees while wringing the moisture out of it, but for the sake of modesty she had tried to hide behind some low shrubs so that no one would notice her exposed legs. He'd noticed, of course.

Hell, yes. He'd noticed.

He'd seen her breasts last night and already knew they were stunning.

Her legs were too, living up to their delightful promise.

"Julian, you'll catch cold if you don't dry off," Nicola chided. "At least take off your shirt and spread it in the sun beside the others."

He glanced at Rose, who still had her backside to him while she fussed with her gown.

Nicola grinned. "She won't mind. I'll warn her not to look. It isn't as though any of us is the model of propriety anyway. Undisciplined little savages is what grandfather used to call us, remember?"

"Ah, quite well. I suppose you're right." They were far from the London gossips and any local prying eyes, so he took off his shirt and wrung it out, then placed it next to those of his brothers.

He'd just spread it out when Nicola—his ever helpful sister—called out to Rose. "Whatever you do, don't look at Julian. He isn't decent."

Of course, she turned and gazed straight at him.

Her light gasp carried toward him on the summer breeze. Her cheeks turned crimson. She was barefoot and still had her gown raised to her knees as she began to stumble backwards, straight into another row of low-lying shrubs. She tripped and fell back into the shrubs, her long, slender legs exposed and flailing in the air as she struggled in vain to right herself. "Damn it, Nicola." He glowered at his smirking sister. "You're a bloody nuisance."

He hurried forward and lifted Rose into his arms to carry her out of the prickly shrubs. "Are you hurt?"

She wrapped her arms around his neck and held tightly onto him. "No, so stupid of me. I hadn't expected you to... and you're not... wearing... you know."

"As long as you're unharmed." He meant to put her down, but his arms chose that moment to wage a mutiny against his brain and refused to take instruction.

Rose sighed. "You have no shirt on."

"It was wet."

"Your skin's still damp. Golden and warm. Julian, you had better put me down before I do something very foolish." She peeked over his shoulder. "We're setting a most improper example for the children."

He followed her gaze. The boys were still chasing Emily and Kendra, this time with worms. "I doubt they're paying any attention to us. Besides, there's never been anything proper about you and me together. Need I remind you? That's why I have to leave. I can't even keep my hands off you during an innocent family picnic."

She smiled. "I'm having the same difficulty."

He set her down abruptly. "Don't tell me that. One of us has to be sensible."

Rose appeared to mull his warning. "It won't be me, I'm afraid. You muddle my heart whenever you're close. So I'll have to designate you as the one to keep his wits firmly in place. Besides, you told my mother you'd protect me. I assume it extends to protecting me from the likes of you as well."

"Damn it, Rose. Of course it does. That's why I have to leave right after supper."

She nodded. "I'm beginning to think you're right. However, there's something I don't understand."

He arched an eyebrow. "What?"

"How can you look at me the way you do if you're supposed to be in love with Countess Deschanel? And if you do love her, then why are you so eager to kiss me?"

ROSE NEVER RECEIVED an answer to her perfectly logical question, for the girls chose that moment to run to Julian begging for protection from their tormenters. He calmed down his younger sisters, scowled at Nicola, and in a very authoritative and viscount-like tone, ordered his brothers to spread a blanket on the grass under one of the chestnut trees beside the pond so they could all sit in shady comfort and eat. Since Emily was rubbing her eyes and complaining that she wasn't hungry, Julian asked her governess to escort her back to the cottage. Emily must have been tired, for she yawned and went along without protest.

A short while later, a line of servants carrying a table, table linens, plates, and silverware strode toward them. As soon as the table was set, Julian began to forage through the large straw basket containing their "simple" repast that now rested atop it. "Ah, good. Wescott thought to include a bottle of wine."

Julian reached into the basket and withdrew the bottle, making a show of holding it up for inspection in the sunlight. "What's wrong?" Nicola asked when he continued to hold it up to the light and frowned.

He shrugged. "Color's a little off."

Nicola rolled her eyes and flashed Rose a conspiratorial glance before turning to her brother and giving him the sweetest smile. *Oh dear.* Was there a new conspiracy that she ought to be aware of? "I'm sure it's just a trick of the sunlight," Nicola said. "May we have some, Julian?"

He glanced over his shoulder at her and frowned again. "No. There's lemonade for you."

Nicola pretended to pout. "But Rolf and I are out in society now. Surely—"

"No. I'll admit Grandfather's complaint was well founded, for we have indeed descended into savagery." He stared at his brothers, who were now hanging upside down on one of the sturdier tree branches trying to catch fireflies with their tongues. He uncorked the bottle. "But to have you and Rose drunk, too? That's a recipe for disaster. I don't think so." He ignored the crystal glassware Wescott had also neatly packed and took a swig straight from the bottle.

Rose liked the way the muscles rippled along his taut chest whenever he moved. She wished that she could touch him and feel his sinewed strength beneath her palms. His skin was golden, as though he'd spent a bit of time in the sun without a shirt, but there were also a number of thin lines of white and a few puckered pink lines on his arms, back, and chest that revealed scarring. One or two might have been from boyish misadventures. The others, she suspected, were acquired on the field of battle.

Her heart tightened in remorse. He was brave and heroic, so how could she and his family punish him by keeping him away from the woman he loved... assuming he loved the countess? Rose wasn't quite convinced that he did.

Drat! Why did love have to be so confusing?

He raised the bottle to take another hefty swallow and she used the opportunity to study his torso. He was quite the appealing specimen, she decided, closing her eyes a moment to trace the outline of his body in her mind. His stomach was flat and sensually lean while his shoulders were broad and muscular. His legs were long, and he had nicely shaped, firm thighs. In truth, all of him was firm and nicely shaped.

He shifted toward her as she opened her eyes. The sunlight caught the dusting of reddish gold hair along his chest and slightly darker red-gold hair below his navel that ran lower but was covered by his pants.

Crumpets! She dearly wished to spend the afternoon conducting a thorough exploration of his body. She didn't need to be tipsy to make a wanton fool of herself. She stifled her uninhibited thoughts and raised her gaze to his face.

Safer.

Oh, my. No, it isn't.

His hair looked more auburn than gold in the sunlight. It was still damp and slicked back from his brow, the ends curling and clinging to the nape of his neck and making her want to put her nose to that spot and nuzzle him. In truth, she wanted to do much more than that, but it wouldn't do to allow her thoughts to wander into more dangerous realms.

But if they should happen to wander on their own despite her best efforts to quell them, then she wouldn't stop them, for the fantasy of taking highly inappropriate liberties with his body in the hope he might respond to her in kind quite appealed to her.

She silently chided herself. What was wrong with her? It was as though the trappings of civility had come off along with his shirt and her slippers. But it couldn't be helped. Julian stood before her, a noble beast in his raw and purest form.

An incredibly handsome and seductive beast that she had neither the strength nor the will to resist.

"Rose, stop looking at me that way."

She wasn't ashamed of her feelings. They were inconvenient, to be sure, but he wasn't immune to her either. "I can't help it."

He groaned and took another hefty swallow. And another, then stopped drinking and gazed questioningly at the bottle.

Nicola shot her a warning glance. "What's wrong, Julian?"

He shook his head. "Wine tastes odd."

"Let me see." His sister took the bottle and sniffed it. "Smells fine to me, but you must have taken in some pond water while playing with Robert and Callum. It must have affected your sense of taste."

He shrugged. "Perhaps."

Rose turned away and began to pour lemonade into glasses for the children. She poured one for herself as well, but set it down abruptly when Julian suddenly began to sway back and forth like a flag caught on a breeze. He groaned and sank to his knees.

Rose rushed to his side and knelt beside him, moving the picnic basket out of his way and angling his body toward the blanket before he inevitably toppled. "Julian, don't drink any more of that wine. It must be a bad vintage. You said it looked odd and tasted odd, so it can't be good for you."

Goodness, had Nicola carried through on her terrible idea to drug him? How could she do this to her own brother? All this plotting to protect him from a miserable marriage didn't seem like such a good plan any more.

He squinted and turned to her, his senses obviously dulled and his gaze unfocused. "What?"

He was swaying quite dangerously now. She moved closer, intending merely to support him in order to ease him gently onto the blanket, but he suddenly enveloped her in his arms and, like a great, toppling tower, brought her down along with him as he collapsed unconscious atop her.

The breath flew out of her in a great, grunting *oof*, for she hadn't expected to fall along with him, much less fall *under* him... or remain embarrassingly pinned beneath him. "Oh. Oh, dear. Uh, crumpets. This is awkward."

She shoved at him, but his big body was too heavy for her to budge. "Nicola, help me up. Your brother is..." *grunt, grunt* "...crushing me."

Her friend was now standing over her, shaking her head and making not the least effort to assist. "You ought to have thought of that before you helped him. You're much too soft-hearted for your own good, Rolf. What are you doing now?"

"What does it look like I'm doing?" Rose shoved at him again and ended with another breathless grunt of defeat, for he was sprawled like a giant, immovable boulder across her chest, the weight of him shamelessly pressed against her, but in a shockingly delightful way. He smelled so divinely good as well, a mix of masculine heat and fresh country air. "Nicola, stop gawking at me and do something." Her first experience with a man was not going to be like this. No indeed! She wanted the gentleman in question to be awake next time and paying attention.

"Honestly, Rolf. I would, but I'm having too much fun watching you." Nicola remained standing with her hands on her hips and making no effort to do anything but gawk and grin.

Rose wasn't sorry that she'd helped Julian, for he would have hit his head against the heavy table and then hit the ground hard. It was bad enough that Nicola had drugged him... hopefully, not too badly... but to injure him as well? That was simply too much. "You've had your sport, now be useful. He's heavier than he looks. His tightly packed muscles are to blame, no doubt." She hadn't realized he was quite so big and hard... or that her body would respond so wantonly to his.

She would be wild beyond measure if he were actually awake and rakishly smiling at her instead of unconscious and drooling out of the side of his mouth.

Nicola finally took pity on her, and with the aid of Callum and Robert, rolled him off her. She took a deep, gulping breath as she slipped free. A little regret mingled with her sudden freedom, for the sensations aroused by Julian atop her were surprisingly intense and at the same time natural, as though they belonged in each other's arms.

However, she wasn't going to admit it to Julian's siblings. Or servants. Or his aunt and uncle who were eagerly rushing toward them now with the assistance of said servants.

Julian's aunt gaped in horror at his prone, unmoving body. "Oh, dear! We haven't killed him, have we?"

The earl patted his wife's hand gently. "No need to worry, my dear. The boy's strong. Perhaps we overdid it a little on the sedatives, but he'll recover. Not too soon, I hope. We still must get him to the hunting lodge. Should we tie him up now or wait until we get there?"

Rose gasped. "Tie him up? What happened to the other ideas? Your gout? Or poachers killing your game? No one ever discussed knocking him out and abducting him. He'll be trapped. You can't treat him like an animal."

Nicola shook her head. "Isn't that the point? We have to keep him away from London for as long as possible. He'll manage well enough, I'm certain. You needn't fret. He's quite resourceful. I'm sure he'll break loose of his bonds in a day's time and make his way back to Darnley Cottage. Hmm, that poses another problem. What if he breaks free too quickly? Uncle, we didn't think about that."

"I did," the earl assured her. "When we get to the lodge, we'll remove his pants. He can't very well escape naked."

Rose shook her head vehemently. "No, it isn't right. I don't think I like this plan at all. Please, you must call it off and confess what you did. He might forgive you if you show some remorse and end the scheme now. But you can't go ahead with... just leaving him tied up and stripped bare... in an old, unused hunting lodge... no food or—"

"Of course, he'll have food and supplies," Lady Darnley chimed in. "To leave him completely without resources would be barbaric." Overlooking that everything they'd just done was barbaric, she turned to the servants. "Help us load him into the carriage. We have a long ride ahead of us and can't risk his waking before he's safely bound and deposited in the woods."

Rose clutched her heart as the footmen almost dropped Julian. "But do be gentle with him," she cautioned. Fortunately, they were still on the grass and not on the hard, stone terrace floor yet.

Lady Darnley smiled at her, obviously believing she was resigned to the plan and ready to abet this mad undertaking. "Take heart, Rose. It will all work out. I'll ask Cook to put some of her currant scones in a basket for him. He does enjoy them."

Rose shook her head in disbelief. "Scones? Then he'll know for certain that we were his abductors." Good heavens, had she just said *we*?

The earl nodded. "Of course, he'll figure it out in time. The boy's far too clever to be fooled for very long. When he does realize it, we're hoping he'll also understand that we acted out of love. Anyway, we're family. He can't be rid of us no matter how angry he's made by our behavior. He was never the sort to hold a grudge, so we expect that he'll forgive us in time."

"I'm not family. He'll never forgive me." Nor would she blame Julian. Yet knowing that he would never wish to set eyes upon her again truly broke her heart. She cared for him. Something had kindled between them, but was it enough to set him free of the horrid countess? What did it matter? She'd lost his trust by participating in this scheme, even though she hadn't realized how far his family had intended to go.

Her punishment for this "good" deed would be to lose him forever.

She watched helplessly as they hoisted Julian's seemingly lifeless form into the waiting carriage. All he had on were his wet pants. No boots. No shirt. Rose's eyes began to tear.

The earl shook his head and sighed. "Come, my dear. This isn't pleasant for any of us, but you appear quite distraught. I've ordered

Wescott to prepare some refreshments for us on the journey, for we all need to calm our nerves after this affair. Would you like to ride along in the carriage?"

She nodded, feeling numb and wishing this were all a bad dream. Riding along with the earl would give her more time to convince him this scheme was folly. She climbed into the carriage and settled beside Nicola while the earl and his wife settled in the seat opposite them. Julian's big body was half sprawled and half twisted on the floor at their feet.

All of them remained silent in the crowded carriage while Lady Darnley reached into the small basket one of the footmen had deposited on the seat between her and Nicola. She took out a bottle of lemonade and poured some into a glass. "Poor Rose. You seem to be the most unsettled of us all. I know we're doing a terrible thing to Julian, but he's driven us to desperation."

Rose was grateful Emily had been taken back to the house by her governess before Julian succumbed to the effect of the drugged wine. She was too young and sensitive to remain unaffected.

"Kendra and the boys might not be taking it well either," the earl said with a sad shake of his head as the carriage rolled down the drive and turned eastward. "I'm sorry they were there to see Julian collapse. But it couldn't be helped. We had no time to come up with a better plan."

"It isn't too late to end it now," Rose implored. She knew the other children had taken this intrigue badly, for they had been unusually quiet, no doubt having second thoughts about it. Even Nicola was nibbling her lower lip in obvious consternation.

"Here, Rose." Lady Darnley handed her the glass of lemonade. "You go first. You look like you need the fortification more than the rest of us."

She nodded, for her throat was parched, and drank it down quickly. Too quickly. Ugh, it wasn't very good and had an unusually bitter taste that stuck to the back of her throat and began to work its way into her stomach. Sour lemons?

"What's the matter, Rolf?" Nicola took her by the arm. "You suddenly don't look so well. Have you taken ill?"

She shook her head. "I don't feel very well. I—I think it's the lemonade." Or too much sunshine. Or too much adventure. Her head was beginning to spin. "I must have swallowed some pond water, too."

"Oh, dear. Honestly, you and my brother are a pair." Nicola took a sip of her lemonade. "Mine tastes fine. Here, try it. Tell me if it tastes as odd as yours."

She smelled it first and then drank it down.

In that moment, Rose realized something was terribly wrong. Her limbs suddenly felt like dead weights and her head was now spinning in earnest.

She stared at Julian's family as their features began to blur before her very eyes. She tried to hold herself up but couldn't. "Nicola?"

Her friend moved the basket aside and leaned close to whisper in her ear. "I'm so sorry, Rolf. I know it isn't fair to you, but we're desperate and have no choice. I'll make it up to you somehow. I promise."

"What? No! Not like this," she attempted to cry out, but her lips and tongue were now as numb as the rest of her body. Her words must have sounded slurred and unintelligible.

"It has to be this way. You and Julian, both. Rolf, please forgive us."

Both? Julian's family had purposely drugged not only him, but her! "Why?"

She received no answer before she fell into oblivion.

Chapter 8

JULIAN AWOKE WITH a splitting headache, the hammer-striking-anvil sort that felt like one's brain was about to explode. He tried to raise his hand to his brow to massage it, but couldn't move it. "What the...?"

He managed to open his eyes to a squint and looked down. His wrists were bound with a cheap, frayed rope and he was tied to a bed—not his bed, but a thin cot fashioned out of rickety wood that would fall apart if he rocked back and forth hard enough, which he immediately started to do.

What the hell is going on?

After a few savage tugs, he freed himself from his bonds. However, sitting upright on the narrow cot proved much harder. It took a long moment and several deep breaths before he managed to roll forward and stand up. As he did so, he felt the chill of the cold stone floor against his bare feet. There was a musky dampness to the room and a sickly sweet aroma lingering in the air that he recognized as the scent of a brewing thunderstorm.

He didn't care if the most violent storm of the century was about to unleash; he was getting out of here now.

He moved his limbs to stretch the ache out of them while he took another moment to survey his surroundings. Where was he? In some sort of crude hunting lodge, and although it didn't look familiar, he couldn't dismiss the possibility that he was still on Darnley grounds or somewhere close.

His steps were unsteady as he made his way toward the door and he had to pause another moment to gather his wits, no easy task to accomplish while his head was pounding with the force of a blasting cannon. His legs were still painfully stiff as well. They'd take a while to loosen up after having been bound for hours. Or was it days already? The last he remembered, he was drinking that odd-tasting wine by the pond. He'd gone swimming and then come out of the water to help set out the picnic fare. He'd taken off his soaked shirt and spread it out with the rest of the clothes his siblings had left in the sun to dry.

His pants had been soaked as well, but he hadn't taken them off. Indeed, not! He glanced down. Good, he still had them on, but he wore nothing else. The pants were a little damp, which meant he'd only been unconscious for a few hours at most.

Where are my boots?

He'd taken them off before swimming with his siblings.

He took another long breath, forcing his muddled brain to think. Were his brothers and sisters safe? And what about Rose? Were any of them hurt? Or held captive along with him?

He needed a pistol. He hadn't left his in his boot, had he? No, he hadn't thought he'd require one at the pond.

The possibility that his loved ones were in danger got him moving again. Using care to be quiet, he attempted to open the door. To his surprise, it was unlocked and opened easily, but it hadn't been oiled in ages and made a loud squeaking noise. "So much for taking anyone by surprise," he muttered, disgusted with himself and the uncooperative door.

But no one responded to the sound. He shook his head, now thoroughly bemused.

Where are the guards?

Am I alone?

He made his way down the narrow hallway toward what appeared to be the kitchen, moving with stealth and stopping to search each room along the way. If his siblings were taken hostage, he might find them tied up in one of these small chambers.

The entire place was small, no more than four tiny rooms in all, none of them locked, and it didn't take him very long to search each one.

Not a sibling to be found.

A good sign? Or did it spell disaster?

He had only the kitchen left to search. The short hairs on the back of his neck immediately began to prickle as he approached. Someone was in there.

Friend or foe?

He hoped it was foe. He needed to pound his fists into some blackguard's face, if only to relieve his own frustration. Who had abducted him and why?

He crept in, keeping to the shadows, which was easy to do because the room was dark and had several nooks and angled walls. He frowned, seeing no one at first, then heard a soft sob emanating from one of the kitchen nooks. He made his way toward the sound. *Rose!* Sparing a mere moment to assess the danger—or lack thereof—he hurried to her side.

Indeed, he wasn't alone.

No, not alone. But this was worse. Rose had been taken, too. And still no guards close by.

What in blazes is going on?

She was tied to a chair, a handkerchief covering her mouth. Her head was craned awkwardly to one side and her eyes were closed. He noted the glint of tears trailing down her cheeks.

"It's me, sweetheart. Julian." He knelt beside her and touched her lightly on the shoulder to gain her attention.

Her eyes widened in fear the moment his fingers touched her skin.

She squirmed and tried to scream, but her throat was obviously dry and the hoarse yelp that sprang from her lips was mostly muffled by the cloth over her mouth. "It's me," he repeated, hoping to calm her before her soft cries alerted the fiends, wherever they were. "Rose, I won't hurt you. I'm going to remove the gag at your mouth first, but you mustn't make another sound."

She recognized his voice and nodded.

He kept talking softly because she was still quite unsettled, not that he blamed her in the least. As he untied the handkerchief from her mouth, she began to tug at her ropes in a desperate struggle to break free. "Hush, sweetheart. You'll only hurt yourself. I'll get you out. Trust me."

"I do," she said the moment she could talk, although her voice was little more than a strained croak.

But at least she was able to talk and he hoped that she knew more than he did about their circumstances. "Did you see what happened to my brothers and sisters? Are they here? I couldn't find them."

"They're safe at Darnley Cottage. I promise." She appeared ready to burst into tears, not that he would blame her, for even he was also on edge and utterly confused.

"You promise? How can you know for certain that they're safe?" He eyed her curiously while untying the bindings at her wrist. She seemed to be as frightened of him as she was of their captors. No, he'd been drugged and was still off his stride. She had no reason to be afraid of him.

"I... I saw them. Those ruffians only took you and me." Her eyes widened and the pulse at the base of her throat began to throb wildly.

He gently rubbed his thumb along that errant pulse in the hope that it might soothe her, but the gesture only seemed to make matters worse, so he stopped. "Why you? Do you believe your pottery ruffians are behind this scheme?"

"I... I don't... I'm not sure. But it makes sense of a sort, doesn't it?" She nodded emphatically.

In truth, it made no sense whatsoever. Sir Milton Aubrey, the fiend responsible for the sabotage of her kiln, could not possibly be so demented as to attempt this abduction. The last Julian had heard, the man had run off to cower in some remote corner of the world.

And why weren't there any guards? Or locked doors?

This scheme had been so incompetently carried out he dismissed the possibility that Napoleon's agents were involved. Nor was this a hoax. So what was the reason? "We have to get out of here before whoever is behind this mischief returns."

"No! I mean..." Rose glanced at the window panes, her attention caught by the patter of rain against the glass. "We can't go out there. We'll be soaked."

He shook his head. "What's a few drops compared to the danger of remaining here?" Obviously, she wasn't thinking straight. Poor thing, she'd had a bad fright. "We must go while we can."

Thunder rumbled in the distance.

"I... I... think we ought to stay. They aren't coming back and there's a storm approaching. Look how dark the sky has become."

He ignored her comment, for there was no telling what their abductors might do or when they might return. Rose may have been drugged well after him, but she had definitely lost consciousness for a period of time, he could tell by the condition of her eyes. Whatever plans she thought she'd overheard could have been changed a dozen times and she wouldn't know it.

He strode to the window and carefully peered out, first surveying the grounds by the door where a guard would logically be positioned. Still no one in sight. He looked upward to the gathering swirls of dark gray and the more ominous purple-black clouds in the distance. "Just our luck," he grumbled, securing the window so that it would remain shut as the wind gusted, "storm of the century."

The strength of the gusts had picked up, forcing air to whistle down the chimney. Rain now pelted the window panes and rattled the jambs with torrential force. Surely their guards would come inside soon. Not even beasts could stay out in this weather. "We'll find shelter somewhere close by. Somewhere safe."

Rose now stood beside him, leaning against the wall for support as she followed his gaze to the more ominous storm clouds in the distance. They would soon be caught in a heavier downpour. "They've gone," she insisted, casting worried glances between him and the rain pounding on the window. "We're on our own... and... we'd hear them if they came back, wouldn't we? They wouldn't bother to be quiet because they'd think we were still tied up."

He sighed and did his best to keep his voice gentle despite his exasperation. "Rose, we're in danger so long as we remain here. I may be able to get the better of one or two of our abductors, but what if there are a dozen men and they're all carrying weapons?"

Her lips tipped upward at the corners in a hesitant smile and her gaze turned soft and worshipful. "I think you could vanquish every one of those rogues. There's no one smarter or braver than you. I feel quite safe and protected when I'm with you."

He groaned and closed his eyes while struggling to contain his urges. He wanted to take Rose in his arms and kiss her into tomorrow. Hell, he just wanted to take Rose... into his bed. Into his heart. No, she was there already. *Bloody nuisance.* When had that happened? "Flattery will get you everywhere, but I beg to differ. You're not safe at all, especially not from me. Do you have any idea what you do to me?"

"No, but I hope you'll show me."

"Rose, don't make this harder than it needs to be. I have no wish to ruin you."

Her smile faded. "I'm ruined already. Alone in a cabin with you? And you're indecently dressed. If word gets out, I'll be as popular as a leper among society. I don't care for my own circumstances. Being shunned will allow me to concentrate on my pottery business, but the gossip will tarnish my sisters, and they've done nothing to deserve the insults they'll face. I fear for them."

"All the more reason for us to leave right now. We'll find our way back to Darnley Cottage before any outsiders realize we were ever gone." He cupped his hand against her cheek, loving the soft feel of her skin and the way she warmed to his touch. "I'd never abandon you to suffer the consequences alone. You know that, don't you? You needn't fret on that account."

Her eyes rounded in surprise. "Are you suggesting that you'd marry me if necessary?"

"You're my sister's best friend and obviously loved by all my siblings. You're kind and talented and beautiful. Lord, you're so beautiful you take my breath away." He lowered his lips to hers and kissed her lightly on the mouth. Thunder rolled overhead. Lightning struck nearby. More thunder and lightning erupted within him. "Don't allow me to kiss you again. I don't think I'll have the power to stop." He tore his gaze away from her beckoning lips and moved away to gather a few supplies to be used for their escape.

Curiously, the hunting lodge was quite well stocked with the sort of fare one might find in a fine country home. He paused a moment and frowned again. Their abductors were remarkably refined. Indeed, their tastes were far too refined for blackguards. "Rose, tell me everything you know about what happened to us over these past few hours."

She let out a soft *eep.* "I don't know anything."

He paused in gathering their supplies and gave her an encouraging smile. "Yes, you do. You've already told me that the villains only took the two of us and left my siblings safe."

"Um, yes. Truly, they are safe."

He smiled again to coax her into talking. "And…"

She rubbed her hands along the fabric of her gown. "And then we were here."

"But they'd drugged me first, which means someone tampered with the picnic basket and got to the wine bottle before it was sent down to us. This was not the work of an outsider. Someone inside the household was involved in this plot. But it still doesn't make sense. If they were after me, why take you? The same is true for the other possibility. If they were after you, why take me as well?"

She now clasped her hands together and swallowed hard. "Perhaps they were afraid you'd follow them and find me."

He arched an eyebrow. "So they brought me along, thereby making certain I would find you? Rose, it still doesn't make any sense." He ran a hand through his hair in frustration. "And what about these supplies?"

She swallowed again. "What about them?"

Was she being purposely dense or had the sedative affected her badly? Or did she know more than she was telling him? He studied the room once more, his gaze coming to rest on the storage chest that served as a window seat. "Do you suppose we might find a shirt and a pair of boots tucked in here for me?"

Rose shook her head in vehement denial and promptly sat down on the chest. She began to nibble her lip. The window seat was an obvious place to sit on a gloriously sunny day, but right now the window was rattling so hard it threatened to break the glass panes. The spot was not safe. Rose was no fool, so why was she suddenly sitting there?

He gazed at her and then shifted his attention to the supplies he'd just gathered and set upon the table. A lantern, matches, bread that was still fresh. So was the cheese. He crossed to the cupboard and began to forage, finding a large tin. He shook it. "Let's see what's in here. Ah, currant scones."

No one made currant scones as well as Florence, the Darnley

cook. He took a bite of one to test it. "Blast."

"What's wrong?" Rose was still fretting, not only nipping at her luscious lower lip but wringing her hands as well.

"Everything about this scheme feels odd. I have no doubt our cook made these. So why would our extremely loyal, would-never-betray-the-family, long-time household retainer happen to bake up a fresh batch and store them here?"

Rose paled.

He eyed her curiously. What did she know that he didn't? "Rose, get up."

She stopped wringing her hands and curled them tightly on the edge of the window seat. "I'd rather not. I suddenly feel quite weak."

He plucked her off the chest, but held onto her on the chance she truly was feeling poorly, which he doubted, for her cheeks that were ashen only moments ago now blazed a hot pink.

He lifted the lid off the chest with one hand and peered inside. "Damn it, these are mine." He released her and knelt down to sift through the contents, picking up his boots, shirt, jacket, and cravat to hold up to her view. He dug down deeper and found a comb, razor, and strop. Unfortunately, no pistol. "What is going on? Everything in here is mine. Even more curious, there's a change of clothes in here for you as well."

Her silence was palpable, cutting through the thick air like a knife. He dropped the contents back into the chest and stood to face her. "Rose? You're going to cut your lip if you chew on it any harder."

"I... I can't."

"What? Betray Nicola's scheme? My aunt and uncle were in on it as well, I assume, for she would have needed their permission to use one of their carriages to transport us here. Perhaps they all rode along in several carriages and made a jolly good outing of it." He tried to stifle his mounting anger for he had no wish to scare Rose. The poor girl was also a victim and deserved his comfort and protection.

Her eyes widened and she gasped. "How can you be certain?"

"They've made no secret of their desperate desire to keep me away from Valentina. Of course I know. The entire family disapproves of her." He groaned. "Rose, you must have suspected something. Were all my siblings involved? Even little Emily?"

"No, she went in to take her nap before the effects of the wine overcame you. She's completely unaware." She began to wring her hands again. "Well, mostly unaware. She might have overheard a snippet or two of the plot, but I'm sure she didn't understand it."

"You must have overheard some of it, too. Obviously not all of it or you would have warned me, even if it was only to save your pretty neck." No, he wasn't being fair to accuse Rose. "Sorry, I spoke out of turn. I know you're confused and trying to be loyal to my sister. Loyalty is a commendable trait, but it is misplaced here. My family is to blame and will be punished."

She frowned at him. "Will you take no responsibility for this situation? Granted, your family might have stepped a little over the line."

He laughed in disbelief. "A little over the line? Surely you jest? They are leaps and bounds across any possible—"

"Them? And what of your behavior?" Rose tipped her chin up in defiance. "Your siblings love you and only wish to see you happy."

"They have an odd way of showing it. Come to think of it, why are you still protecting them? You ought to be furious about what they did to you. Or have you not been quite truthful with me?"

She emitted a huff of indignation. "Me? How am I to blame for your poor judgment?"

"My..." He raked a hand through his hair. Of course, they all had to be wondering how he could be so idiotic as to worship Valentina. He knew his family loved him, but it was a little frightening to realize the extent to which they'd go to protect him from himself. They'd drugged and abducted him! No wonder their grandfather had referred to him and his siblings as little savages.

In truth, they were, but so was his uncle, that old badger. Julian had dismissed the wild stories he'd heard about the earl's exploits in his younger days as mere exaggeration, but no longer. "Rose, I need to know all of it now. Were you in on this scheme to some extent? Perhaps hoping to trap me into marriage? Tell me the truth and I'll go easy on you. But you must tell me everything. You must have been aware that something was going on. Nicola adores you. She'd keep nothing from you."

Her eyes widened and her chin began to quiver. *Oh, hell.* He'd pushed her too hard and she was about to cry. "Not this!" she said with a gasp. "Not drugging you and bringing you here. And I would never agree to being stranded here with you. How dare you presume such a thing! How dare you believe I'm a base creature who would scheme to trap you into marriage! I'd never do such a thing."

She was working herself into a temper and he was fully to blame. Now that she was riled, not even his attempt at apology slowed her down.

"What's happened is a mere inconvenience to you, but the consequences are disastrous for me," she said, her hands now curled into fists. "Surely, you understand this. I wish to marry for love, not out of necessity and shame. I wish to marry a man who loves me with all his heart and looks forward to sharing the rest of his life with me, not one who'll feel resentful whenever he looks upon me."

He expected tears, for he had been a bit harsh with the girl. Instead she frowned, regarding him as though this mess was one of his own making and entirely his fault. "If you knew how much they disliked your icy countess, then why did you continue to court her? You obviously love your family and care very deeply for their feelings. More important, why did you kiss me? Or tell me that I take your breath away?" She appeared to grow angrier as she spoke. "You have a scheme as well." Her chin was no longer quivering but tipped upward in defiance. "Kindly keep me out of your family disagreements. I don't wish to be hurt by whatever game it is *you're* playing."

He raked his fingers through his hair again, irritated that she'd managed to cast the blame on him and not his outrageously impulsive family. "It's no game." But he couldn't tell her the real purpose of his courtship of Valentina. "Rose, you'll just have to trust that I know what I'm doing. I promise you that I shall make things right in due course."

He sighed and shook his head. "I know you're angry with me and although you're still protecting them, I expect you're furious with my family for dragging you into their nefarious plot."

She studied her toes for a long moment, then raised her pained gaze to meet his steely stare. "I'm sorry I ever met you. I wish none of this had happened. I was managing quite well on my own and didn't need you to further complicate my life. And I certainly don't need to marry you to validate my own worth."

Rose was right. He'd unfairly judged her, assuming she'd gone along with his family's scheme in order to trap him into marriage, but it wasn't so. Rose wasn't that sort of girl. She had spirit and talent and so much heart. "I'm truly sorry for what I said. I had no right to accuse you. It's obvious you're innocent in all this and merely trying to protect my loved ones from my wrath."

She opened her mouth to respond and then snapped it shut, so he continued. "It's commendable of you. I know you like my family, but what they did to both of us, especially you, is unpardonable."

He crossed his arms over his chest and stared down at her. She was of average height and he stood a head taller, but he liked the way she still managed to stand her ground. "They went to a lot of effort to accomplish very little. They would have delayed my return to London for only another day or two at most."

Rose nodded. "They would have come up with another plot to detain you by then."

"I suppose I'll find out soon enough what it is they intend to do next. But getting you safely back to Darnley Cottage is the problem at hand. How do I accomplish it without causing scandal? We'll have to be careful and keep out of sight. Can't have a villager or a gentleman walking these scenic trails recognize us."

"Um, do you know where we are?"

He nodded. "On Darnley property. My uncle's hunting lodge, no doubt. He hasn't used it in years, but it has obviously been dusted and restocked. Recently." He returned to the chest, donned his boots and the fresh shirt conveniently provided for him, and then stared out the window again. "Since the blackguards turned out to be my own family, I suppose there's no need for us to escape until the weather improves."

He lit the lantern as the darker clouds approached, turning the late afternoon sky as black as night. "Make yourself comfortable,

Rose. Are you cold?" He held out a chair and motioned for her to sit. When she did so, he returned to the chest and grabbed his jacket to tuck it over her trembling shoulders.

He was furious, but also elated.

A night alone with Rose.

Could he keep his hands off her?

Hell no.

CHAPTER 9

"WHAT WILL YOU do to your siblings?" Rose asked, taking a seat at the kitchen table while Julian tossed some more logs into the hearth to stoke the fire, for a chill had set in with the arrival of the storm. It was nearing supper time she supposed, but couldn't be sure because they had no clock and the midsummer sun that might have guided her was nowhere to be seen. The rain was still coming down in buckets, and the flashes of lightning and thunder rumbling in the distance would be upon them soon. "They meant you no harm."

Rose moved her stool closer to the hearth, eager for the warmth of the flames to chase away the damp ache still in her bones. The jostling she'd received during the carriage ride had left bruises on her arms and legs, and her attempts to free herself from her bindings had left chafe marks on her wrists. All in all, the damage was not serious, but Julian had noticed these marks immediately and been angered by them.

Perhaps they wouldn't have been so obvious if her skin wasn't such a delicate shade of pink. She'd had to assure him they were nothing of consequence, because with each passing moment, he appeared to grow more tense.

"No harm? Other than almost killing me with that overdose and setting you up for ruin?" Julian set aside the andiron and returned to her side, a furious expression on his face. He groaned and ran a hand along the nape of his neck. "Hell, Rose. This is a mess. The younger ones aren't so much the problem, for I know they didn't think up this idiotic plan." He absently rubbed the nape of his neck again, a sign of his consternation. "Nicola must have concocted it, and I don't know if I can ever forgive her for that."

Rose's stomach began to churn, for she had been the original instigator and had helped Nicola come up with their first plan as well as propose other options. But this wasn't the time to confess her involvement to Julian. He was clearly enraged, but not at her. Thank goodness. She couldn't blame him for being on edge and angry with his entire family, including his aunt and uncle. However, since an earl outranked a viscount, there wasn't much Julian could do by way of punishing the elders in his family. For this reason, he was focusing his anger on Nicola. "You must forgive her," Rose insisted, although there might have been a little pleading in her tone as well. "Losing your love would devastate her."

"Still loyal to Nicola despite all she's done to you?" He set the last of the currant scones on a plate and settled his large frame on a stool beside hers. He offered to cut it in half to share but she declined. She'd had one a few moments earlier and couldn't handle any more to eat. Her stomach was still unsettled because of the effect of the drug still in her veins. As well, she was fretting over being part of this misguided plot they'd hatched. What would Julian do to her when he found out the true extent of her involvement?

She declined the tea he offered her. "Yes. She's my best friend and always will be. She wishes we were sisters, she's told me so quite often."

"I know how much she cares for you, but there is no excuse for what she's done. Her affection for you doesn't make it right."

"I know." Rose stifled a yawn, not yet able to shake off the effects of the drug, but there was more to do than think of sleep. In truth, attempting to sleep while her body was so lethargic held no appeal for her. Besides, there were things to occupy her time in the lodge. The place was well stocked with food, blankets, and other useful supplies to peruse.

Thinking of sleep would force her to think about sleeping arrangements, and since Julian had broken the cot in the room where he'd been bound, there was only one other cot left in the small chamber beside it. Only one narrow, rickety bed for the two of them to share. Of course, not at the same time. They'd either have to take turns sleeping in it or Julian would have to make a pallet for himself beside the kitchen hearth and sleep on the floor along with the mice and other vermin that had taken up occupancy while the hunting lodge sat unused.

The thought of those creatures creeping up Julian's boots as he slept on the floor caused a shiver of disgust to run up her spine. She couldn't allow him to spend the night in such discomfort.

They'd have to share the cot.

Not at the same time, of course, she reminded herself, refusing to consider the possibility of sleeping in his arms, their bodies entangled as she lay atop him, her head nestled against his golden chest. Should she suggest it? Never! She simply couldn't. But would he?

"You're tired," he said, staring at her when she yawned again. "Come along, I'll set up the cot for you. We haven't discussed sleeping arrangements."

"Is there a need?" She blushed, never considering that he had the power to read her mind. But he must have known what she was thinking or he wouldn't have raised the matter now. Were her thoughts so clearly written on her face? "Separate arrangements, of course."

"Of course." The corners of his eyes crinkled as he smiled. "Did you think I'd suggest otherwise?"

This was a moment when she ought to keep her mouth shut and allow the question to quietly disappear into the night unanswered, but most Farthingales were not discreet—in truth, the word did not appear in the Farthingale vocabulary—so she attempted to respond with full knowledge that it was a terribly wrong thing to do. "Um, considering your past behavior toward me... and your lack of... because you kissed me in places..."

"On your body?" He was still smiling and his eyes were now dark and gleaming, or was it merely a trick of the firelight?

"I meant *places*... such as the library... and again here in this lodge."

The man was now shamelessly grinning at her. "Ah, I thought you were referring to the parts of your body. All quite glorious, by the way. My mistake."

"Yes, indeed. You are quite mistaken." She swallowed hard,

because the memory of his lips against her skin was making her hot and decidedly uncomfortable. The mere thought of what he'd done to her in the earl's library was sending her into improper spasms of elation. "My body parts, specifically my breasts, are not your property. Neither the right one nor the left one. You may not touch either of them."

"That's quite specific. Any other instructions about what not to do with your breasts? Do they have a vote in the matter or is your edict irreversible and final?" He stood quite close now, close enough for her to feel the heat radiating off his big body. Or was all the heat coming from her own body, which was now a liquid pool of fire?

Hot, buttered crumpets!

She was in deep, deep trouble. Not from Julian, of course. Despite his jest, he was a gentleman to the core and would keep his hands off her if she requested that he do so. But she didn't wish him to do so, and therein lay the problem, for all she wanted to do was grab him by the lapels and sprinkle hot kisses down his body and… and… then set him loose to do whatever he wished to do upon her body.

She didn't know what he would do, only that she was certain to like it. "I'm not in the habit of giving any of my body parts a say, other than my brain, of course." *Which isn't functioning at the moment.* "Or my heart." She emitted a soft, shattered sigh. "Too often, my heart."

"Rose," he said with a tender ache to his voice, "I'm a beast for teasing you when you've been nothing but sweet and generous to me and my family."

"No, I'm silly and frivolous and quite at fault. In truth, I'm uncomfortable trapped here alone with you. Or rather, I ought to be uncomfortable, but I'm not." She glanced at him in desperation. "What I mean to say is… I ought not be feeling safe and protected with you. It's going to get me into trouble." She stared down at her hands, which were clasped together and resting on the table top.

He set his large hands atop hers, fully enveloping them in the warmth of his rough palms. Despite being raised in elegance and refinement, he had a wonderful ruggedness about him that distinguished him from the London dandies. "Look at me, Rose."

She shook her head furiously. "I can't."

His thumb began to move in gentle, stroking swirls across the top of her hand. "Why can't you look at me?"

She closed her eyes and stifled a sigh. "Because I'm not that strong. I can't resist you, Julian." She licked her lips. "Obviously this is the reason why unmarried young ladies are warned never to be alone with handsome gentlemen such as you. You're irresistible."

He choked lightly and then chuckled. "Thank you."

She kept her eyes closed, still afraid to open them and fall prey to his allure. "I didn't intend it as a compliment."

"It doesn't sound like an insult."

She nodded. "I didn't mean it as an insult either. It is simply a statement of fact. You're every young woman's dream and you're here alone with me. Were you to set your mind to a nefarious purpose—"

"Such as seducing you?"

She nodded again. "I'm afraid you'd succeed."

He tipped her chin up and urged her to open her eyes, which she did reluctantly. "Rose, I find you irresistible as well, but I will sleep right here on the kitchen floor and not make any untoward advances. It won't be easy for me. In truth, it will take a monumental effort because I think you're beautiful in every way."

She *eeped*.

"I want to take you in my arms and hold you through the night. I want to do much more than simply hold you through the night. All sorts of things. Naughty things to your delightful body."

Her eyes widened in surprise. She meant to chastise him for his presumption, but she was curious to find out about these forbidden intimacies. She'd had a brief introduction in the earl's library and quite liked it. "Such as?"

He laughed. "Oh, no. Not telling you. Perhaps in time I'll have the pleasure of showing you. But not tonight. No. And stop looking at me that way or I'll never be able to keep my hands off you. Let's speak of safer topics."

She arched an eyebrow. "The weather?"

"Yes, that's suitably dull."

This time she laughed. "Very well. Um, it's frightfully wet outside. Now your turn. Give me a dull comment in return."

"Your gown is still damp from our earlier frolic in the pond. You ought to change into the dry clothes our 'abductors' conveniently provided for you."

That didn't sound very dull. In truth, it sounded quite dangerous for it involved taking off her clothes, and even though it involved putting fresh, dry clothes back on, she wasn't certain that she'd ever get that far while Julian stood on the other side of the door. A door that had no lock. "I can't."

"Why not?" His expression was one of innocent concern, which made her wonder whether she was the only one having these indecent thoughts. He had teased her and complimented her, and made an occasional suggestive comment, but not actually behaved improperly in any way.

In fact, his proper manner was beginning to grate.

If she was so irresistible, why was he able to resist her?

More to the point, why was she irritated by his desire to be noble and protective? "I can't reach the buttons down the back. These gowns are designed for ladies who have maids at their beck and call."

He cleared his throat. "I'll act as your maid. Just the buttons you can't reach. And I'll close my eyes the entire time."

"It won't work. How will you see the buttons to unfasten them if your eyes are closed?"

"I'll feel around for... ah, I see. You're right. That obviously won't work." He rubbed his hand across the back of his neck. He was doing that a lot lately.

"You see? That's why I'm in so much trouble. I refuse to consider what might happen if you touched me. I'm afraid it would be something wonderful that would lead to something else wonderful and—"

"Rose, you're getting off our dull conversation. Kindly steer yourself back to it. No more talk of taking off your clothes. I'm sorry I mentioned it, but I don't like that you're still wearing a wet gown."

"It's merely damp now. I'll sit close to the fire until it dries. It's early yet. I won't go to sleep before then."

He nodded. "That's a workable solution. Keep my jacket tucked over your shoulders. You'll need the warmth."

She smiled. "It carries your scent. It's a nice scent. Clean and manly. I like being surrounded by it."

His hand went to his neck again and began to rub. "Do you enjoy needlepoint? Tell me what you're working on that can be described to me in yawn-inspiring, lengthy detail."

She laughed heartily. "You are a glutton for punishment, but I'm afraid I must disappoint you. I'm dismal with needle and thread, and not working on any needlepoint designs at the moment. Or ever. But I will happily list all the designs my aunt Hortensia has completed and describe in very dull detail where each one is on proud display throughout our townhouse."

She raised her hands and grinned as she prepared to count them off. "She's a tigress with *petit-point* and spends much of her day in that endeavor when she isn't otherwise occupied in meddling. My family happens to have a talent for meddling that rivals yours."

"Which explains why you accepted my family's outrageous actions with equanimity." He took hold of her hands once more and again began to absently trace circles on her skin with his thumbs.

They were supposed to be engaging in dull conversation to keep their minds on safe topics, but Rose knew their attempt was doomed to failure. There was a spark between them, a natural affinity that drew them closer no matter how determined they were to resist. In truth, she wasn't determined at all. "It is a sign that they care."

"Is that supposed to be a gentle reminder? That I should go easy on Nicola?"

"Yes, since you ask. I'm not condoning her actions, mind you." *Since I was the instigator.* "But people make mistakes. There's a difference between actions taken out of love and those taken out of malice."

"I know," he said quietly. "My family means everything to me. But I'm not an infant in leading strings. I'm a bloody viscount. I ought to have their trust and respect."

"Because you're a viscount? It's merely a title."

"They ought to respect me for *me*. I've earned it."

She knew of his prowess on the battlefield and the lives he'd saved because of his intelligence and bravery. She also knew that he was adept at business and had worked hard to maintain the family's holdings after his parents had suddenly died. "Your father would have been very proud of you."

He was admirable in so many ways. For this reason, if there was something to be learned about what went on between a man and a woman, she wanted Julian to be her teacher. In truth, she couldn't imagine feeling this way about any other man. How could she when he overwhelmed her senses?

Everything about him was a jolt to her composure, the way his body moved with the grace and sleek power of a wolf, the way his eyes shone with kindness and humor, the way his mouth curved in a slightly lopsided smile that was at the same time boyish and quietly seductive.

What confused her was his connection to Valentina. Despite his good looks and obvious charm, he wasn't the rakish sort. She sensed he was a man of honor and would be loyal and true to the woman he loved.

So why was he holding her hands?

Why had he kissed her with the force of storm waves crashing to shore? Goodness, he'd completely swept her away on a tide of passion. No prim kisses for her. No, indeed. Each touch of their lips sent her reeling and each time he put his arms around her, she felt drawn into a swirling pool of pleasure.

Even now, his eyes were a maelstrom of smoky desire, as though he wanted to swallow her up whole and do all those naughty things to her he'd hinted about a moment ago. Not for one night, but for a lifetime. She understood expressions; she had to in order to capture the essence of a person when drawing portraits.

Julian was looking at her in an I-want-you-as-my-mate way.

She shook her head to clear her muddled thoughts. He couldn't be. He was on the verge of proposing to Valentina. His actions simply didn't make sense.

What was she missing? "Julian, I think we must speak of an unsafe topic."

He was instantly wary. She felt his tension through his fingers that remained entwined in hers. It was telling that he hadn't drawn them away. "Such as?"

"Your countess." There had to be a logical explanation. He

couldn't possibly love that woman. So why was he courting her? That he was so attentive and fawning over her like a doting dandy simply felt amiss. Was she blackmailing him?

"That topic is out of bounds."

"Why?" He wasn't the sort who would care if sordid secrets about him came out in the open. Nor did he seem the sort to allow the person who'd leaked those secrets to go unscathed.

"Enough, Rose. I will not discuss it." Until this moment, Julian had been gentle with her, but there was no mistaking the hard, lethal edge to his words. She was stepping into forbidden territory, and he would not indulge her trespass.

She'd seen that flash of steel in his gaze when he'd taken it upon himself to deal with the saboteur of her kiln. Those who crossed him would not escape punishment. That's why she was so worried about Nicola. Julian loved his sister, but he was going to make her suffer before he ultimately forgave her.

Would he do the same to her when he found out about her involvement in their scheme? She shook out of the thought and concentrated on him, and that brought her back to Valentina.

Why pretend she was the love of his life? What hold did she have over him? Since Rose had ruled out the possibility that it was a deep, dark secret about himself, it had to be someone else's secret he was protecting. Someone he loved. A family member? No, it didn't seem likely. A friend, perhaps? A good friend, one he held dear to his heart and felt honor bound to rescue.

Oh, dear. That friend must have gotten himself into serious trouble.

But what sort of trouble? Murder? She dismissed the possibility. Julian would not condone cold-blooded killing. Still, this secret was something dire, something so awful that his friend had begged for Julian's help.

It still didn't explain why Julian had agreed to sacrifice his own happiness and chain himself to the horrid countess for the rest of his days. How loyal did his friend expect him to be?

"You're nibbling your lip," he said with a groan, interrupting her concentration.

"I'm thinking about you." This mystery merited investigation.

She'd talk the problem over with her sisters as soon as she returned to London. They'd come up with a plan. She'd invite Nicola into the discussion, assuming Julian allowed his sister to return to London as well. Right now, he seemed inclined to banish her to the Scottish highlands, to a remote family property where she might never be seen or heard from again. "Your actions simply don't make sense."

"Rose, I will not discuss it." He drew away and began to pace across the kitchen like an agitated wolf locked in a cage, silently stalking from end to end in an obvious attempt to subdue his anger.

What had she done? Poked a finger into a raw, open wound? She wasn't about to stop. "There is an attraction between us that cannot be denied."

He glowered at her. "Don't make too much of it."

"I'm not. You forget that I'm an artist, that I understand the nuances of a person's expressions. That's how I distill the essence of a person and capture him or her on canvas. I know what's fake and what's real."

"And?"

She groaned softly. "You're real. Everything wonderful about you is real. There's a natural valor that emanates from within you, shining outward with a golden warmth. As for your countess, there's a brutal coldness that pours out of her in icy waves. The sun dies in her presence."

"That's rather dramatic. You don't know her." He sounded unconvincing.

"Nor do I wish to know her. More important, I sense that you would have nothing to do with her unless there was a compelling reason. Whose life are you trying to save?"

He strode forward and loomed over her, his face so close to hers that she was almost blinded by the flash of anger in his eyes. "Stop. I'm not your bloody concern. My friends are not your bloody concern. The discussion is over."

His warning was even more proof that the situation was dire. She returned his glower.

"Rose, you cannot speak of this to anyone. Not my sister. Not your sisters. Not anyone."

"We Farthingales are mostly wonderful, but we do have some

irritating qualities. For one, we don't like to be ordered about or told what we can and cannot do or told to stop looking at a puzzle when it's so obviously begging to be solved."

He was still looming over her, his every muscle straining. She wanted to set her hands on him and feel every flex and tug. However, he looked angry enough to bite her hand if she dared raise it to touch him. "That's more than one irritating quality. I believe you've mentioned at least three."

"I understand that you're hoping to intimidate me by hovering over me in that imposing and frowning manner, but I must tell you that your nearness is quite thrilling to me and is shooting delightful tingles of desire up and down my spine." She sighed. "I know you won't hurt me, Julian. You may kiss me, if you wish. I'd rather like that."

He drew away as though scalded and cursed under his breath as he resumed pacing like a caged wolf. "For pity's sake, Rose. You mustn't tell me such things. You don't even realize what the word *desire* implies. Desire is..." He was furiously rubbing the nape of his neck and still stalking from one end of the kitchen to the other. "Desire is hot and sweaty, it leaves you breathless and spent."

"In each other's arms?"

He shot fireballs at her with his angrily blazing eyes. "I am not going to teach you about desire. Not tonight, that's for damn certain."

"But you will another time?" She knew that she was pushing him over the edge of his endurance, but someone had to break through his wall of reserve and find out what was really going on. She understood that he was involved in something dangerous. But he wasn't the danger, certainly not to her. The countess was. She knew to keep her distance from that heartless woman.

"Not if you continue to irritate me. Go to bed, Rose. Take whatever you need to make yourself comfortable and then barricade your door."

"Against you?"

A muscle twitched in his jaw.

She shrugged. "Very well, but there will be no barricades between us, Julian. My door and my heart shall always be open to you."

ROSE WAS A snoop, and Julian knew she was going to interfere in these last few weeks of his investigation unless he dealt with her now and stopped her misguided attempt. He had two choices. The first was to tell her the truth and swear her to secrecy, which wasn't a choice at all since he didn't have the authority to disclose the details of the investigation or even reveal that one was being conducted.

Even if Prinny gave him the right to disclose certain details to Rose, what assurance did he have that she wouldn't tell her large and intrusive family? Or, heaven forbid, his?

The second choice was to push her away, to dash all hope of there ever being something between the two of them. It was the only sensible solution, but could he feign disinterest when every thrumming part of him ached to have her? This wasn't merely a passing fancy, but a throbbing, pulsing ache that spanned universes and would not be restrained by the boundaries of time.

Bloody nuisance.

This was Rose, his annoying sister's best friend. A young innocent who had yet to complete her first London season and had never been kissed by any man except him. He suppressed the surge of possessive pride that swelled within his chest at the mere thought.

No, he refused to give the girl any power over him.

Love was an impossible complication. How hard could it be *not* to fall in love? He'd endured severe hardships on the battlefield. He could manage this.

"The girl's a bloody nuisance," he muttered under his breath, watching Rose gather her blankets and the dry gown that was still neatly folded inside the window seat that served as a storage chest.

She must have heard his grumble and glanced up at him. "Did you say something to me?"

His heart tugged at the hopeful look she cast him. "No." Now he was just being surly. In his own defense, the less he said to her the better. He had very little resolve when it came to Rose, especially now that she was regarding him with a forlorn look in her big blue eyes. *Damn it.* They were glistening with unshed tears.

Had he been too gruff with her?

He could apologize and sweep her into his arms, kiss her soundly on the lips.

No! What was wrong with him? He was about to botch a yearlong investigation because of this innocent.

"Good night, Julian."

He sighed. The bundles in her arms were almost as big as she was. "Let me help you with those."

She drew away. "I can manage on my own. They aren't heavy."

"I know." But they were bulky and awkward. He took the blankets and gown out of her arms. "I'll set them on the bed and then take my leave of you. Simple enough."

"I suppose that's how you want your life to be, nice and simple," she retorted, obviously still stinging from his words. "You'll never have it if you marry the countess."

"Message received, Rose. You needn't repeat the warning." They entered the spare room containing the cot and he dumped the blankets on it. Taking more care with her gown since it was the only decent change of clothes she had, he set it neatly over the back of the one chair in the small room. "Go to sleep. Stop meddling."

"I'm sorry. You're right, of course." She turned to face him as she hastily shrugged out of his jacket. "Here, you've given me all the blankets so take this back for yourself."

"I'll be fine, Rose. I don't need it."

She continued to hold it out to him. He caught her sweet scent on the fabric, the scent of sunshine and warm breezes and meadow flowers. "Then take one of the blankets," she said, noting his hesitation although she couldn't have understood the reason for it. She was a torment to him. He'd never have a peaceful night's rest while the scent of her clung to him. "You must have something to keep you warm."

He did—the fiery heat of his desire.

He grabbed his jacket out of her outstretched hand and strode out of the chamber, slamming the door behind him in his haste to leave. He needed to be out of there before he was overcome by the temptation to remain. Rose had an inviting way of looking at him that drove him wild.

He tossed his jacket onto the table and went in search of the whiskey bottle he'd noticed tucked away on one of the pantry shelves. He grabbed a glass and the bottle and set both down on the table. He then knelt beside the hearth to stoke the fire once more.

The room was now hot and dry.

Rose was safely abed and knew better than to come out again.

Alone with his turmoil, he unbuttoned his shirt and rolled up the sleeves, deciding against taking it off completely on the chance Rose came out of her room for whatever reason. He poured himself a whiskey and leaned his shoulder against the mantel while he sipped his drink and lost himself in thought. The glass was empty before he knew it so he poured himself another.

The liquid was an opalescent amber under the fire's glow and glistened as he absently twirled it in his hand. The gem-like beauty of the whiskey was illuminated by the flames and somehow reminded him of Rose's beauty, for there was an exquisite, shimmering quality to her features, her hair a luminescent gold, her lips as red as rubies, her eyes as dazzling as sapphires. *Blast!* He was no better than a mewling boy spouting odes to Rose's beauty.

Women did not affect him like this. Never. Why now?

Why Rose? He'd asked the question of himself before and each time ended up scratching his head, for the answer was elusive. He simply felt the way he did because his heart willed it. Not that he was ever in the practice of following his heart. Quite the opposite, he was a creature of reason and logic, save matters concerning Rose.

She wasn't a classic beauty in any sense. Beautiful, to be sure, but in a warm, embracing way that made him want to reach out and hug her. He usually reserved that affection for his family, especially his youngest sisters who were growing up without the attentive care of a doting mother and father.

Rose was naturally welcoming and expressive. A chuckle quietly burst from him as he thought of the girl's attempts at seductive glances, so adorably inept. It was obvious that she'd never known a man's touch, had never felt passion before. She'd tried to look sultry, but instead looked like she'd stepped on a worm. Yet her paltry attempts had done the job, arousing him to fiery heights, only she didn't realize it.

He poured a third drink and then stuffed the cork back in the bottle because the effects of the drug had not completely worked through his system. He'd already passed out once today and had no intention of doing so again.

"Julian?"

He groaned. "I thought you were asleep. You ought to be by now." He dared not look at her in his weakened condition. Lusting and drunk was never a good combination.

Thunder once more rumbled in the distance, a harbinger of the next wave of rain and lightning from the tempest that seemed to be swirling overhead with no intention of abating or moving on. It matched the torment now swirling within his chest and causing his heart to pound in a rampant, tumultuous beat.

"I meant to sleep, but you're right. I ought to have changed out of my damp clothes. They didn't feel quite so bad while I was up and moving about, but the dampness crept into my bones and left me cold once I settled between the sheets. Not even the blankets were enough to warm me." She walked to his side. "I can't reach these last buttons. Will you help me? Here, I'll move my hair out of the way."

He groaned again. "You let down your hair?"

She quirked her head in confusion. "Yes, isn't it obvious?"

Of course it was. His fingers itched to wrap themselves in those long, silken waves. He longed to caress the vibrant curls and watch them spring back softly against her perfect shoulders.

"I couldn't sleep with the pins in it. I would have braided it, but I needed my brush and it's at the bottom of the window chest. Um, I knew you didn't want me to come out of my chamber, so I didn't think there would be any harm in leaving it loose. I intended to fix it in the morning. Then I grew cold and nothing seemed to warm me up. I had to ask for your assistance." He could feel her soft breaths against his shoulder as she rattled on in explanation, obviously feeling as uncomfortable in his presence as he was in hers.

"Um," she said again, sighing, "I'll fetch it now."

"Don't bother. It can wait until morning." He closed his eyes a moment and swallowed hard. "Here, turn your back to me." He set down his empty glass on the mantel. It had been full a moment ago. He shouldn't have drained it so fast.

Drunk.

Lusting.

Soft woman who sparkled like a gemstone standing before him.

With her gown unfastened.

Begging for him to finish the job.

His body heated with such intensity it felt as though the flames crackling in the hearth had leaped out and engulfed him. They hadn't, of course. The heat came from within him, kindled by his own fiery desire.

This will not end well.

Rose made the mistake of turning to face him once he'd accomplished the simple task. He was amazed that he'd managed it, for his hands began to shake the moment his knuckles brushed across her soft flesh and had yet to stop shaking. He was worse than a ten-year-old lad peeking into one of London's pleasure houses. "Thank you." She made the further mistake of smiling up at him.

The gown was loose and falling off her creamy shoulders. Her hair was wild and tumbling down her back in golden waves.

The front of her gown slipped lower, exposing the tops of her breasts. Most women of fashion wore their gowns cut that low, but this was Rose. She had the most beautiful breasts he'd ever seen, and he'd seen many in his wild younger days. Rose's weren't your average sort of beautiful breasts, but the Holy Grail of breasts. Men went on odysseys to search for such perfection, and here she stood before him.

His for the taking.

He took a deep breath. "Good night, Rose. I'll see you in the morning."

That might have been the end of it if the tempest overhead hadn't chosen that moment to unleash its fury. Lightning cracked and thunder boomed almost simultaneously, the strike coming so close it shook the rafters. Rose let out a startled cry and jumped into his open arms, which shouldn't have been open, but somehow were. He'd reached for her the moment the roof had swayed, ready to protect her with his body.

Now she was crushed up against him, the gown slipping even lower as she let go of it to throw her arms around him. They were now skin to skin, hearts pounding and entwined in each other's arms.

As the storm broke loose and wild, so did their passion.

He wasn't so far gone that a simple no would have stopped him. Instead, Rose was whispering yes and "don't you dare stop," so he didn't. He slid the gown off her, leaving her clad only in her camisole, which was sheer and damp. He realized she was tugging at his shirt, so he tossed it off as well and in the same motion lifted her by the waist to balance her on the table while he positioned her legs around his hips and bent his head to sample the Holy Grail.

He hadn't stripped her of the camisole, intending for that flimsy fabric to act as a protective barrier between them, but it was too easily nudged aside by the tug of his finger so that the sleeves fell off her shoulders. A second tug brought the rest of the delicate bodice down with it around her waist. His knuckle grazed over one of her exposed nipples, causing it to pucker into a hard bud. His heartbeat came to a crushing halt. "Sweetheart, you're so beautiful."

She seemed surprised. "Thank you."

He loved how unaffected she was about her striking good looks. "Polite, too," he said with a grin, lowering his head to trail light kisses down the curve of her throat.

Her skin felt satin soft and tasted lightly salty. He moved lower, taking one nipple between his teeth and gently scraping across it, then letting his tongue and lips take over, suckling and swirling over one and then the other until she was hot and writhing and her pink peaks were as hard and erect as he was. "Julian, oh my! Oh, ooh…"

Overhead, thunder and lightning continued to shatter the evening quiet with pounding intensity, but he didn't care and Rose didn't seem to either. Her eyes were closed and mouth slightly parted as she took in each sensation with avid delight. He watched her, drank her in, worked his lips and fingers over her incredibly responsive body and wanted more because he couldn't get enough of her and knew he'd never have his fill of this perfect beauty. She was his.

She had to be his, for all the days of their lives.

His.

No other man's Rose.

His Rose.

His fingers stroked between her thighs. She was already slick and aroused, near to slipping over the edge. So was he, but he wanted her to experience this womanly pleasure, to be guided by his touch, his and only his ever after.

The forces of nature clashed and crashed in a roar, as though a fierce battle were being fought in the sky, but Julian felt oddly at peace. He was with Rose and nothing else mattered. He felt her begin to tremble and swell around his stroking finger and knew that she was about to reach her climax.

"Julian," she said in a throaty whisper, her eyes as wild and beautiful as her glorious mane of golden hair that tumbled over her naked shoulders. She didn't understand what was happening to her, only that his hands and lips were roaming everywhere on her body, guiding her with purposeful abandon to unexplored heights. He loved that she trusted him so completely, that she willingly followed wherever he led, that she trusted him enough to hold nothing back.

He watched in fascination as she responded to his touch with a passionate innocence that stole his breath away, that aroused him and left him as hard as a blacksmith's anvil. He wanted to drive himself inside her willing body. He ached to feel her close around his throbbing member, but he wasn't so far gone as to take that last, irrevocable step.

Not this time. Not while he held back secrets from her.

She dug her fingers into his shoulders and tossed back her head. Soft, breathy moans escaped her lips. She arched her back, allowing him unhampered access to every inch of her body, and then she shattered into a thousand pieces of splendor, a thousand sensations of delight. His heart swelled as he gathered her in his arms and held her close against his chest for an endlessly long moment, his feelings for this innocent so powerful they shattered the walls surrounding his heart.

Rose was now in his heart.

Irrevocably and permanently.

This was the Emory curse, to love once. To love forever. He'd chosen Rose.

But he was still on assignment.

How was he to keep Rose away from Valentina?

How was he to keep himself away from Rose?

Chapter 10

ROSE FELT THE steady beat of Julian's heart against her cheek and the warmth of his strong embrace. His fingers stroked up and down her back, gently caressing her until she floated down from the celestial heights he'd sent her to. Is this how it would always be between them?

She'd tasted whiskey and traces of currant scones on his breath as he'd kissed her on the mouth, his kisses deep and probing and unrestrained. Despite the wild heat in his eyes and the coiled tension in his body, she had not been afraid that he would force her to go beyond what she was willing to do. In truth, she was willing to be led anywhere with him because of the way he held her, his touch always gentle and protective despite his superior strength.

Knowing she was safe with him had allowed her wanton urges to break free, and as he'd kissed a scorching path down her body, she'd done the same in return, making her way along the muscles and musky heat of his chest and shoulders.

The two of them were still in disarray. His shirt was off, his muscled torso in full view, including the scars that again brought an ache to her heart. But those imperfections were what made him perfect. Heroically ideal. There was a wondrous, bronze sheen glowing from him, surely an effect of the firelight.

Her camisole was wrapped around her waist, her own pale body open to his full view. Not that the sheer fabric would have covered much in any event.

His eyes turned smoky green as he studied her. "Trust me, Rose. No matter what you may see or hear once we're back in London."

She hesitated.

He sighed. "I know. I don't deserve it. My actions have been unforgivable, but they're not dishonest. I can't abide dishonesty, for it reveals a mean and petty spirit. You wouldn't understand it. You're too kind and noble in purpose."

She glanced down at herself. "Does this look noble to you?" She tried to straighten her clothes, but he stopped her with the gentle grasp of her hands.

"Yes, in fact it's the most beautiful sight I've ever beheld. Don't cover yourself up just yet. I love the way you look. The pink of your breasts, the cream of your skin, the deep blue of your eyes, and the fiery gold of your tumbling hair. There isn't anything lovelier than you on this earth."

"And you're not being dishonest?"

He lightly brushed back a lock of her hair. "No, sweetheart."

She leaned into the gentle touch of his hand across her brow. She wanted this for the rest of her life.

She wanted him.

I love you, Julian.

But how could she admit it to him now? They were trapped here because of the scheme she'd set into motion. It mattered little that his family had carried it out well beyond the bounds of reason. To drug them and trap them in this hunting lodge together was madness, but she'd lose him if she confessed the truth now.

No, don't tell him. Hang on to him a little while longer.

She'd tell him all in the morning when her head was less muddled. Indeed, there were a hundred reasons not to spill all yet, most important among them a purely selfish one. She wanted to hold on to the magic of this night a little longer.

She wanted forever, but knew she would have to be satisfied with this one moment.

The truth would come out along with the rise of tomorrow's sun. She rested her head against Julian's chest, soothed by the strong, steady beat of his heart and the protective warmth of his arms wrapped around her.

Tonight she'd revel in the magic, even if it was a lie.

"ROSE, YOU'RE AWAKE. I'm glad. We must talk," Julian said, hearing her quiet footsteps as she tiptoed into the kitchen the next morning. She was trying not to disturb his sleep as she wiped the fog off the window and peered out.

She turned to him in surprise. "I didn't mean to disturb you."

"You didn't." If only she realized just how badly sleep had eluded him. Despite the drugs and whiskey that ought to have put him in a stupor and left him loudly snoring through the night, he'd been up and pacing into the wee hours thinking of her. "This thing that's happened between us—"

"I know," she said, her voice laced with ache as she eased from the window she'd just cleaned with the sleeve of her gown. The sun was now streaming in and it took a moment of squinting against its brilliance for his eyes to adjust. When they did, he saw just how fragile she appeared, for her gaze was uncertain and filled with doubt, as though she knew he was about to break her heart. "Please let me speak first, Julian. There's something important I must tell you. It's been weighing heavily on my heart."

He rolled to a sitting position and groaned as his muscles rebelled against his slightest movement. As dawn broke, he'd finally stretched out atop the kitchen table, preferring it to the floor that he would have had to share with a family of field mice who'd been forced to seek shelter from the rain. "Rose, I—"

"Truly, it's important and if I don't confess now, I don't think I'll have the strength to do it later."

"Confess?" He arched an eyebrow, at first certain she was in jest but realizing her expression was anything but mirthful. Now he was curious as to what this enchanting innocent could have done that was so devastating. "Go on," he said with a nod, unable to imagine that Rose held any deep, dark secrets.

She remained standing beside the window, unwilling to approach him, and took a deep breath before she began to speak. And then another. "I plotted against you. In fact, I instigated the entire affair."

He shook his head and laughed. "Rose, you don't have to lie to me to protect my family from my wrath."

"That's the thing. It isn't a lie. I came up with the plan to lure you to the Cotswolds and other schemes to keep you here for the entire week. Oh, not the part about knocking you out and dragging you to this hunting lodge or bringing me along with you, but... everything else... mostly everything, was mine." Having started, she now blurted the rest. "So I completely understand if you never wish to see me again. Or speak to me ever again. I deserve it. I'm so sorry, Julian. I never meant for all this to happen. It's all my fault that it did."

He stood and took a step toward her. "So you weren't an innocent victim?"

She skittered back, falling onto the window seat as the backs of her legs struck it and knocked her off balance. "No. As I said, I came up with the original scheme... with the help of my sisters." She swallowed hard. "I'm not that clever, but I told them about Nicola's worries about you and Valentina and I understood immediately when Lily explained about lions and tigers and other such animals who roam across the African plains. You know, hunting beasts, and how they separate their prey from the herd and then pounce on that poor, defenseless creature."

He took another step toward her.

"Only, you're rather big and not so defenseless, but that's neither here nor there. The point is, that's all we contrived to do with you at first, separate you from your London friends. For some reason Nicola thought I would be bait for you. It was ridiculously easy—all we had to do was request that you escort us all to Darnley Cottage." The little nub of her throat was madly bobbing up and down. "But your siblings and dear aunt and uncle—they're quite delightful, by the way, if one overlooks this barbaric stunt—worried that it wasn't enough, so apparently they decided to... to... well, this." She waved her arms to encompass their situation. "So I was also abducted— quite by surprise, I had no idea that was coming—and dropped here with you."

"You were completely unaware?" He tried to stem his anger but wasn't doing a very good job of it.

"Of course! What sort of girl do you take me for?" He had no need to respond to the question, for her cheeks turned a bright shade of pink and she began to stammer an answer to her own question. "A terrible girl, I know. That is, I do understand that I've behaved abominably in…" She sighed and her cheeks now turned to crimson flames. "But the passion I felt last night under your expert tutelage was exquisitely real." She cleared her throat. "Yes, but that doesn't excuse my actions. Abominable in every possible fashion. I completely understand if you consider what happened last night a mistake."

Having been up to her eyeballs in schemes, having lied to him, was he now expected to believe that her response to his touch was honest? Was she even a virgin?

Hell, yes. She hadn't faked that.

Still, it didn't excuse her other behavior.

"It was a mistake," he said, trying to sound unaffected, but the girl had gotten to his heart and getting her out of it was not going to be easy. He drew close, but ignored her hopeful gaze as he peered out the window. "Now that the storm has passed, I'll return you to Darnley Cottage and then I'm heading straight to London."

"You're still going to London?" At first she appeared incredulous, then her chin began to quiver and her eyes watered as she realized that he meant it.

He nodded. "This afternoon."

"Oh." Her chin was still quivering and her eyes were now glistening. He wasn't certain he could remain angry if she broke down and cried. Damn, she'd burrowed herself that deeply into his heart. All a lie. Were those tears she appeared about to shed also a lie?

"It's for the best."

"Back to your countess?" She took a deep, ragged breath and let it out slowly.

"Yes. Nothing's changed. I apologize if I've misled you. No harm done. You were mostly faking anyway. As was I."

"You were?" She gasped. "Not about *that*. You couldn't have been. It was real. It felt so right. I'll treasure the moment always. Won't you?"

He arched an eyebrow. "What? I've offended you?" She deserved his anger, but he felt no glee in distancing himself from her. Even if she were telling the truth about her response to his touch, which had been spectacular in every way, he still had to keep her safely out of the way while he dismantled Valentina's spy operation. Once that was done, he'd decide if he ever wanted to see her again. "Forget it, Rose. I assure you that my family will keep this incident quiet and you'll have nothing to fear going forward. I'll return to Valentina, and you—"

"No!" She shook her head and then her fingers curled into fists at her sides and her eyes began to blaze. "Are you jesting? I know you don't love her. I know there's something mysterious going on that forces you to remain with her. My behavior may have been unpardonable, but that doesn't change the fact that this woman is wrong for you and that she'll make you miserable for the rest of your days if you... if you... I don't even dare say it. Simply put, you don't belong with her."

He reached for his shirt and slipped it on, not bothering to adjust the cuffs that were still rolled up from the night before. "We'll give it another hour or two for the sun to dry the wooded footpaths and then we'll go."

"The footpaths will take much longer than an hour or two to dry out." She shook her head again. "That's it? Will you say nothing more to me?"

He shrugged. "We can't stay here, Rose. And we can't take the high road. The local villagers will see us." He eyed her up and down. "One look at you and they'll know that you sacrificed your virtue in the hope of trapping me into marriage."

"How dare you!" She glanced around the kitchen, no doubt looking for objects to hurl at him. "Is this all you have to say to me? That my wanton behavior is now branded on my face for the rest of the world to snicker at? Did last night mean nothing at all to you? Was it merely a frolic to ease your boredom?"

Hell, last night had meant everything to him. "I wasn't bored. I had a good time, I readily admit it. But I'd gone through half of that bottle of whiskey and you ought to have known better than to—"

She gasped. "Are you blaming me?"

"Hell, Rose. There's blame enough to spread everywhere."

"You *are* blaming me," she said, once more incredulous. "So you think you're excused because you were drunk, but I was sober and therefore should be the one to suffer the consequences. Is that it? You must realize that being alone with you, no matter your condition, has left me hopelessly compromised."

"Not hopeless. No one has seen you, and..." He paused meaningfully, ready to duck the moment she tossed a frying pan at his head. "We didn't... you're still a virgin. I didn't take complete leave of my senses."

"Thank goodness for that." She spoke with such an ache to her voice that he knew he'd mercilessly trampled her heart. *Hell, blast, and damn.* He couldn't bear hurting her, even if she did lie to him.

In truth, it was a ridiculously foolish and dangerous scheme that she and his family had concocted, but she'd confessed her part in it. He could see the relief in her eyes as she unburdened herself, for the girl was not a practiced liar and her remorse was obvious. Just as she saw the essence of a person through her artist's eye, he had the same ability to tell a person's character through his soldier's instincts. Rose, this misguided foolishness aside, had a generous and honest heart. He hated having to trample it. "You are a virgin, aren't you? Or should I say that I've left you in the same condition as you were before this night?"

Her gasp was filled with pain. "Right, I'm still a virgin despite my best efforts—perhaps no effort at all on my part to protect my virtue," she amended. "I allowed you to take advantage. I'm such a fool, but I wanted to feel your arms around me and your lips on mine. I knew I'd melt when you kissed me. I did melt." More heat shot into her cheeks as she spoke.

"Rose, I—"

"Please don't say another word. I suppose my behavior must seem awful, but I never meant to trap you into marriage. I would never do such a thing. Truly. I understand that you can't forgive me. I don't know if I can ever forgive myself."

He nodded, knowing this is what he'd wanted and stayed quiet. But the long moment of silence between them played havoc with his resolve and almost destroyed it. He took a deep breath and held firm, knowing the only thing that would be destroyed this morning were Rose's beautiful memories of last night.

Once Valentina and her cohorts were arrested, he'd make amends with Rose. One more week, perhaps two, until Prinny issued the orders to round them up. "Do what you need to get ready. Are you hungry? I think there's still some cheese and bread left from last night. I'll set it out for us."

She shook her head. "Tend to yourself. I can manage on my own."

He sighed. "You'll need help fastening your gown. And pinning up your hair. I'll put the kettle on for tea. We have a long walk ahead of us. I know a little about long marches under a hot sun. You'll never make it on an empty stomach or without water to drink. I'll pour out the last of the whiskey and fill the bottle with water. We'll walk in the shade as much as possible and stop to rest whenever you feel dizzy."

Her eyes rounded in surprise. Did she think he'd be an utter ogre? She pursed her lips and hastily turned away. "I'm used to taking long walks in Coniston. You needn't concern yourself with me. I'll put on the kettle."

But her fussing and the clang of the kettle as she noisily attended to it could not hide the sound of her sniffles. "Rose..."

He crossed the kitchen to reach her side.

She pushed him away. "Set out the bread and cheese. I don't need your help."

"You're crying."

"No." But she was still sniffling and her shoulders were rising and falling as she shed silent tears. "Yes, perhaps so. But it's no concern of yours."

Wordlessly, he took her into his arms.

She ached too badly to fight him off; he could tell by the way she slumped against him, her beautiful body curled in defeat. "I'm so sorry I plotted against you. I'm sorry I didn't do more to prevent your abduction, but I'm not sorry about kissing you or the rest of it. I thought last night was magical," she said with a sob.

He sighed and stroked her hair. "It was, Rose. Don't let me or anyone else tell you otherwise."

CHAPTER 11

"ROLF! THERE YOU are!" Nicola called out from the earl's carriage the moment it drew to a halt beside the copse of trees where she and Julian were hiding. They'd been forced to walk closer to the main road than planned because most of the wooded footpaths were either flooded or too muddy, just as she had predicted.

"Nicola! Thank goodness!" Rose eased away from Julian to run toward the carriage, her relief at being found quite sincere, for she and Julian had been walking for over three hours, much of the time buried up to their ankles in mire and thorny brambles that slowed their progress to a crawl.

They were still another three hours on foot from Darnley Cottage and despite her assurances to Julian that she was fine, the truth was that she was exhausted and sad and humiliated enough to crawl into bed and hide for the rest of the summer. Whatever hold Valentina had over Julian was still firmly in place. The misguided plot Julian's family had contrived had failed, except that she was now ruined for any other man, not because Julian had touched her or because they'd been alone overnight, but because she'd fallen in love with him.

Hopelessly in love.

He would never reciprocate, not after what she'd done to him.

Nicola swung open the carriage door. "You poor thing! How's your ankle?"

"It's held up just fine." In truth, it hurt like blazes and felt swollen, but she wasn't about to admit it within Julian's earshot. The effort of slogging through the flooded woods had left her spent and she had simply refused to ask Julian for help or accept it when he offered, something he had done with irritating constancy.

One would almost think he cared.

She knew that he didn't. Love might conquer all, but not for her and Julian. She'd gotten her moment of magic last night, but with the morning sun came a painful clarity. He could never love a liar, even a well-intentioned one such as her.

She had to get Julian out of her heart.

Could she?

Being with him these past few hours had been a torment, especially agonizing each time he lifted her into his arms to carry her across a particularly bad stretch of stagnant, dirty water that had yet to dissipate under the hot sun. His arms were perfect and she was meant to be held in them.

She ought to have been glad Nicola had rescued them. Now if they were seen, no one would think anything of her and Nicola going out for a carriage ride with her brother. Perhaps an eyebrow would wag for their lack of an elderly chaperone, but no horrific scandal would erupt.

Rose paused to wipe her mud-stained shoes before climbing into the carriage, but Nicola waved her in. "Don't worry about that. I'm so glad I found you! I went to the lodge first, but you were already gone. I've packed up the belongings you left behind and stowed them in the carriage."

"Good," Julian muttered from behind her. "Saves me a trip back to clean up the mess you created."

Nicola swallowed hard. "We've been creeping along this road for hours hoping to find the two of you. I'm so sorry for what we did to you, Rose."

Julian came to Rose's side, his large hands on her waist as he effortlessly lifted her inside, and then climbed in after her, taking the empty bench across from her and Nicola. "You damn well ought to be," he said, settling against the leather squabs and glowering at his sister. "Are you demented? Leaving Rose behind with me? Anything might have happened, none of it good."

His sister looked suitably contrite. "Did it?"

"No," she and Julian shouted at the same time, their protestations only confirming that something had indeed occurred. Rose felt her cheeks burning.

Julian cast her an exasperated glance. "No, nothing happened," he said more gently. "But something will the moment we reach the cottage."

Nicola's eyes brightened. "Really?"

Julian groaned. "Yes, I'm going to take you to the woodshed and give you the long overdue thrashing you heartily deserve. I'd do the same to our aunt and uncle if they weren't so old and fragile. Where are they now? Still at the cottage, or have they run off to hide from my wrath?"

"Oh, I thought you meant something good was going to happen between the two of you. Honestly, Julian. You needn't thrash me or any of us. We're all terribly ashamed of what we've done." She sighed and took Rose's hand in hers. "My uncle and aunt are at the cottage waiting to offer you their sincere apology. We should not have dragged you into this family matter, but we were certain that you cared for Julian and believed he was growing to care for you. It isn't your fault that my brother is the greatest idiot who ever lived."

Julian growled to mark his displeasure. "Definitely the woodshed, Nicola."

Rose drew her hand away. "I'm not ready to forgive either of you just yet."

Julian emitted a bark of laughter. "You? I'm the injured party in this scheme. You two are the conspirators." He raised his gaze heavenward. "My entire damn family conspiring against me."

"You brought it on yourself," Nicola retorted. "Do you think we enjoyed doing this to you?"

Julian leaned forward, his brow furrowed in obvious anger. "I don't care what you think. I don't care what anyone thinks. I'm never speaking to any of you savages again. Indeed, I'm cutting off all ties with every last one of you."

Rose gasped. "You can't mean to abandon the children."

His frown deepened. "Keep out of this, Rose. You and Nicola have done quite enough."

"I don't deny it. But it doesn't make your hurting little Emily or Kendra or the boys acceptable, just because Nicola and I were in the wrong." Her heart felt heavy and her eyes were once more turning watery, for she truly adored Julian's family, all of them, and wanted to patch things up with them. She was angry with Nicola for putting her in an unthinkably scandalous situation, but she still loved her. They were best friends. "Nicola meant well."

"Hah!" He rolled his eyes. "Did she mean well when leaving you with me overnight?"

"Yes, I did," Nicola insisted. "Rolf loves you."

"Stop calling her that. Her name is Rose. She lied and schemed and I'm supposed to believe she did it all for love?"

"Yes." Nicola scowled at him. "And if you had any brains, you'd love her back. And even though you appear to have no brains, you do have an ingrained sense of honor. I knew you would have accepted to marry Rolf had you been discovered, so there was little real danger to her. No harm done. And hopefully she will understand my motives and forgive me in time, even if you never do." Nicola turned to her, looking as though she were about to cry. "You must, Rolf. I couldn't bear it if we were no longer friends."

Julian snorted. "You ought to have considered that before you drugged her. Or me."

They rode in silence much of the way to the cottage, that silence occasionally broken by Nicola's attempts at contrition. "I'll have refreshments and a warm bath brought up to you, Rolf. Whatever you desire. You have only to ask. You, too, Julian."

"Don't bother about me," he said with a grunt, scratching the stubble of beard that had grown overnight. "See to Rose's comfort. I'll be off for London within the hour."

Nicola blinked. "What?"

"You heard me. Your disastrous plan has failed. I'm returning to London today." He leaned forward and cast both of them a warning glower. "You're to remain here for the rest of the week. Rose, too." He then turned his gaze solely on Rose, cupping her chin in his hand and gently forcing her to look at him even though she wanted to turn away. "You must stay here. I don't ask this of you lightly because I know how uncomfortable it will be for you, but I want you to remain at the cottage until I return to escort you home."

Rose slapped his hand away. "And when will that be? You can't possibly expect me to stay here with your family. How will I face them every day? After what they've done to me?"

He nodded and ran a hand roughly through his hair. "I know I'm not being fair to you, but it can't be helped. I'm sorry, Rose. I will not allow you to contradict me in this. I'll collect you next week. Or soon after. I promise. I can't return for you any earlier."

"What rubbish! I'll write to my parents," she said in exasperation, for why should he care what happened to her next? He was running back to Valentina. "My father will come for me. I'll make up some reasonable excuse."

"We'll all return," Nicola interjected, trying to be helpful. "No one will doubt us if we tell them the cottage suffered damage during the storm and requires immediate repairs that can't be completed while we're in residence."

"That isn't the point." Julian leaned forward, now noticeably angry. "Haven't you meddled enough, Nicola? I want the two of you out of the way until I come for you. I don't want you anywhere near London. How much clearer can I be?"

Rose put a hand on Nicola's shoulder when she appeared ready to continue the battle. "It's all right. I'll stay."

Nicola eyed her curiously. "You will?"

Julian drew back, his gaze never leaving her face. "You will?"

"Yes." She wasn't certain why she suddenly trusted him, but his cruel behavior this morning now made perfect sense. He was planning something dangerous and didn't want her underfoot. She wasn't usually this dense or stupid, but neither was she familiar with relations between men and women, having never had any relations whatsoever with any man until Julian.

His response to her last night had been real, only he couldn't admit it to her yet. More important, she had to go with her instincts about his supposed relation with Valentina. His feigned adoration for the countess was just that… feigned.

Nicola, obviously not thinking beyond their friendship, threw her arms around Rose and hugged her fiercely. "Thank you, Rolf. I'm so glad you'll stay. I'll make amends. We all will. You'll see. I'll be the best friend to you… and I promise never to embroil you in anything so foolish again."

"At least for another week," Rose teased, hugging her back. She was still angry, but had always been terrible at holding grudges. Nicola and her family had done an awful thing to her, thinking to force Julian into marrying her instead of Valentina. But their hoped-for outcome wasn't so awful. They understood Julian's sense of honor and thought he would marry her.

Perhaps he would have, but she didn't want him to offer marriage out of necessity, only out of love. She wouldn't accept him any other way.

Did he love her? Last night it had felt as though he did, but men were good at faking such things. Loving her wasn't quite the same thing as wanting to bed her. She knew he'd wanted to do that. No, indeed. Lust wasn't at all the same thing as love.

But neither did he love Valentina. Had his family truly understood Julian, they would have seen into his heart and known he could never willingly choose someone like Valentina as his wife.

Rose squeezed her eyes shut and continued to hug Nicola, who was still openly sobbing tears of relief and contrition on her shoulder and giving it a thorough soaking. "All will be well, Nicola. You'll see."

Indeed, she and Nicola would repair their friendship. Julian would return to London and do whatever he needed to do concerning Valentina. Just not marry her. *Please don't marry Valentina.*

That was the greatest danger, that he would somehow be forced into an unwanted marriage with the countess to rescue… a friend? She still didn't know any of the specifics.

She'd have to trust that Julian knew what he was doing.

And trust that he'd overlook her lies and schemes and forgive her.

And trust that he'd somehow fall in love with her even though she'd given him no reason to do so.

Her heart sank, for it all seemed so hopeless.

JULIAN EASED BACK in his seat as the carriage rattled toward Darnley Cottage. He wanted to grab Rose and kiss her soundly on the lips, for he'd noticed the precise moment when understanding had dawned upon her. She'd finally seen through his charade and appeared to trust him to do whatever necessary while in London even though she had no idea what it was that he needed to do.

Did she understand how much he truly cared for her?

Last night had been anything but a mere frolic for him. She'd called it magical. Indeed, it had been because she'd made it so, even for someone as experienced and cynical as he.

She trusted him.

But for how long? Trust had to be earned, and all the news she might hear this coming week would send her reeling. In truth, the news could get much worse before it got better. "Nicola, you'll crush her if you continue to squeeze her so hard."

"No, I won't," Nicola insisted, still soaking Rose's slender shoulder with her tears. "Rolf is tougher than she looks. She has a wonderful inner strength and a forgiving heart."

He hoped Rose was the forgiving sort. His plan was to go to the jewelers as soon as he returned to London. Everyone would think he was choosing a ring for Valentina.

Only he knew it would be for Rose.

Yet, Rose wouldn't. Nor would he tell her in advance, not without Prinny's permission, which there would be no time to obtain.

No, he'd simply have to make amends with Rose once the mission was over. He'd offer her the ring along with his heart. *Bloody nuisance.* How had he gone from questioning whether he would court her to deciding to offer marriage?

He'd keep offering no many how many times she flung the ring back in his face.

He'd keep offering no matter how long it took her to accept him.

Even if it took him into his dotage.

An Emory loved once and forever.

No one but Rose would ever wear his ring.

CHAPTER 12

"I WAS BEGINNING to think you'd forgotten about me," Valentina purred, greeting Julian when he called upon her shortly after his return to London. He'd stopped by his townhouse long enough to change out of his travel-stained clothes and bathe, and then he'd completed one more errand before venturing to her residence.

Her arms snaked up Julian's chest to draw him closer for a possessive kiss. He tried to imagine that he was kissing Rose, but failed miserably. The only saving grace was that Valentina was as insincere as he was and didn't particularly care how he felt. Nor did she truly understand love or passion, so how could she know that his passion had been faked all along?

A greater difficulty would present itself later this evening when they returned to her bedchamber after a night at the gaming hells. Arousal couldn't be faked.

Nor could he dismiss his own nature, the traits of loyalty and faithfulness to the woman he loved. It was of no moment that Rose had no notion of how he felt. His actions, a duty for the sake of the Crown, still felt like a betrayal of his principles. "My love, I rushed back to your side the moment I settled my family at the cottage. You knew I'd be gone for a few days."

She was never the understanding sort. "You ought to have returned sooner. Or did Nicola's pretty friend delay you?"

Damn. "My uncle delayed me. He wasn't feeling well. In truth, he's been ailing for weeks now and I was concerned that he'd taken a turn for the worse and needed to be brought back to London. Only the best doctors will do for him."

She stroked his jaw. "The earl? But you returned alone."

Julian nodded. "I couldn't wait to race back to your side."

"And how was dear Lord Darnley when you left him?"

"Much improved."

His stomach churned at the flicker of disappointment in her eyes. He would inherit the earldom upon his uncle's death. Once he was earl, did Valentina truly believe he'd make her his countess? She'd already duped one earl into marrying her and he'd died under suspicious circumstances. Of course, she'd been with friends in Bath when her husband had cocked up his toes, and later she had done a commendable job of pretending to be the distraught widow.

At the time, no one had suspected her involvement in Lord Deschanel's death because she had little to gain, but Julian, along with others in Prinny's elite group of special agents, knew better now. By killing off her husband, she'd gained a foothold in society and a manor house conveniently close to one of the most important shipping lanes along the English Channel. Toss in a smuggler's cove or two, and she'd set herself up quite nicely to welcome Boney to England if and when he chose to invade.

"When does your family intend to return to London?" Although she casually tossed off the question, it was obvious there was nothing casual in her bearing and she was quite on edge. Was something important about to happen?

He shrugged. "They'll send word when they grow bored listening to bullfrogs croak among the willows. Perhaps by the end of this week or next."

"Will your sister's friend remain with them all the while?"

Damn again. Why was she asking about Rose? "The two are inseparable. I expect that she will." He took Valentina into his arms and began to nuzzle her neck. "Why bother with the girl? Who cares if she stays or goes?"

Valentina drew away. "She's very pretty."

"You're jealous, my love!" He shook his head and forced a laugh. "You needn't be. The chit comes from a family of merchants. They're barely fit to go about in society. She has no polish, and do you know that she spends her days buried up to her elbows in clay?" He took hold of Valentina's smooth hands. "I want a lady, not a rustic bumpkin for my wife."

She arched an eyebrow. "You're thinking of taking a wife?"

He returned to nuzzling her neck. "Yes, you know I am. Should I be angry that you've had me followed ever since I returned to London? How else could you know that I'd been to the jewelers?"

"You wound me, Chatham." She pursed her lips in a practiced pout. "Who said anything about jewelers? Not I. You're the one who mentioned it."

"And you, my love, are avidly staring at the pocket of my jacket, obviously aware of the little box tucked in it."

"As it happens, one of my friends noticed you entering Asprey's and rushed over here to tell me." She had stiffened slightly, enough to confirm that she was indeed having him followed by a hired ruffian or a Bow Street runner, although he didn't think she'd risk hiring a runner for they weren't the sort who could be made to vanish without a trace if the task turned sour.

Some runners had connections among the Upper Crust, not to mention among their own business circle, so if a runner suddenly disappeared, questions would be asked. No one would ask after the scum who haunted the dockside.

"Oh? Which friend?" He'd been on alert even at Darnley Cottage and didn't think anyone had followed him there or seen him alone with Rose in the hunting lodge. A lurking stranger would have been noticed at once on Darnley property or in the nearby village. Someone would have reported this unknown person to him.

The Cotswolds was nothing like crowded London, where a scoundrel could be hired to follow a gent and never be noticed. Still, his decision to keep Rose away from London gave him pause. He feared for his uncle as well, although Valentina would not be so foolish as to poison him now, not before she was securely married to Julian and able to call herself Viscountess Chatham.

It would never happen.

"Valentina?" he prodded when she didn't immediately answer. "Which friend?"

"Why should it matter to you? He isn't an acquaintance of yours."

"A man? What connection is he to you?" This was the opening he was hoping for. "Can I not leave London even for one day without your entertaining another gentleman? Do you not love me?"

"Of course I do! How can you think anyone else holds my affection?"

He moved away and feigned agitation by striding to the window and peering out of it. "Is the bounder out there now? Waiting for me to leave? What have you offered him? Your body?" He turned back to glare at her. "Or has he claimed your heart?"

"Really, Chatham! You go too far." She appeared more frustrated than hurt. "You're the one I chose. There's no one else but you."

He returned to her side and took her by the shoulders. "Prove it. You know my feelings for you, how ardently and completely I worship you. But I have yet to believe those feelings are returned even in part. Yes, I bought the ring, but it signifies nothing. Is your heart pledged to me, Valentina? I know you're holding something back. What is it?"

"Don't be a fool. What would I have to hide from you?" Her eyes were now blazing, a sign of her anger. Despite that blaze, she was still a cold-hearted—Damn, Rose was right. The woman sucked all warmth from a room.

"You tell me. I won't move forward without the truth." His fingers tensed on her shoulders to emphasize his earnestness, then he gentled his hold. "What is it, my love? Are you in trouble of some sort? I'll protect you, whatever it is. You can trust me. You can tell me anything."

"Get out, Chatham. I don't want your ring. If you don't trust me, then I'll have nothing more to do with you." She tossed her chin up imperiously and motioned toward the door. "Get out now!"

Damn, had he just blown a year's worth of investigation? "Valentina, please. Forget what I just said. I want you. No one else can have you."

"You ought to have thought of that before you insulted me! Go! I'm through with you. Cry on that Farthingale girl's shoulder for all I care."

He backed away slowly toward the door, cursing himself for overplaying his hand. Did she suspect something was amiss? Had someone warned her that she was under investigation concerning

Napoleon? Or was she merely in a jealous fit because she suspected him of liking Rose? There was malice behind her cruel smile. He saw the venom and spite in her eyes as he backed away, but he remained in character, still feigning the desolate lover, for whatever it was worth.

Nothing now, he feared.

What had he just done? Somehow turned Valentina's vicious attention on Rose?

He'd put an end to the investigation right now.

"SIR," JULIAN SAID, his concern growing as he was kept standing in the presence of the Prince Regent, enduring his questions for the last half hour, "we must act now. As I've explained repeatedly, Countess Deschanel knows something is amiss and even now must be alerting her agents to flee."

Prinny arched an eyebrow and glanced at the ormolu clock perched on his elegant desk. "No one else has noticed any movement out of the ordinary these past three days while you were in the countryside and not a single agent has sent warning today. No, you're needlessly fretting. Despite your suspicions, I believe the incident is nothing more than a lover's spat. You were caught enjoying the company of a sweet young thing and the countess became enraged. Tell me about the Farthingale girl. I hear she's beautiful."

He didn't wish to discuss Rose with anyone, especially not Prinny, who was known for his roving eye. "I suppose," he said with a shrug. "Mostly she's headstrong and unsophisticated."

Prinny arched an eyebrow. "No wonder the countess is worried about you. It's obvious that you like the girl. Don't bother to deny it."

Bloody nuisance. Could everyone see straight into his heart?

"Forget her for now and attend to your mission. You've hurt Countess Deschanel's feelings and now must soothe her."

Julian snorted. "That woman has no feelings. She has discarded me and—"

Prinny slapped his hand down on the desk. "Enough, Chatham! Do you expect us to leap into action on your mere say so? What's happened is nothing more than a squabble between you and your jealous countess. Set it right and go on about your business. We're too close to shutting down Boney's entire operation to stop now. I'm not about to let you toss it all away because your affections have strayed."

Julian gritted his teeth but knew better than to provoke Prinny any further. Fortunately, their argument was halted by a sharp rap at the door. "That will be Lord Malinor come to lecture me on the woeful state of our treasury."

Julian frowned. He wasn't fond of England's newly appointed finance minister, a self-important prig if there ever was one. "He shouldn't see me here. I'll go out the back way."

"Stay. He can help put you back in the good graces of your countess. The man has a penchant for gossip to rival that of the dreaded Lady Withnall. No one keeps secrets from her. Perhaps you ought to enlist her services for this investigation." Prinny laughed at his own remark, but Julian didn't find it witty in the least. "Stop scowling at me, Chatham, and do as I say. We'll turn Malinor's loose tongue to your advantage." Now enamored of his idea—one that Julian didn't like at all—Prinny smiled as he turned toward the door. "Enter!"

The royal steward strode in, followed by Lord Malinor, who strutted in like a peacock. His silk trousers were a striking mint green and his silk brocade jacket a blinding clash of colors including mint green, violet, and azure blue, all shot through with gold thread. He wore a fanciful powdered white wig and too much perfume. French, no doubt. Smuggled into England, no doubt. Such goods had been embargoed since the war began. "Your Royal Highness," Lord Malinor intoned with breathless gravity as he performed an obsequious bow.

Prinny glanced at Julian and grinned before returning his attention to the finance minister. "Malinor, you've come at just the right time. I require your assistance."

He bowed low again. "I'm ever at your service."

"Good. Good, for this young pup requires your guidance. You'd be doing me a great favor if you helped him out."

Malinor straightened, his expression flustered. "Of course, anything to please Your Royal Highness. How can I be of assistance to Viscount Chatham?"

"He's lovesick and the countess in question has just spurned him. He came to me hoping I might sway her, but my schedule is too busy these next few days and I fear Chatham will expire from a malady of the heart if his problem isn't addressed immediately."

Lord Malinor looked at him askance. "I assume we are speaking of the beautiful Countess Deschanel? Has she tossed you aside, Chatham?"

"Let's just say we had a spat." Julian noticed a swirl of expressions in Lord Malinor's features, some he understood and others he thought odd. Malinor obviously thought his predicament amusing, curious, surprising. But there was also a flash of fear, just a momentary glint in his eyes and then it was gone.

"Did you give her cause?" Malinor eyed him a little too avidly.

"None, I assure you." The old man was still eyeing him intently. What was his interest in Valentina? Julian didn't think they knew each other beyond a passing acquaintance. They were invited to many of the same society functions, but that signified nothing. Those in the nobility were often invited to the same events.

However, Malinor and Valentina never attended the same intimate dinner parties or joined in the same excursions to the theater or gaming hells. No, Malinor would not be seen with Valentina's fast crowd, but neither was he a pillar of sainthood. Quite the opposite, he had an eye for the ladies, especially the young, beautiful ones. Julian always kept close watch on Nicola whenever that old hound was about. He always seemed to be leering and in his cups.

Malinor's jowls wobbled as he shook his head and sighed. "But she must have had a reason to toss you out on your ear."

"I left her side to escort my uncle to his country estate. She didn't appreciate that I was gone for three days." He put a hand to his heart, doing his best to appear a distraught suitor. "I assure you, Malinor. I never strayed. I love her."

Malinor eyed him even more intently. "You do?"

He nodded. "I even bought her a ring. I wish to…" Damn, he couldn't say it. "Her rejection has gravely wounded me. I must win her back. I'll do anything she asks of me."

Prinny let out a bark of laughter. "See, the man is lost without her. Do help him out of his misery. I can't bear to see him like this. But he's under the Emory curse and can't help himself."

"The Emory curse? Sire, I don't believe I've ever heard of it."

Prinny laughed again. "Calm yourself, Malinor, it isn't the pox. Every Emory male falls hard for one woman and loves her forever. That's their curse." He turned to Julian. "Run along now and lick your wounds at home. Lord Malinor will correspond with your countess and soothe her hurt feelings. Hopefully, she's the forgiving sort."

Julian bowed, but he wasn't grateful to Prinny for this attempt to put him back in good stead with Valentina. She would now have more time to warn her agents. He cursed silently. Now Malinor was involved. He hoped Prinny had more sense than to confide in that pompous oaf.

True, he was England's finance minister, but that didn't mean he could be trusted. For one, the man drank too much. Secrets could be pried out of him and he'd be none the wiser. For another thing, Malinor and his son were arrogant, ambitious men. They put their interests before those of anyone else and would never extend a helping hand to another unless it served to benefit them in some way.

"Be gone, Chatham! The finance minister and I have more important matters to discuss than your romantic woes."

Julian strode out of St. James Palace in worse temper than when he arrived. Not only had Prinny dismissed him, but he'd now assigned Malinor to assist him in rekindling a romance he was desperate to extinguish.

On Prinny's command, he was obliged to accept Lord Malinor's invitation to share a drink with him at White's later that evening. Reluctantly, and still in ill humor, he strode into the club at the appointed hour. He'd long been a member at White's, but tonight he found the elegant establishment oppressive.

The gleaming, oiled wood bookshelves and tables, the well-worn leather chairs, and even the elegant carpets that muffled all sound in the private rooms made him feel as though he were walking into a mausoleum. The heavy scent of cigar smoke filtered into the entry hall, and not a sound could be heard except for the occasional rustle of newspapers coming from the club's reading room.

Indeed, he felt as though the walls were closing in on him. He wanted nothing better than to ride back to Darnley Cottage and spend the rest of the summer rusticating in those idyllic surroundings, his hair tousled by a pine-scented summer breeze while he enjoyed the laughter of his brothers and sisters at play in the garden... while he held Rose in his arms and kissed her with the same abandon as he'd done last night. Was that too much to ask?

Lord Malinor harrumphed as Julian entered their private room, escorted in by a stodgy, white-haired footman. "Have a seat, Chatham. Let's get down to business."

The overstuffed brown leather crackled as Julian settled into his chair and stretched his long legs before him. "Let's not," he said, declining the brandy Lord Malinor was about to pour. The man was dressed in yellow silk this evening and sported a large, flame-red ruby ring on his plump middle finger. "I don't require your help in wooing Countess Deschanel and I would appreciate your not getting involved."

Malinor shrugged and poured himself a glass. "Much as I would like to be rid of this duty, I must see it through on Prinny's orders. So, let's speak frankly, one man to another. You can tell me if you're involved with another woman."

"There is no other woman," he said, irritated to have to play the part of wounded lover. "That's what has me so distraught. How can I prove what doesn't exist?"

His companion winked at him. "Well said, now let's get to the truth. What have you been playing at, Chatham?"

Julian sighed. "I'm no rake, nor have I ever had a roving eye. I will speak no more on the subject. You may tell Prinny whatever you wish. I've done nothing wrong and I hope in time the lady in question will come to realize it."

"How much time will you give her?" he asked, arching his powdered eyebrow.

Julian withdrew the small box containing the ring he'd purchased earlier and toyed with it in his fingers. "As long as she needs. This ring won't turn to waste and I expect it will take me quite some time to find another lady who might have more respect for me," he paused and nodded toward the box, "or for this gift I'd happily bestow on her."

Lord Malinor gazed into the amber liquid in his crystal glass. "You speak like a heartbroken lover and yet there are rumors of your dallying with that Farthingale girl. Not that I would blame you, she's a tempting bauble—"

Julian jolted up in his seat. "With all due respect, Lord Malinor, you are treading on dangerous ground. You may say whatever you wish about me, but I shall call you out if you ever insult my sister's dearest friend. Whatever slanderous gossip you've heard is nonsense. If you ever treat her or speak of her as anything other than a lady, I shall stuff your entrails—"

"Egads, Chatham!" He set down his glass and raised his hands in mock surrender. "If there's nothing to the rumor, then why are you so protective of the girl?"

"Surely you've heard that I saved her life." Not quite true, for Rose would have made her way safely out of the demolished shed eventually, whether or not he had been present. Still, he'd carried her out and tended to her injuries. That counted for something, didn't it? And he'd scared the stuffing out of Sir Milton Aubrey, the perpetrator who'd sabotaged her kiln. The dastard knew better than to show his face in England again, on pain of death at Julian's hand.

"She must have been grateful."

"She and her family thanked me. That's it. She's a nice girl from a decent family but has very little social polish. She's very pretty, but Countess Deschanel is dazzling. Surely, you agree. How can the two compare? Miss Farthingale is a quaint pearl, but the countess is a diamond of the first water."

"Very well," he said with a chortle. "I'm duly chastened."

"Since we now understand each other, I'll be off to the theater with friends." He rose to signal an end to their conversation. "Care to join us, Malinor?"

"Who are you going with?"

"Lord and Lady Chester, Lady Bainbridge, and her nephew, Lord Randall."

Lord Malinor rolled his eyes. "No. What are you doing in the company of those old fossils?"

"Randall's my age."

"He behaves like a doddering old man. John Randall is one of the dullest men I've ever met. All he talks about is hunting grouse in Scotland or wild boar in the forests of Saxony."

Julian nodded. "I thought I'd invite him to Darnley Cottage when I return there at the end of the week to escort my family back to London. He enjoys fishing and our stream is well stocked with—"

"Spare me, Chatham. No wonder the countess wants nothing more to do with you. I never realized you were so deadly dull." He sighed and rose with him. "I'll put in a good word for you should I happen to see her, but otherwise I'll keep out of your business. However, the blame is on you if Prinny finds out I've done nothing to advance your cause."

"Agreed." Julian nodded. "Thank you."

He left White's and hopped in his carriage to join his friends at Vauxhall Gardens before they all headed off to the theater on Drury Lane. He was late. He and John Randall had much to discuss, for John was one of the most respected agents in Prinny's royal circle of spies. The elders in their entourage served as a cover for their activities, lending an air of genteel respectability and allowing them to plan their next steps under cover of social engagements.

John tossed him a questioning glance as he approached. "Got rid of Malinor?"

Julian nodded. "For the moment. Hopefully, for good. There's something about the man I don't trust."

"I never thought much of him either." John grinned. "He detests me, thinks I'm a crushing bore."

Julian shook his head and laughed. "You've perfected your cover, the dull nephew who's devoted to his elderly aunt, your only pleasure being hunting, which is something you drone on and on about until everyone present is put to sleep by your aimless blather."

"My aunt," he said, nodding toward Lady Bainbridge, "quite enjoys the charade, although she worries that I'll never find the right girl while I'm forced to remain in character. I haven't minded so far. Haven't yet come across the young lady who knocks the breath out of me. Why are you suddenly frowning?"

"I have a favor to ask of you."

John shrugged. "Of course, whatever you need."

"Good, because I need you to protect a girl for me."

John crossed his arms over his chest and eyed him warily. "If you mean the black widow spider, forget it. She's all yours."

"No, I'm talking about Nicola's best friend, Rose Farthingale. Long story. You don't need to know all of it. What you do need to know is that she's in danger. Valentina is jealous of her. She's gotten it into her head that I like her."

John's eyes rounded in surprise. "Do you?"

He ignored the question. "I need you to watch over Rose. More than that, I need you to pretend to court her. I can't think of another way to keep her safe. *Pretend*, John. Your role is to defuse an explosive situation. Nothing more."

"And if I should happen to fall in love with Rose?"

Julian clenched his jaw and curled his fists. "I shall have to kill you."

The gesture was noted by his friend, who grinned and, in jest, ran a finger along his suddenly too tight collar. "Ah," he said with a chuckle. "I'll keep that in mind."

CHAPTER 13

ROSE'S BREATH QUICKENED as she peered out the window of the bedchamber she and Nicola shared at Darnley Cottage. It overlooked the lovely front gardens that were abloom with lilies, daisies, and daffodils, a daily reminder of her sisters. The garden afforded a clear view of the drive leading up to the cottage. "I see two riders approaching."

"Two?" Nicola stopped sorting clothes for her maid to pack and joined her by the window. They weren't scheduled to leave until tomorrow, but since the family would depart early in the morning they needed to accomplish as much as possible today. "The one on the black gelding is definitely Julian, but I don't recognize the gentleman on the roan... oh, yes, I do. It's his friend, Lord John Randall." She turned to Rose, groaning and rolling her eyes. "Crumpets, as the twins would say. The man is such a bore. I can't believe he and my brother are friends."

Rose continued to peer at the approaching pair, studying them as they reached the cottage and casually drew up their horses to dismount with the easy grace of experienced riders. "He looks pleasant enough."

Nicola groaned again. "He'll put you to sleep within five minutes in his company. All he ever talks about is hunting. Or fishing. Or the proper gun for hunting. And the proper rod for fishing. Nothing else ever rattles around in that limited brain of his." She pursed her lips suddenly and quirked her head.

"What's the matter, Nicola?"

"It's just struck me that my brother has the worst taste in friends.

First Countess Deschanel and now Lord Randall. I must have a serious discussion with him, make certain he didn't fall off his horse and strike his head some time over this past year."

Rose giggled. "Don't be silly."

"I'm being quite sensible for a change. He must have suffered a serious blow to the head around the same time that he met that horrid woman. How else can his sudden execrable choice in friends be explained? For pity's sake. One is an ice queen and the other a eunuch."

"Nicola! That's not a nice thing to say. Your brother can't be too pleased with your choice of friends either." Of course, Rose was referring to herself and the wanton night she'd spent... no, she'd worked hard to suppress the memory of that exquisite encounter that had ended so badly. Julian believed her to be an untrustworthy young lady of loose morals and even looser character.

As though sensing he was being spied upon, Julian chose that moment to glance up.

Rose quickly moved away, but she knew he'd seen her because he suddenly frowned. "Your brother is still angry."

Nicola tossed back her auburn curls. "Let him be. We're angry too. He's given us just cause."

Rose moved to the mirror and studied her reflection. Her cheeks were a hot, bright pink. Pinker than the demure pink hyacinths in the weave of the muslin gown she'd chosen to wear today, the choice of gown purposely designed to make her appear innocent—which she was—except for the wanton thoughts about Julian that continually rattled in her brain. It wasn't her fault that her body's response to his nearness was to instantly heat and become lustily wild and rampant. She'd never experienced these unwholesome urges until she'd met him.

He was the bad influence.

She was the unsuspecting innocent.

She cleared her throat and patted her prim bun. Well, perhaps she could no longer be considered innocent, not after the night they'd shared at the hunting lodge. "I've almost finished packing. Have you?"

Nicola nodded and playfully bumped her from her spot in front of the mirror. "My turn."

Rose grinned as she watched Nicola primp. "I thought you didn't care for Julian's friend."

Nicola blushed. "I don't. The man is dull as dishwater."

"And yet, you're fussing with your gown and hair. Interesting." She took pity on her friend as she continued to protest, taking her arm and nudging her toward the door. "We may as well go downstairs and get the uncomfortable greetings out of the way."

Nicola held her back a moment. "Rose, are you glad to be going home? It's been almost ten days since you've last seen your family."

She nodded. "I do miss them, very much. I've never been apart from my parents or sisters this long before."

"I hope you won't end our friendship once we're back in London." There was a sudden, quavering catch to Nicola's voice. "I'll never forgive myself for what we did to you. I was so certain Julian liked you. More than liked you. And I knew you were falling in love with him. I wanted so badly for the two of you to end up together."

Rose put up a hand to stop her, for she'd received this apology daily from Nicola and knew she was sincerely suffering over her mistake. "I do care for your brother, probably more than is wise. But he doesn't care enough for me to change his intentions, so that's an end to it. The incident is over. No outsiders are the wiser. I'll move on and so must you."

Nicola was now wringing her hands. "But will we remain friends?"

What Nicola had done to her was unpardonable and yet her actions had been born out of love, so Rose knew she would forgive her in time. Also, Rose had gone along with tempting Julian and it wasn't merely because she was selflessly devoted to Nicola. She *had* been falling in love with Julian, and her feelings were obvious to all in his family. "Yes, but you must give me a little distance. There's much I must still think about."

Nicola eagerly agreed. "Of course. Take all the time you need... but not too long, please. I shall miss you terribly once we're back in town. You're the only friend I have there. In truth, you're my only friend anywhere."

Rose gave her a quick hug. "That's because you're a meddlesome, opinionated, brash, and headstrong... wait, that's me, too. And my sisters. Not Daisy, though. She's sweet and perfect, but we love her anyway."

"I suppose that's why you and I get along so well. We're odd ducks. I'm glad neither of us fits society's constraining mold."

They swept downstairs, arm in arm and heads held high, and entered the salon. Lord and Lady Darnley were seated on the sofa, about to offer the new arrivals tea and cakes that had already been rolled in on a silver cart. Julian and his friend were standing beside the unlit hearth, Julian resting his broad shoulder against the mantel and John perusing a painting of a fox hunt. "I told you," Nicola whispered. "Hunting on the brain."

"Ah, there you are, girls." Lady Darnley looked up and smiled at them. "Your brother made excellent time and arrived earlier than expected," she said after introducing Rose to Julian's companion. "He and Lord Randall thought they'd do some fishing today."

Nicola nudged her again, a silent I-told-you-so. "Where will you fish? Rolf intended to sketch by Puffin's Bend, but we'll—"

"That's where we'll be fishing," Julian said, still not smiling at either of them.

His friend, however, had a genuinely amiable expression on his face. "We'd be delighted to have your company, Miss Farthingale." John Randall was taller and more muscular than she'd expected, and although he wore spectacles and had the reputation of being boring, there was a glint of mischief in his gray-green eyes that hinted of more going on in his brain than Nicola credited him for.

Nicola fidgeted beside her. "What about my company, Lord Randall?"

He removed his spectacles and slowly rubbed them with his handkerchief, and then even more slowly returned the handkerchief to his breast pocket and his spectacles to his nose, quite aware of the silence that filled the room in expectation of his response and in no apparent rush to accommodate by hastening to respond. "If you must, Lady Nicola."

Rose bit her cheek to stifle a wayward bubble of laughter. The fiend! He was teasing Nicola. Did he like her? Because despite

Nicola's protestations, Rose knew that she liked Julian's friend. The manner in which she angled her body toward his gave her away.

"Of course I must! If Rolf is to join you, then so must I. It wouldn't be proper for her... alone... never mind. Stop casting me those smug, disapproving glances, Julian. You've little to recommend yourself either." Nicola stuck out her tongue.

Lady Darnley groaned. "Children, both of you behave yourselves. Most of all you," she chided, pinning Julian with her most imperious scowl. "After all, you're a viscount and your sister is barely out of her leading strings."

Julian grumbled.

Nicola pouted.

John winked at Rose, catching her by surprise. At first, Rose ignored the gesture, for it seemed quite forward considering they'd just met. What had Julian told him about her? Did he also believe she was a woman of loose morals?

"Miss Farthingale," John said, ambling to her side, his manner quite deferential and not at all leering, "I would be honored to escort you to the fishing spot. Permit me to carry your sketchbook and pencils. I understand you're an accomplished artist. My friend," he said, glancing at Julian, "speaks highly of your ability. Have you had formal training?"

"No, my lord. My learning is solely from art books I've received as gifts from my family over the years. No tutors. Just my own attempts to put into deed all the ideas I've read about."

His hair glinted gold as he stood beside her in the sunlight. "You've taught yourself. Then I'm even more impressed. I understand you also work with clay."

She nodded. "But that's had to come to a halt for a while."

He nodded sympathetically in return and glanced at Julian. "I was told my friend had to teach one of your detractors a nasty lesson after the bounder damaged your kiln."

"Seems you know a lot about me, my lord."

He grinned at Julian. "Lord Chatham spoke of you the entire ride. Chewed my ear off about you, if you must know."

Julian crossed his arms over his chest and grumbled again. "Will you waste the entire day chattering or do you intend to fish?"

"Ah, I've been duly chastened." He took Rose's hand in his and politely bowed over it. "A pleasure to finally meet a young woman of your intelligence, talent, and beauty. Shall we all meet on the terrace in half an hour and walk to the pond together?"

"An excellent idea," Lord Darnley remarked. "You ought not waste this beautiful day indoors."

Rose watched in silence as Julian and his friend strode out of the salon, their gaits arrogantly confident and showing not a whit of weariness despite their hours in the saddle. Nicola began to huff and puff as soon as the men could be heard climbing the stairs, their deep voices and occasional laughter resonating through the hall as they shared a private jest. "Uh-oh. Nicola, what's wrong?"

She emitted a ragged breath. "Lord Randall likes you."

Rose frowned, for her friend sounded pained and she certainly had no wish to hurt her feelings. "No, he's merely being polite. He's never met me before. It signifies nothing."

Nicola shook her head vehemently. "It means *everything*. He paid attention to you."

Rose opened her arms to her friend and offered her a comforting shoulder. "Isn't that what gentlemen are supposed to do?"

"Yes, but... but, he's a eunuch. He shouldn't—"

Lady Darnley gasped. "Nicola, watch your language."

Nicola shrugged off the admonition and huffed again. "Only he wasn't acting like one around you. He only acts that way around me. Bored and disinterested. He barely tolerates me. I've never been so insulted in my life."

Rose patted her gently on the back in a vain attempt to calm her before she worked herself into a temper. She was afraid her friend would begin to hurl objects at Lord Randall's head the moment he reappeared. "Why do you care what he thinks about you? I thought you didn't like him?"

"I don't." She eased back and crossed her arms over her chest in imitation of her brother's stance moments earlier. "At least, I thought I didn't."

Rose arched an eyebrow. "And now you're not sure?"

"This must be my punishment for what I did to you. Now I'm to be made to suffer knowing that Lord Randall has eyes only for you.

And I can't even blame him because you're wonderful and I'm not. I'm a wretchedly scheming wretch, and I deserve to have a wretchedly pitiful and lonely life after the wretched thing I did to you."

Rose stifled her amusement, for her own family had a tendency toward the dramatically theatrical as well. "Honestly, Nicola. You deserve to be happy. We both do. It isn't our fault that eligible gentlemen are not flocking to us like geese."

Nicola turned to Lord and Lady Darnley. "What are we doing wrong? Why isn't courtship as easy as it's made out to be?"

The elderly pair gazed and each other, love evident in their eyes, before turning to face her and Nicola. "Love is never easy," Lady Darnley responded gently. "It's much more than a pleasant tea among friends or a round of balls and soirees. Love is about finding the one person who appreciates your strengths and weaknesses. Someone who understands you better than you understand yourself."

Lord Darnley nodded. "A flock of bachelors will do you no good. All you need is one. The right one. The special man who encourages you to flourish. Oh, how can I explain it better? Help me, my love."

Lady Darnley tossed him a smile as she effortlessly picked up on his thought. "You and your beloved are two halves of a circle, together making a perfect whole, but neither of you ever overshadows the other."

"Love doesn't travel a smooth course," Lord Darnley added, clearing his throat. "Ours certainly wasn't, was it my love? No, indeed. There are plenty of bumps in the road along the way, but you'll appreciate the journey more because of those bumpy parts."

Although Nicola nodded, she wasn't quite satisfied. "It has all been bumps so far."

Rose nodded in agreement. "Lots of them. Is finding love as difficult for men?"

"Indeed, yes. Much more so," Lord Darnley said, reaching for a piece of raisin cake and popping half the slice into his mouth. He washed it down with a sip of tea and then continued. "Men are not domestic by nature. They tend to run wild until the right woman comes along and tames them. But they are never eager to be tamed and so they resist."

"Uncle, you'll never convince me that Julian has found the right woman to tame him. Countess Deschanel is an evil witch and she's obviously cast a dark spell on him. As for Lord Randall, he isn't wild. He's as mild a gentleman as any woman could ever meet. Any milder and he'd be in a stupor."

Lord Darnley sighed and shook his head. "Fine, Nicola. Hold to your opinions. What does this old man know?"

Rose remained a few moments longer chatting with Nicola, the earl, and his countess. "Well, I had better fetch my sketchbook and pencils." She skittered upstairs, hastily gathered her supplies, and was about to make her way downstairs when Julian emerged from his room at the same moment.

"Rose," he said in a husky murmur, his breath seeming to catch. "Here, let me help you with those."

He reached for her book and pencils and took them out of her hands before she could utter a protest, his fingers grazing hers and instantly setting off tingles everywhere on her body. "We parted badly. I was in a temper because of all that happened, but I took it out on you most of all. You have every reason to be angry with me."

She shook her head. "Not at all. My part in what happened to you was inexcusable. But you will be relieved to know that I hardly thought of you. Not once in the seven days and fourteen hours you were gone." It was of no moment that her heart yearned for this man.

"Seven days, fourteen hours, and thirty-two minutes, to be precise. But who's counting?" He grinned wryly, almost mirthlessly, and then his gaze turned serious. "Despite my best intentions, nothing has been settled yet. I wish you could remain here for another several weeks until this matter of concern to me is addressed, but it is not to be. Your family expects you home, and Lord and Lady Darnley have obligations in town that cannot be put off any longer."

She tipped her chin up. "We've managed quite nicely without you, my lord. So do feel free to go about your business without concern for me."

"I shall, but it's good to see you again, Rose. You look beautiful, you always do."

"You're merely being polite. Have you not noticed? I have a bee sting on my chin." How was she ever to fall out of love with Julian when her heart leaped joyfully whenever he was near? She liked that his compliments weren't flowery or obsequious, but appealingly direct and simple. Indeed, simple words that came straight from his heart.

He had a way of looking at her that made her feel beautiful.

He paused on the steps and turned her to face him. "A bee sting?" He tucked a finger under her chin to raise it to his view. "It must have faded. Your skin is perfect, not a single red welt to mar your creamy complexion." His thumb moved lightly across her lips. She closed her eyes and swallowed hard because his touch felt so good. "Rose, I—"

"Ah, there you are, Julian. Wait for me. I'll join you in a moment." John caught up to them near the bottom of the stairs and held out his arm for Rose. "Since Julian has his hands full carrying your supplies, may I have the pleasure of escorting you?"

Bumpy is right.

Nicola would not be happy to see her enter the salon on John's arm. Curiously, Julian didn't appear very happy about it either. So why wasn't he doing something about it? Outwardly, he seemed to be resigned and approving of his friend's attentions toward her, but there was a tell-tale twitch to his jaw and a stormy heat in his dark green eyes that gave away his underlying tension.

Why is love so complicated?

Shakespeare wrote comedies about love and its entanglements. In truth, she felt as though they were all characters in one of his plays. Misaligned pairs. She loved Julian, but he loved the wicked countess whose icy stare could freeze entire oceans. Nicola was infatuated with John, but he seemed to be more interested in hunting and fishing than her. Nobody was happy.

She paused at the doorway of the salon and slipped her hand off John's arm. "I think I prefer to carry my pencils," she said, taking a step back so that she was now walking in beside Julian and leaving John to march ahead. She turned to Julian. "I think we ought to walk together to the stream so that we may discuss your portrait."

"You're going to draw him?" John turned to her, a broad smile on his face. Obviously, he thought the notion quite humorous. "I can't wait to see the final sketch. Will you capture his arrogance and pomposity?"

"Is that even a word?" Julian remarked with a growl.

"Pomposity? It is," his friend assured him.

Rose shook her head and chuckled. "I shall capture his every scornful nuance and disdainful glower. Or shall I draw you as a bright red poppy and hang your portrait next to Emily's? She'll adore that."

She glanced at Julian and was surprised to see him smiling back. Finally! A smile!

"Don't you dare!" He laughed heartily. "I shall be teased mercilessly by my family and friends for the rest of my days. But speaking of Emily, where is she? I couldn't find her or the other children upstairs."

Lady Darnley waved off his concern. "They and the governesses have gone to a birthday party at Squire Melton's home for his twins, Geoffrey and Caroline. They're Kendra's age, but his youngest is Emily's age and his other children are close in age to the boys, so they'll all have companions to keep them entertained. We expect them home sometime late this afternoon."

Julian remained obviously concerned.

"They've taken two of the carriages and four of my best footmen," Lord Darnley assured him, noting his nephew's continued frown. "Is something wrong, Julian? It isn't a far trip to Birdslip. We can collect them at once; you have only to give the word."

"No, Uncle." He shook his head and smiled, although Rose sensed it was forced. "I wouldn't intrude on their party. I had hoped to see them upon my arrival, that's all."

After more polite exchanges with Lord and Lady Darnley, the four of them set off for the stream, John and Julian carrying their fishing poles, Rose's supplies, the picnic basket, and a blanket to spread out under a shade tree for her and Nicola. A light breeze rustled through the trees and the sun shone brightly upon them, gleaming down from a deep blue sky dotted with gentle white clouds.

Robins and sparrows chirped out their songs, redheaded woodpeckers knocked on gnarled tree trunks with their beaks, and butterflies flitted across the green meadow, occasionally stopping to rest on the colorful wildflowers growing in profusion along the sweep of grass.

Even the breeze was light and warm, marking a perfect day.

Rose shook her head and sighed. It was a perfect day if not for the fact that the wrong man was paying avid attention to her. "It's beautiful here," she remarked, unable to ignore John, who refused to leave her side and insisted on making polite conversation.

Nicola also walked beside her, making for an uncomfortable stroll because John only addressed his comments to her and appeared to be purposely ignoring Nicola. She felt trapped between the two of them and desperately wished to be anywhere but in the middle. "Do you look forward to seeing your family again, Miss Farthingale?"

"I do, but I shall be sad to leave this place. It's a little slice of heaven here, don't you think?"

"All the more delightful because you're here," John said, seeming to hang upon her every word.

What a nuisance!

She and Nicola exchanged glances. *Oh dear.* Although Nicola professed not to like the man, she was obviously irked by his behavior. Rose didn't know what to do. How was she to get him to pay attention to the right girl?

Perhaps if she pretended to be busy. Rose settled on the blanket now spread out on the grass beside the bank and picked up her sketchbook. "Do go on about your business, gentlemen. I don't wish to delay your fishing. Lord Randall, would you help Nicola bait her hook? I'd be ever so grateful if you did. She has a dislike of worms."

"Of all varieties," Nicola added, tossing back her vibrant auburn curls. However, she allowed John to lead her away.

Rose waited for the pair to move out of earshot and then turned to Julian, who was still at her side, looking like a veritable Greek god with the sun beaming down on him and illuminating his dark gold hair. "Try to forget that I'm watching you." She tried to sound indifferent, but her words came out soft and slightly breathless because he always did have the ability to steal her breath away. Had he noticed? "I'd like to capture you in your natural state. No forced poses or stiff expressions."

He immediately struck a stiff pose, but his chuckle gave him away. "Shouldn't my portrait be a formal affair? I ought to look aristocratic. How's this?"

"With your nose stuck in the air?" Rose teased. "Nostrils regally flaring? Rest assured, you'll be depicted in all your noble arrogance, but you do have one or two commendable aspects that I would like to capture as well."

"Such as?" John asked, his ears perking at what should have been a private exchange.

She stifled a groan, knowing she had to dissuade this man once and for all. "I'm better at expressing myself in drawings than in words, but Julian has a certain elegance and valor about him that inspires confidence in those who meet him. He's quite magnificent, really. In every respect. Don't you think?"

Julian regarded her in obvious surprise.

"Well, you are. I hope I can capture those qualities on canvas. Your mouth and eyes are the hardest to draw accurately because they're so expressive. Same for most people. A line drawn with just the wrong slant will completely change the character of the man I hope to convey in your portrait."

He arched an eyebrow, still remaining silent.

"You see, it's this very expression that defines you. In the curve of your lips and the arch of your eyebrow. The crinkle in the corner of your eyes as you're about to laugh."

He laughed and shook his head. "Now I'll be acutely aware of all my movements while under your trained eye."

"Perhaps for the next few minutes, but I'll fade into the background and you'll soon forget about me and my sketchbook."

Julian's gaze turned tender and indulgent. "I'll forget your sketchbook," he said in a husky whisper, leaning close to pick up one of the fishing poles resting beside her, "but never you."

A ripple of excitement coursed through her body, but she quickly tamped it down and composed herself. Julian, as far as she knew, had not broken off his courtship of Countess Deschanel. Until he did, every compliment he paid her was meaningless. He could not have his countess and her as well. He would have to choose between them, but Rose knew that he still meant to choose the countess even if he did not like the woman.

Or was her intuition wrong about that?

She sighed and turned away from him, pretending to concentrate on her tin of pencils as though she had not yet decided which one to use for the preliminary sketches. She knew very well which to use. The slate gray graphite was just the right color to convey his hard-edged strength as well as the loving warmth he held for his family, even if said family had turned lunatic and abducted him.

She had gone mad right along with them. Goodness, she'd encouraged them and led the way.

"Rolf, I'm going to walk by the stream," Nicola said, setting down her fishing pole and sounding quite forlorn when John left her side to once more return to the blanket and intrude on the conversation she and Julian were having. Nicola tried her best to hide her disappointment with a pert smile.

Rose knew Nicola very well, and she was many things but never pert. Enthusiastic, headstrong, and passionate perhaps. But pert? No, she wasn't the sort to accept failure and cheerfully press onward, chin up and optimistic that tomorrow would bring a better day. Poor thing! She was falling in love with a man she'd always thought of as a eunuch and not liking that loss of control over her heart one bit.

As her friend slowly ambled away, so did the men, but they walked in the opposite direction and began to fish along the bank of the stream. Rose fixed her attention on Julian and began to study him. He seemed at ease, his stance casual and shoulders relaxed; however, Rose couldn't help but notice that Julian's gaze was fixed on the trees and overgrown foliage across the stream and not on the water itself.

She glanced at John and noticed that he was doing the same.

She'd spent many mornings fishing with her family when at home in Coniston, and while her gaze was never constantly on the lazily rolling currents while she dipped her bait in and out of the water to lure the fish, it did rest there often enough. These men weren't looking at the water at all. That struck her as odd.

Had they noticed something in the woods that merited their attention?

There were deer and game fowl aplenty in the Darnley park grounds, but nothing more sinister. No, whatever they'd noticed hiding among the trees and underbrush was not a woodlands creature. She glanced at Nicola with concern, for she had strolled well away from them all. Suddenly, the advice Lily had spouted when speaking of separating Julian from the herd to make him more vulnerable was raising alarm bells.

Nicola stood a good distance away and not aware of whatever danger lurked on the opposite side of the stream, assuming there was any danger at all.

Acting on impulse, Rose dropped her sketches and pencil and scrambled to her feet. "Nicola, I need your help in setting out the picnic lunch!"

Her friend turned upon hearing her shout and started toward her with a shake of her head. "Are you hungry already? It's early yet."

"I'm famished," Rose lied, waving her forward and unable to shake the feeling that something terrible was going to happen to Nicola if she didn't return to her side immediately. It was the oddest sensation, completely illogical, but she was desperate to have her friend back on the blanket as though the square patch of cloth spread out under the shade tree was a magical safe harbor for both of them.

She held her breath, only releasing it when Nicola reached the blanket and knelt beside the picnic basket. "What's the matter, Rolf? You look ashen, as though you've just seen a ghost."

Rose laughed shakily and sank down beside her. "You'll think me mad, but I had a sudden, impending sense of doom. I didn't like that you'd strolled so far away from us. You're not a child, but a sudden dread washed over me, and I needed to bring you back to me urgently. Silly, of course."

"Not at all." Nicola threw her arms around her and hugged her fiercely. "I understand perfectly. We're friends forever and you just realized that we must remain friends when we return to London. Your heart was speaking to you and telling you that you must forgive me."

Rose laughed. "Perhaps."

Nicola released her and eased back. "There's no 'perhaps' about it. You and I were physically standing apart, but your metaphorical fear was that we would remain apart as friends. Do you see?"

"Odd as it seems, I do," Rose admitted, throwing her hands up in surrender. "Very well, we are friends once more. You're forgiven, but no more dragging me into your schemes. In fact, no more scheming at all. Promise me."

"Gladly!" But Nicola slumped her shoulders. "However, that means Julian will be lost to us."

Rose reached out to pat her hand. "Trust him." She turned to study Julian, wondering whether she had faith enough in him to know he'd come to the right decision about his frosty countess before it was too late.

"Trust him," she repeated with a little less confidence, "but perhaps I was a bit hasty about no more schemes. Your brother's awfully dense."

Nicola rolled her eyes. "Dense as a block of granite, for certain."

"Agreed." Rose nibbled her lip. "What harm can there be in one more scheme? But that will be the end of it."

"Unless we require another," Nicola added hopefully.

Rose groaned. No, they couldn't meddle more than they already had. They shouldn't meddle even one more time, but it was only the once and they couldn't allow Julian to march down the wedding aisle to his doom, could they? After that, they'd leave him to his fate. He was a grown man and capable of making his own decisions.

She intended to say no. She would say no. She and Nicola had to stop meddling in Julian's life. "Heaven help me, but yes. Whatever is needed to keep him out of her wicked clutches."

CHAPTER 14

JULIAN NOTICED A metallic glint coming from the copse of trees across the stream only a short distance from where he and his companion stood fishing. "Did you see it, John?"

"Yes, it's probably nothing. A gardener walking with a shovel over his shoulder, no doubt." Although by his expression, John obviously didn't believe his own words. "Dash it, now Nicola's wandered off. I can't protect her from here. She's standing too far away from me."

Julian arched an eyebrow. "Let me worry about my sister. Rose is your assignment."

John snorted. "But Rose is closer to you and Nicola's closest to me. Damn, did you see? Another glint, this time further downstream. He's moving toward your sister."

Julian reached for the pistol hidden in his boot, noting that John was about to do the same, although neither would shoot before making certain this stranger posed an imminent threat. It wouldn't do to shoot an innocent local whose only crime was to sneak a peek at the earl's niece.

Rose's sudden call to Nicola seemed to alarm whoever was lurking in the copse and send him running off. He and John lowered their pistols, both of which had been aimed at the stranger and ready to fire before he could get off a shot. "Bloody good fortune," John muttered as Nicola hurried toward Rose, blissfully unaware of the peril now averted.

Julian nodded, his gaze fixed on Rose. "How did she know?" The girls were now kneeling beside the picnic basket, hugging each other and unaware that he and John had weapons drawn. As he tucked his pistol back in his boot, Julian caught snatches of their conversation, which consisted of an exchange of vows to be friends forever. Lord, the pair were such innocents! He hoped they would never change.

"She couldn't have known." John stowed his pistol as well. "You think she did?"

"The girl has good instincts."

"Shall I go after the bounder?"

Julian frowned and then shook his head. "No, as you said, the man was probably harmless. Our poles are floating away." He waded into the shallow water to retrieve them before joining his sister and Rose. A summer breeze blew through the trees and stirred the stream currents. He noticed the gentle sway of branches and heard the rustle of their silvery green leaves. Nothing amiss.

"The fish aren't biting today," he said when Rose cast him a quizzical glance that got him wondering again whether she'd noticed the danger and acted quickly to rescue his sister. That sort of cleverness took training. No, it must have been a matter of chance.

"Is that what you were doing? Fishing?" She still had her big blue eyes trained on him. Her mouth was pursed and she was nibbling her lower lip, something she often did when unsettled.

"Of course. Pole. Bait. What else do you think we were doing?" Julian groaned inwardly. Breaking up a spy ring was hard. Resisting Rose's kissable mouth was even harder. Diverting her suspicions would be harder still. He loved that she was clever, but that agile mind of hers was also a great inconvenience to his assignment. He changed the topic before she had a chance to respond. "Have you completed any sketches? Let me see."

He reached behind her to grab her sketchbook, ignoring the sudden jolt to his bodily organs the moment he grazed her soft shoulder. He was used to these heart-stopping jolts to his system by now. The only problem was they had grown stronger instead of abating. The more he knew Rose, the more desperately he wanted her.

She blushed as he inspected her sketches. "I've only done bits and pieces. They're merely rough drawings of your eyes. Your mouth. Different aspects of your face in profile. They're early attempts. Far from perfect."

"These are excellent." Pride for her swelled within his chest. "I knew they would be." Pride and a yearning to protect her from the envy and petty jealousies she would face as a woman competing among men. She'd already experienced their nastiness and not been daunted. But how many times did her work need to be destroyed before she gave up? He wouldn't allow it ever to happen again. "Truly splendid, Rose."

"Thank you," she said quietly.

All the more reason he had to be the man to claim her. She needed to flourish and could only do so in proper surroundings, with a husband who respected her talent and would stand beside her as she fought for proper recognition.

Bloody nuisance.

He couldn't seem to think of Rose without wanting her in his life forever.

Rose was aptly named, for she was the most beautiful blossom in any garden of flowers, her petals vibrant and her colors so intricate and delicate they stole one's breath away.

"Quite talented," John said, studying them as well. "My aunt, Lady Bainbridge, will be interested in your work. I'll introduce you to her when we return to London."

Julian coughed to stifle his unreasonable anger. John was merely following his orders to protect Rose. That Julian wanted to pound the stuffing out of him whenever he came near the girl was a ridiculous response, but he felt the urge anyway.

Rose poured him a glass of lemonade. "Why the dark scowl? Are you all right?"

Julian ignored the question.

"Lord Randall," Rose said, turning away from Julian with a sigh. "Nicola and I would love to meet Lady Bainbridge. I'll ask my mother to invite you all to tea at our home once we've settled back in London, then you can inspect my work. I've done portraits for most of my family."

"Sounds delightful. My aunt and I look forward to it."

After devouring the food set out for him, for it was better to keep his hands occupied with food than give in to the urge to pound his fists into his friend's face, Julian returned to fishing. John remained with Rose and Nicola, his manner irritatingly charming, for the three of them were chatting and laughing as though this outing was a lark.

Perhaps it was to the girls, but not to him. Nor should it be for John.

He was being unreasonable again, for John was an experienced agent of the Crown and ever on alert. John's assignment was to protect Rose, and Julian knew he would do so even at risk to his own life.

He glanced at Rose as he cast his line into the water. She had caught the attention of some very nasty agents and Julian was truly concerned for her safety. He needed to draw their attention away from her. In truth, John was doing his part in playing the attentive suitor. This ruse was the best way to keep Rose safe. He was the fool for having a problem with his own plan.

He couldn't keep his eyes off Rose.

Or keep his heart detached.

But he had to.

The person across the stream may have been an innocent passerby, but Julian doubted it. He was certain Valentina's agents had followed him here as well as trailed him around London. It was imperative to keep those blackguards away from Rose. Having John pretend to court her was the best solution. But could Julian feign disinterest once they were back in London?

What if Rose decided that she preferred John to him?

Bloody nuisance.

"The ladies wish to return to the cottage. I'll escort them," John said with a grin, enjoying his assignment far too well. "Wouldn't want to interfere with your fishing."

Julian clenched his jaw, knowing his friend was teasing him, purposely goading him now that he believed their lurker had run off. But the man hadn't run far and now appeared to be back. Julian noticed a movement once again amid the lush foliage. "John," he said, discreetly keeping his gaze on the copse.

"Got it."

Before either of them had the chance to move into position, Rose accidentally dropped her pencils. "Oh, drat." She rushed forward to gather them before they rolled down the bank into the water.

"Rose, get back!"

Two shots rang out as Julian shouted his warning and lunged for Rose, managing to pull her down onto the soft grass and cover her with his body. The first shot whizzed overhead and lodged harmlessly in the trunk of the shade tree. The second shot struck his arm with an unmistakably hot sting as the ball of metal tore through his flesh.

Fortunately, it probably was only a graze. No bone struck, he hoped.

Out of the corner of his eye, he saw John grab Nicola, lift her into his arms, and deposit her behind the stone wall separating the cottage garden from the stream. "Stay down, brat," he commanded with a growl and took off after the assailant.

Julian intended to do the same, but not before he made certain Rose was unharmed, for the bullet might have struck her after it tore through his arm. "Rose, are you hurt?"

All his years of training flew out of his head as rage overcame him. He wanted revenge and didn't give a damn if Prinny would have him clapped in irons for the rest of his days. He was going to take down Valentina's operation the moment he returned to London.

They'd lose the man at the top, the elusive spy in Prinny's inner circle, but how effective could the man be without his web of agents to deliver English military secrets to Napoleon?

"No damage done," Rose said with a grunt, finally responding. "However, I'd appreciate your getting off me." More grunts as she fought to catch her breath. "Your body is big and it's crushing me."

He rolled off her at once. "Sorry."

"Don't be. You saved my life." She put a hand on his shoulder and then drew it away with a gasp. Her palm was covered in blood. "You're injured!"

"Just a bee sting. Nothing more."

"Julian," she said in an agonized whisper. "Please tell me what's going on."

ROSE STOOD IN the Darnley kitchen, quietly watching while Julian's aunt tended to his injury. He'd removed his shirt upon his aunt's command and sat stiff and impatient in one of the hard wooden chairs as the adept older woman fussed over him. He'd also removed about a half dozen weapons that were hidden on his person, and those were now set out on one of the kitchen tables within arm's reach of him.

Knives, pistols, and a garrote.

"Rose, hand me that damp cloth." Lady Darnley pointed to the clean white linen cloth and small basin filled with warm water that were atop the oak table beside her.

Nodding, she quickly dipped the cloth in the water, twisted the excess moisture out of it, and handed it to Lady Darnley. "Thank you, my dear."

She smiled wanly at the efficient older woman, but her hands were violently shaking and she doubted she'd fooled anyone.

She'd never seen anyone shot before, and despite Julian's stoic expression, she knew that this was more than a mere flesh wound. If he was in pain, he refused to show it. Rose wanted to appear brave as well, but she was crying on the inside and her stomach was twisted in knots.

So was her heart. Julian could have been killed!

She wanted to throw her arms around him and weep on his shoulder—the uninjured one—and feel the warmth of his arms wrapped around her.

"You're going to need stitches, Julian," his aunt muttered, cleaning the blood off his arm. "Rose, dear. Dip the cloth in water and continue to cleanse his wound. I'll return in a moment with needle and thread."

Rose swallowed hard.

She clutched the edge of the table as her head began to spin. "Yes, of course."

Ordinarily, a young lady of good breeding would not have been permitted to remain alone with any man, much less one who'd removed his shirt. However, the Emory family, with her instigation and participation, had already behaved so scandalously that this new situation seemed to be nothing out of the ordinary and quite tame in comparison.

Propriety had long since been trampled. She'd already seen Julian in this state of undress and he'd seen her in a worse state.

Besides, he had saved her life and she was not going to leave his side until he was safely on the mend.

Julian studied her intently as she dipped the blood-soaked cloth into the basin and gagged as the water turned red. "Rose," he said in a gentle murmur, "sit down. I'll do it."

"I'm fine. Truly." Her stomach was still churning and her head still spinning, but she refused to admit that she was having any difficulty. A few inches to the left and the shot would have killed him... or her, if that was truly the villain's intent.

Why would anyone want to kill her? She understood about the pottery ruffians wishing to scare her, but murder? These men were artisans for the most part, not cutthroats. Or was she wrong about that as well? They had proved themselves to be knaves and scoundrels.

Julian drew one of the kitchen stools closer to him. "Come sit by me. You look as though you're about to faint."

She was indeed. He must have noticed that she'd rested her hip against the table's edge for support. "No, I'm quite fit." She cleared her throat. "But I shall sit beside you. The better to tend to you."

Her hands were still shaking as she took the offered seat and then raised one hand to his shoulder and began to wipe away the remaining blood around the wound. "Twice now," he muttered.

She looked up at him. "What?"

He reached out and tucked a stray curl behind her ear. "You're hardly two months into your debut season and already two attempts have been made on your life."

"I know." She emitted a long, ragged breath. "And I've spent a night alone with a man—you. And I've behaved wantonly with a man—again you. My parents will be so disappointed."

He laughed mirthlessly. "They love you. They'll be worried, not angry, and will want to keep you safe. John's tracking the blackguard now. We'll soon find out what this latest intrigue is about."

"Do you think it's more of Sir Milton Aubrey's mischief?"

He pursed his lips in displeasure. "It's a possibility, but I doubt it. The man fled England in abject terror after I had a little talk with him."

She arched an eyebrow as she gently dabbed the cloth around his wound. "That must have been quite some chat you gentlemen had."

"It was." There was an icy glint in his eyes and Rose suddenly realized that he must have frightened the wits out of Sir Milton. These pottery merchants were rough, but apparently Julian, despite his outward polish, could be even rougher when the occasion called for it. "If he isn't behind this latest incident, then who is?"

"I don't know."

Her eyes suddenly rounded in surprise. "But you have your suspicions. Is Valentina somehow involved? She's dangerous, isn't she? This hold she has over you has nothing to do with courtship. She isn't merely jealous and keeping you for herself."

Julian glanced at the weapons on display before her. "Rose, I'd tell you more if I could. I'm not at liberty."

"Will John have answers for me? Or is he also not at liberty to speak? Nicola's anxiously awaiting him by the front entry. I know he's a hunter and no doubt an excellent tracker, but this isn't merely a deer or wild boar he's after."

"He knows to be careful."

"What else does he know? There appears to be a side of you gentlemen that none of us has ever seen."

"Nor will you ever," Julian said, intending to put her at ease, but his assurance was having the opposite effect.

Her eyes rounded in alarm. What was he involved in? "The assailant is carrying weapons. Are you quite certain John will be safe?"

"He's one of the best."

She took no pains to hide her frustration. "One of the best at what?"

"I'll go after him once I'm properly stitched up." He glanced once more at the weapons on the table. "He won't come to harm. He knows what he's doing."

"You seem awfully confident in his abilities. I suppose I ought to be as well, especially if he's carrying an armory on his person just as you are." She lightly pressed the cloth to his arm in the hope of stemming the flow of blood. Thankfully, it was slowing. "Tell me more about Valentina."

He merely blinked.

"Because I realize now that you don't love her. I don't think you ever have. In truth, you don't like her at all. You can't possibly. However, you need to remain close to her for some reason."

"Stop, Rose."

She frowned, although she remained more frustrated than angry. "Still won't tell me what all this is about? Why do men always believe they're protecting the fairer sex by keeping them ignorant of what is really going on? Let me assure you that you're not. We're much safer understanding the danger and doing our best to avoid it."

He caressed her cheek. "I agree, but I still can't tell you. Trying to uncover the truth on your own will only place you in greater danger. I don't have the resources available to protect you."

"What makes you think I can't protect myself?"

"Are you daft? There have been two attempts on your life already." He stiffened his spine as he sat up sharply. "Protect yourself? Leave that to me. As soon as we're back in London I'm hiring Bow Street runners to watch you from sunup to sundown and all the hours in between. And you're not to go anywhere near Valentina."

Rose did not appreciate being called daft, but she'd gotten some useful information out of Julian at last. "So this latest bit of mischief was her doing?"

"I can't say."

"Can't or won't? But you don't love her. Please tell me that you don't."

His gaze turned tender. "What do you think?"

She resumed lightly wiping the blood off his arm. "I can only say what I wish, and that is to fervently hope you don't love her." His lips tipped up at the corners in the hint of a smile. It was all the encouragement she needed to continue, although a wiser girl might not have spoken at all. Keeping one's mouth shut was never a Farthingale strength. In any event, she wanted Julian to know what was in her heart. "I've fallen in love with you," she said in a whisper. "I love you with my whole heart."

She paused to give him the opportunity to respond in kind, but he didn't say a word. Indeed, he looked stricken.

That wasn't promising at all.

"You don't have to love me," she continued, her heart sinking as he remained silent. "In truth, I don't expect that you do, nor do I expect you ever to entertain the notion of marrying me after all the trouble I've caused you. I'm sincerely sorry for that. However, I wish that you might one day change your mind. The point is, loving me isn't nearly as important as your not loving *her*."

His lips slowly turned upward at the corners once more in an almost smile. "Are you quite through pouring out your heart to me?"

She nodded. "I could go on, but it would only be a repetition of what I just said. Unfortunately, we Farthingales tend to run on at the mouth when we're uncomfortable and this admission has made me most uncomfortable. Awkward, really. Quite humiliating, truth be told. Especially if you don't reciprocate my feelings."

She licked her lips. "And I suspect you do not. You've made it painfully obvious by the look of shock on your face. You have a very handsome face." *Groan.* "Just order me to stop talking and I will. I can't seem to stop on my own. But you're a viscount and —"

He kissed her on the lips with exquisite urgency, his hand lightly poised on the back of her head to ease her closer and keep her from backing away, as if she would ever do that. She never would, for she ached to be in his arms and hungered for his kisses, eager to accept as many as he was willing to bestow on her.

She loved the possessive warmth of his mouth against hers, loved his heat and coiled tension. His kisses were never prim. There was always an undercurrent of danger, as though he were a beast on a fragile tether that might break at any moment and unleash his wild passion.

He appeared about to intensify the kiss when he suddenly eased away with a soft, laughing moan. "Bloody bad timing. We have an audience."

"What?" She followed his gaze and found Lady Darnley standing by the kitchen door, her mouth agape.

Rose drew away with a start, almost tumbling off her stool. She would have fallen if Julian hadn't caught her by the waist to steady her. It escaped no one's notice that he did not release her once she'd steadied. She tried to pass along a silent hint that he ought to let her go, first gazing at his arm that circled her waist and then discreetly gazing up at him in silent pleading not to make matters worse. All she managed to do was make herself dizzy by shifting her eyeballs rapidly back and forth, a gesture that he was clearly ignoring.

He grinned at her. One of those conquering warrior, smug sort of grins that she would have found irritating if he weren't every bit as brave and handsome as that grin conveyed. "I ought to go," she said in rush, now thoroughly humiliated.

"Stay, Rose." Julian continued to hold her by the waist, his grasp gentle even though she was halfheartedly struggling to break free. "I don't want you out of my sight."

She would have been elated had he made the request because he loved her, but it was a command given merely in order to protect her. He'd kissed her to shut her up. He wasn't besotted by her beauty. In truth, he was frowning at her again.

How could he kiss her like that and still not love her?

She really needed to talk to her sisters, for she was utterly confused about men. Not that any of her sisters were any wiser, but perhaps together they might figure out whether Julian loved her or was simply keeping her close because he felt responsible for her.

Were men able to pour heart and soul into a kiss and not mean it? Was every man a base creature capable of taking advantage of a girl who'd just admitted that she loved him? "I wish to return to my room. I'm only in the way here." She finally squirmed out of Julian's grasp.

Lady Darnley gave her a pitying smile. "My dear," she said gently, "I think you and I must have a talk."

Rose blushed. "No lecture required, Lady Darnley. You can't possibly berate me more than I'm berating myself. The fault is mine completely and I take full responsibility. I can't seem to behave myself around your nephew."

Julian grabbed her hand before she could dart away. "I can't let you go," he insisted, looking quite serious and not at all doting or loving, so she knew he wasn't about to fall on bended knee and declare he loved her madly. "John is still tracking the assailant. You're my responsibility until he returns."

Rose couldn't stop her chin from quivering as she struggled to hold back tears. She'd just admitted that she loved him. Went on and on about it, truth be told. Declared herself a wanton in front of Lady Darnley. Was her humiliation to continue? "I release you of your so-called responsibility. I release you of every obligation you may feel toward me."

"Rose, you're twisting my words."

"What words? You haven't said anything to me other than that I'm an obligation to you. I just told you that I loved you."

Lady Darnley gasped.

Rose was still too ashamed to look at her. "Can you not say it to me, Julian? If you can't, then just say so. Don't worry about sparing my delicate sensibilities. I'd like to hear the truth for once. Just tell me what's in your heart."

She finally glanced at his aunt. "I don't mind if you stay, Lady Darnley. You and Lord Darnley knew my feelings for your nephew even before I realized them. You wouldn't have thrown us together at the hunting lodge unless you were certain that a love match could develop. I do love your nephew. My heart soars whenever he's near. But he doesn't love me. There you have it."

Lady Darnley began to back out of the kitchen. "I'll leave the two of you alone a moment longer. Julian, you must tell her. Stop being an idiot."

Rose gazed at him in expectation.

He ran a hand roughly through his hair. "I'm sorry, Rose. There are things I cannot say to you." He strode across the kitchen and summoned his aunt. "Stitch me up. John will return soon. He and I will have to pay a call on the local magistrate."

"Your uncle has already gone off to fetch him." Lady Darnley regarded him askance. "And what of Rose?"

His gaze remained cold and indifferent. "She needs to trust me."

CHAPTER 15

ROSE FELT AS though eons had passed, for every *tick, tick, tick* of the clock stretched out with excruciating slowness while they awaited John's return. She, Lady Darnley, and Julian were still in the kitchen, which had been cleared of servants to lend privacy for the minor surgery Julian was about to undergo.

They would be allowed back in once Julian's wound was stitched and he had once more donned his shirt. Not the blood-soaked one, but a fresh one brought down by Lord Darnley's valet.

Rose ought to have been tossed out as well, but Julian refused to let her out of his sight for even a moment. Did he not trust her? Or was he worried that another assault could be in the offing? He'd ordered the footmen to arm themselves and sent two of those armed footmen off to the residence of the local squire to escort the children home once their party was over.

Rose thought it was a good idea to leave the children where they were for the moment, especially delicate Emily, who was easily frightened. She doubted Julian would reveal to the children what had happened, but Emily was likely to sense something was wrong. She would immediately pick up on the tension in the room and burst into tears. Her distress would affect her sleep as well.

Rose had taken the girl into bed with her twice already during the week and would do so again if the poor little thing needed comforting. She'd do the same for Kendra, although she was a hardier sort and would likely drop off to sleep without a care after a busy day at the squire's party.

The matter of the children now resolved in her mind, her

thoughts returned to Nicola. "I ought to check on your sister. She hasn't left her position by the front entry since we ran back to the cottage."

"No." Julian motioned for her to sit down when she attempted to rise. "She'll be fine. It's you that the blackguard decided to shoot."

Lady Darnley put a hand to her ample bosom. "Oh, dear. What if the villain has given John the slip? Will my dear Darnley be all right?"

Lord Darnley, upon being told of the incident, had roared like a bull, summoned his carriage, and immediately stormed off to fetch the local magistrate, intent on personally fetching the man, for he was incensed that anyone would dare put his family in danger, especially on the grounds of his beloved cottage. "Rose, you're family, too," he'd said before climbing into his carriage. "We love you as we do our own nieces and nephews."

That had warmed her heart.

If only Julian felt the same way.

She stared at the clock again. Only ten minutes had passed. Ten interminably long minutes.

Where is John?

His absence cast a pall over all of them.

The kitchen now reeked of whiskey, for Julian was liberally pouring the contents of an excellent vintage onto his wound to thoroughly cleanse it before his aunt began to stitch his arm. Rose jumped to her feet. "Let me help you with that."

He laughed and took a hearty swig, offering one to her in jest.

She frowned at him. "How can you be so casual at a time like this?"

His expression softened, allowing her to see the pain he'd been hiding all the while. "I'm not," he said quietly.

She closed her eyes while Lady Darnley dug her needle into his flesh. Her stomach was in such a roil she didn't think she could manage watching her loop the thread in and out of his raw, puckered wound without losing the contents of this morning's breakfast or bursting into tears.

Her cold hands were clasped in front of her. Resting them on her lap and even rubbing them together did little to ease her sudden chill. In truth, her entire body was cold and shivering.

"Rose," Julian said in a husky murmur, "hold onto me." In the next moment, his warm palm fell atop her small hands and his fingers entwined with hers. Her first thought was that he needed a human touch to ease his pain as Lady Darnley worked needle and thread, and then she realized that he wasn't afraid and his spirits did not need bolstering.

She opened her eyes and inhaled lightly in surprise. He was worried about her and trying to soothe her. It was extraordinary. He was injured and yet his thoughts were on her comfort.

"Done," Lady Darnley said finally, taking a step back to admire her handiwork.

Julian ran his thumb across the top of Rose's hand in slow, gentle circles. He hadn't let go of her all the while his aunt stitched his wound. "Rose? Are you all right?"

She didn't think it possible for love to grow deeper. Until now, she simply thought that one loved or one didn't. But Julian's gesture revealed how wrong her supposition had been. She smiled at him.

He gave her a lopsided grin in return. "No longer angry with me?"

Her response, which would have been an embarrassing stream of blather about how much she truly did love him, was cut short by a commotion at the front door. Julian released her and grabbed one of the pistols lying on the table, aiming it at the kitchen door as the sound of running footsteps drew nearer.

Rose jumped to her feet and gasped. "What are you doing? Nicola's out there."

"Get behind me. You too, Aunt Bess."

Rose knew better than to disobey his instructions. Julian was not about to shoot before knowing his target, and the last thing he would ever do was shoot Nicola, no matter how willful or exasperating she could sometimes be.

"It's me," John called out before slowly entering the kitchen. His shirt was stained with a dark circle of red just below his heart.

Nicola followed him in, obviously distraught. "Will one of you louts please tell us what's going on? John, whose blood is that? And if you dare tell me it's only animal blood, I'll pick up one of the weapons on this table and — good gracious, how many weapons can one hide on one's person? And why would you feel the need to carry so many of them?"

"Enough, Nicola." Julian said, finally dropping his arm. But he did not set down his pistol. "What happened, John? Are you injured?"

"No, it isn't my blood. We ought to speak in private." His gaze shot from Nicola to Lady Darnley and finally to Rose.

Julian motioned for him to take a seat at the table and nodded for the ladies to do the same. "Much as I would agree, it's hopeless. They'll only eavesdrop and I'd rather have Rose where I can see her. She's in danger so long as they think I care for her."

"Think you care? Don't you like her?" Nicola had just sat down and was now back on her feet, incensed and sputtering in indignation. "How can you be so dense? Are all men this stupid? You and John are certainly proving it so." She turned to scowl at John. "Yes, you too. You're as bad as my brother. Possibly worse."

Julian nudged her back into her seat, speaking to her with surprising patience. "Nicola, you're overset and with good reason. There's more going on than you understand. Let me hear what John has to say."

"Can't tell you anything useful, I'm afraid." John shook his head and sighed. "The man was dead by the time I tracked him down, which means he had a partner. Or he was reporting to the man in charge, no doubt expecting to collect his reward, and received a musket ball to the chest instead."

Rose's heart beat faster. These men spoke so casually of death. No doubt they'd seen it all too often before.

John rested an elbow on the table and continued. "I tracked that other man, but lost his trail when his horse turned onto the London road. He's taken the dead man's horse as well. Apparently the beast has more value to him than his companion."

"The pair must have followed us here from London," Julian said.

John nodded. "I'll have an easier time tracking him back to town. There can't be many travelers with two horses to feed and water. Hopefully one of the ostlers will provide me with a decent description of the villain."

Lady Darnley's brow furrowed in obvious concern as she regarded both men. "You're leaving?"

"Soon as I wash up and change my clothes," John said. "I don't want to fall too far behind the blackguard."

Julian glanced at the clock. "Where's the body? I'll take the magistrate to inspect it once he arrives. Perhaps I'll get a clue or two off it."

"You'll find it... him... just outside Birdslip, in the glade to the right of the main crossroads." John slapped his hand on the table to mark the end of the conversation. "If you'll excuse me, ladies. I have more hunting to do."

Rose had a thousand questions she still wished to ask, but had no desire to delay John. She'd try to pry the answers out of Julian since he would remain with her until the magistrate arrived.

John paused as he reached the door. "Julian, er, do I... keep up the pretense?"

Julian rubbed a hand across the back of his neck and cast Rose a look of chagrin. Why was he staring at her? What did she have to do with any pretense? "No, don't bother. No one was fooled by it."

Nicola, obviously more nimble-brained than Rose was at the moment, was back on her feet and mad as a wet hen. "What are you saying? That you ordered John to *pretend* he liked Rose?" Her hands curled into fists. "Do the two of you dolts have no care for her feelings? Do you make it a practice to lead young ladies along by their heartstrings and then break their fragile hearts?"

Rose groaned. Nicola ought to have been relieved that John was faking his affections. Rose certainly was delighted by this turn of events and Nicola would be too once she calmed down and gave it thought. John was not attached to any young lady and would now be free to court her, assuming her tirade hadn't scared him off.

In truth, he didn't appear the timid sort, but Nicola looked angry enough to fire off a cannonball straight through his chest.

"It was the best plan we could come up with to protect Rose," Julian tried to explain. "One of us needed to watch over her and it couldn't be me."

"Protect her from whom? Her pottery ruffians?" Nicola seemed more confused than ever. "Were they behind this latest attempt?"

"No," Rose said. "This is something far more serious. It involves Valentina, only I haven't figured out what her role is exactly and your brother won't tell me. No, that isn't quite right. He *can't* tell me. Which means he must be under orders from a higher authority and—" She gasped. "How stupid I've been! This involves Napoleon. She's spying for him, isn't she?"

"Holy hell," John muttered. "What now?"

Rose shook her head emphatically. "Nothing. Do you seriously think I'd ever give away you or Julian?"

Julian groaned. "Never purposely. I know that. But this is a high stakes game and the smallest gesture, the slightest glance, could give our hand away. Bollocks, I dare not take any of you back to London now."

Lady Darnley had remained silent all the while but spoke up now. "I think you must take us back as planned. Lord Darnley and I have obligations in town, and if what you say is true, I don't think any of us will be safe if left behind here. We're better off staying close to you so that you may more easily watch over us."

Rose added her opinion when Julian didn't seem persuaded. "I have to get back as well, for I must start work on the Runyon pottery contract. The documents are likely at home awaiting my signature. I'm to submit several more designs by next week."

Julian rubbed a hand across the back of his neck and emitted a long, slow sigh. "Very well, I know how important those designs are to you. In any event, John and I have gathered as much information as we can on our investigation for the Crown. I've wanted to end it since last week and arrest Valentina and her cohorts, but Prinny's been getting some bad advice from one or more advisors in his inner circle."

"Purposely?" Rose understood that poor judgement could be as destructive as any intentionally treasonous act. "Do you think there's a spy in the highest echelons? Someone interfering with your work?"

Julian nodded. "But we have yet to discover who he is. That's why Prinny won't allow us to close the investigation. He's desperate to find out which minister is working for Napoleon. But by insisting that we ferret out the traitor, he's given Valentina the time she needs to make her escape. I doubt she'll be in London by the time we return. That attempt on Rose's life was her parting gift to me."

"Horrid woman," Lady Darnley muttered.

Julian nodded. "We won't catch her this time around, but we know who her underlings are and will round them up over the next few days. She has the resources to flee, but most of them don't. The best they can do is go into hiding, but we'll easily find them. Who knows, with his web of spies gone, the traitor in Prinny's inner circle might be forced into the open."

Rose's thoughts were awhirl. How could she and Nicola have been so stupid? They almost destroyed a year of Julian's important work with their idiotic scheme. "I'm so sorry, Julian. I'm to blame for ruining your investigation."

"You weren't at fault." He arched an eyebrow and grimaced. "I underestimated the determination of my own family. I'm still shuddering over just how far you all were willing to go to save me from myself. Next time, kindly trust me and do nothing."

"Then you're not angry?" Rose held her breath in hopeful expectation.

"I'm bloody furious with all of you, but just as much with myself."

Rose drew up her stool and sank onto it beside him. "Perhaps there's a way we can make it up to you. I think we can help. Oh, not in the physical aspects of your investigation, but if you give us the details that still have you stumped, we might come up with an answer. Valentina is a woman, after all. An odious one, for certain. We can look at the clues from a woman's point of view and perhaps come up with some fresh leads for you."

Nicola and Lady Darnley were eagerly nodding, so she continued. "Even if we don't come up with anything, we might still stir something tucked away in your memory that might help."

Julian did not hold the same enthusiasm for her proposal. "I wish I could, Rose. But even this conversation could be viewed as treason. I dare not involve any of you further."

"I understand, truly I do. But someone tried to shoot me today. They could have taken aim at Nicola as well." She nibbled her lip, wondering whether to reveal that sudden sensation of dread that had come over her earlier. Yes, she had to tell him. "In truth, I think this villain contemplated shooting her instead. When she walked away from us by the stream, I had an overwhelming sense of fear that something bad was about to happen to her. That's why I called her back with that excuse to set out our picnic fare. So you see, we're embroiled in your investigation whether or not you like it."

She fixed her gaze on him. "Are you going to let us help?"

He was saved from responding by a commotion at the front entry hall. "Lord Darnley and the magistrate are here."

JULIAN HAD LITTLE trouble finding the body of Rose's assailant. It was situated in a thicket off the main road into Birdslip exactly as John had described. A hot breeze already carried the smell of death, and all three men had only to follow their noses through the hedgerows and underbrush to reach the grim spot.

Sir Hubert, a portly, gray-haired man of equal age and vigor as Julian's uncle, took a step back and pressed a handkerchief to his nose to ward off the odor. "Damned hot weather. The man's insides will soon turn to pudding."

Julian held his breath and knelt beside the body.

His uncle hesitated a moment and then approached to stand over him. "Do you notice anything worthwhile about this villain?"

"Other than his deplorable bathing habits?" Julian nodded. "The expression frozen on his face is one of surprise, which means he and his accomplice weren't mere cohorts. They were friends and this murdered man trusted him." Julian carefully leaned over the body for a closer inspection. "Sir Hubert, do you recognize him?"

The magistrate shook his head with vehemence. "No, my lord. He isn't from these parts, that's for certain. But I'll ask around at the local inns and taverns. He might have given a name or spilled some useful information while having a pint. Perhaps he stayed the night and—"

"No, if he isn't a local, then he must have followed us from London today." Julian carefully searched through the man's pockets but found no clue as to his identity. More important, no clue as to the identity of his slayer.

Sir Hubert nodded. "The maggots will have at his body soon. He'll have to be buried quickly. I wonder if he has family? Anyone who might miss him?"

Julian's mouth tightened in a grim line as he handed the magistrate a few silver coins. "I'll leave it to you to take care of the burial arrangements."

The magistrate stared at the coins Julian had deposited into his palm. "What shall I do? Have him buried in a pauper's grave?"

Julian nodded. "Make note of where you've put him and let me know if anyone comes around asking for him. I doubt it will be a grieving family member, if anyone at all. Men such as he never leave loved ones behind to weep."

He turned the last of the man's pockets inside out. Empty. Someone had rifled through them beforehand, no doubt his companion to ensure no trace of his identity would remain. His clothes were of good quality but worn and faded. They might have belonged to a gentleman at one time and then been given away to a seaman's charity. The man had a weathered look to his sun-bronzed face that indicated long hours in the sun.

In truth, he could have worked on a farm, but there was a sallowness to his features that indicated scurvy, a common ailment for those at sea for extended periods. This man was likely hired at the docks by one of Valentina's cohorts.

Bloody nuisance. Another futile lead, for he'd get no reliable answers from the scum who frequented the dockside taverns. Any wharf rat who might be inclined to talk for a reward of a few coins would understand he'd be risking his life to do so. Knowing one's throat would be slit if ever he was found out tended to keep a man quiet no matter how much gold or silver was dangled before him. "Sir Hubert, I'll be returning to London on the morrow along with Lord and Lady Darnley and my family. I'd appreciate your conducting a discreet investigation and dispatching your report to my London residence as soon as possible."

"I will, my lord." He nodded emphatically.

Julian rose and stepped away from the body. "If anyone did notice this man and his companion, make certain you get a thorough description of his companion and forward it to me immediately."

"You may rely on me," Sir Hubert assured him, his words muffled by the handkerchief pasted to his mouth and nose.

Within the hour, the lifeless assailant was taken to the local mortuary, the magistrate's clerks were dispatched to the local stables, inns, and taverns in search of information, and Julian and his uncle were on their way back to Darnley Cottage.

The women, who were waiting for them in the salon, leapt to their feet in anxious expectation as he and his uncle strode in. Was it merely afternoon? He'd ridden from London on a hot, damp day that seemed to stretch into eternity, except for the moment he'd been shot, which had passed in a lightning blur.

The only thing that cheered him was Rose's beautiful face with the welcoming smile on her lips. He wanted to take her into his arms and kiss her into said eternity, but he'd been around a dead body for the better part of an hour and didn't think she'd appreciate his getting too close.

"Nothing to report," he said with a shake of his head and then excused himself to wash up. He returned to the salon soon thereafter and was surprised to find Rose seated with her sketchbook and pencil in hand, drawing something for his uncle. "What are you doing?"

She smiled up at him again with one of those light-up-the-room smiles that he had grown quite fond of in the short time he'd known her. "Being useful, I hope. Lord Darnley is providing me with a description of the villain you found murdered. I'm trying to draw his likeness."

He strode to her side and sat next to her on the sofa to inspect her work. It was excellent, as he knew it would be. "If the Runyon Pottery Mill doesn't want you, I'll snatch you up and put you to work for our war effort." He'd meant it in jest, but her eyes rounded and filled with hope, for the girl had no sense regarding a woman's place in the home or other twaddle taught to young women in preparation for their debut. He didn't know whether Rose had been taught differently, but he suspected that she had been. Her parents must have nurtured her talent.

Her love of art transcended all.

He liked that she didn't restrict her dreams to what society deemed proper and was not surprised that she'd won the Runyon contract. Her talent would lead her in unusual directions, and it would be her choice as to which paths she'd follow. She couldn't have expected that her ability would land her in the middle of a military operation, but her sketch of the man was quite useful to him. "You managed this on a mere description provided by my uncle?"

She shook her head. "It's merely a rough drawing."

"Can you make about a dozen more just like it?" He took the sketch and perused it.

"Of course. The original is the hardest. After that it's simply a matter of copying the lines."

He eased back in his seat and chuckled. "Sir Hubert is searching for someone who's seen the companion. Hopefully, he'll find him before we leave for London. If so, I'll have you draw that scoundrel as well."

She turned to face him, her eyes aglow with starlight sparkles once more. "I'd love to be of help. I feel awful for meddling in what was obviously a matter of the highest importance to every English citizen. We ought to have trusted you. I'd feel so much better if I were able to make it up to you in some important way."

She was referring to the sketch in her hand.

He nodded, but he had other ideas for how she might make it up to him, none that he could propose without getting his face roundly slapped. Nonetheless, he would follow up on a few of those ideas once his business for the Crown was completed.

He wanted Rose.

He admired her for her generous heart and artistic talent.

But he'd practically ruptured his eyeballs in excitement when he'd stripped her out of her camisole that night at the hunting lodge and seen her naked by firelight, her golden hair tumbling wildly down her back and blue eyes aglow with passionate wonder.

She was the Lorelei who sent men crashing against the tidal rocks in frenzied and fiery spasms of lust.

Yes, he *wanted* that.

Chapter 16

"IT'S SO GOOD to have you home, Rose!" Laurel cried, rushing through the gate as soon as Lord Darnley's carriage pulled up to the Farthingale residence on Chipping Way. Rose hardly had time to step inside and take off her bonnet before Daisy and the twins stampeded down the stairs, the three of them chattering and squealing as they swallowed her in hugs.

"It's good to be home." One would think she'd been gone ten years instead of a mere ten days.

Within moments, she was taken into the arms of her parents and given more hugs. Her aunts and uncles soon joined them, her Uncle George laughingly ruffling her hair and then ordering their butler to bring out tea and cakes. "Pruitt, this calls for a celebration. Lily bring down your harp—"

"No!" everyone shouted at once and burst into laughter, including Lily, who detested that instrument even more than the family detested having to listen to her play it.

"Only jesting," Uncle George assured her, tossing Rose a wink. He then turned to greet Julian, who had stepped down from the carriage along with her in order to escort her inside.

Her father also stepped forward to welcome him into their home. "My lord, thank you for returning my daughter to us. Or should I express relief that you managed to survive her visit?"

Julian arched an eyebrow as he glanced at her. "Suffice it to say that I survived, although barely." He spoke lightly, but Rose knew that her father would be aghast to learn what had truly transpired. "I hope to chat at length with you soon, Mr. Farthingale. I have some important work to finish over the next few days and would like to stop by once I'm done, if that is agreeable to you."

Rose heard her mother's soft gasp. No doubt she believed Julian was about to offer for her hand in marriage. If only her parents understood his true purpose, they wouldn't be nearly so amenable. He was going to tell them about the attempt on her life, which was bad enough, but what if he insisted on telling them about the night they'd spent together in the hunting lodge?

No, he wouldn't be so foolish.

He'd have no choice but to marry her then.

She wanted to marry him, but only if he offered of his own accord. He ought to want her because he loved her, not because he'd bedded her... although they hadn't done anything on the bed. No, it had all taken place on the kitchen table.

The mere thought of it brought heat to her cheeks.

Julian grinned and arched an eyebrow as though understanding her thoughts. Was she that transparent? He seemed to know her mind as well as she did.

As the footmen brought in her trunks, Pruitt quickly set up tea and cakes for the family in the salon. "You and your family are most welcome to join us, my lord," her mother offered.

"Very kind of you, Mrs. Farthingale, but Lord and Lady Darnley are quite spent. I'll be dropping them off next." He bowed over her mother's hand and looked exceedingly handsome with his boyish smile as he once again promised to return at his first opportunity. "But I must take my leave of you now."

While the rest of the family ambled into the salon, Rose walked him to the door. "Thank you, Julian. Especially for not saying anything to my parents about... well, everything."

His expression turned serious. "I'll have to tell them about the attempt on your life."

"But nothing more, I hope." She blushed. How could he possibly say anything about the hunting lodge? There was nothing to be gained and all to lose by revealing that little secret.

"Let me give it thought, Rose." He glanced behind her to the demi-lune table beside the front door. "Runyon."

"What?" She followed his gaze and saw the brown envelope that could only be her pottery design contract. "They've sent it!" She smiled up at him, feeling as though her heart might burst with happiness.

He gave her the tenderest of smiles. "Go on, I know you want to open it."

"I do." She grabbed it off the table and excitedly ripped open the seal. "I'll ask Father and Uncle Rupert to look it over. They're brilliant negotiators and—"

She suddenly found herself struggling for breath.

"What's wrong?" Julian frowned, obviously noticing that her effervescent joy had crumbled and turned to agony before his very eyes because she hadn't the ability to hide her feelings, especially from him.

"This must be a mistake." What she held in her shaking hands was no contract but a rescission letter. The Runyons didn't want her to design for them.

"Rose?"

She clasped the letter to her chest, not wanting him to see the full extent of her distress. Her dreams were shattered. What could she do? She forced herself to smile back even though her eyes were misting. "Nothing serious. You mustn't worry about me." She didn't want him distracted by her petty problems when he was about to save England.

She took another moment to catch her breath and then shook her head as she tossed him an even brighter smile. It didn't work. He took the letter from her hand. "Give it back, Julian. Truly, it's nothing." She cast him an imploring look.

"Rose, I can almost hear your heart ripping to shreds. Do you expect me to shrug my shoulders and walk away?" He held the letter out of her grasp when she tried to snatch it back and then turned away to quickly read it. Once done, he set it down and turned back to her, his expression exquisitely tender. "I see."

"I'll get over it."

He caressed her cheek. "You will, because you have a beautiful, fighting spirit. I'm sorry, Rose. I know how much this meant to you. These men are cowards. Your work is brilliant."

"They've given the job to someone else." A tear rolled down her cheek. "It's my fault for getting my hopes up. I never expected them to rescind their offer." She tipped her chin up and tried to sound casual, but the wobble in her voice gave her away. "An important lesson in life now learned. Runyon will never have a female as their managing designer, not while old Mr. Runyon runs the shop."

He caressed her cheek once more, his touch divinely gentle and comforting. "I know you're disappointed. I would be as well. What they did was cruel and unforgivable, but no matter what they do, they can't take away your talent."

She nodded, but another tear fell onto her cheek. "I'll survive, Julian. You needn't worry about me."

"But I do worry." He tucked a finger under her quivering chin. "I must go now, but I'll see you as soon as I can. We'll work this out together."

"There's nothing to work out. It's done. No, I—"

"Together." He gave her chin an affectionate tweak. "You'll see. We make a good team, even though we often work at cross purposes."

Rose shook her head and laughed softly. "Yes, we must work on that."

He gave her a smile that simply melted her bones. "We will."

"I HEAR CLINKING crystal," Uncle Rupert said three days later as they prepared to head off to Lord Carlisle's ball. "Pour me a tall one, George. What a day I've had. I'm off to Coventry first thing in the morning for more negotiations with those damn woolen merchants. Unmitigated thieves is what they are."

Drink in hand, he crossed the room and took a seat beside his aunt Hortensia, who looked quite regal and daunting in her gray bombazine. "What did you do while at Darnley Cottage, Rose? With all the family and friends paying calls on us, we've hardly had time to speak of your visit there. Did you have nice weather?"

A safe topic. "Oh, yes. It was exceedingly pleasant weather. We fished and swam and hiked. I drew portraits of Nicola and her siblings that were quite well received. Lord Darnley would like me to paint a portrait of his nephew, Viscount Chatham, and one of the viscount's friends would like to bring his aunt, Lady Bainbridge, to tea with us to discuss commissioning a portrait as well."

Her mother frowned lightly. "My dear, this is your debut season. You mustn't overextend yourself with obligations. I had hoped that when your kiln was… er, damaged, that you might slow down and simply enjoy the balls and other social entertainments."

"I'll manage, Mama. I'm under no obligation to finish these projects by a particular date. In any event, the viscount is a busy man," she explained, thinking of the spy ring Julian was in the process of destroying. It was a dangerous assignment, and she would not take a calm breath until it was all over and he stood before her, safe and sound. "I doubt he'll have much time to give me for his portrait over these next few weeks. Perhaps no more than half an hour a day, if that."

Her mother's ears perked. "You'd see him every day?"

Rose smoothed a nonexistent wrinkle out of her white satin gown. "I'd have to until I completed the final sketches and that might take a while."

Hortensia chuckled. "Oh, I think you ought to take as long as you need to get it perfect. Don't let anyone rush you. No, indeed. Stick close to the handsome viscount."

Laurel and Daisy giggled. "Aunt Hortensia, would you be as insistent if he were a lowly baronet?" Laurel asked.

She waved her hand with an air of nonchalance. "If Rose loved said baronet? Of course. Love is what matters. When one is fortunate enough to find it, one must not be coy about seizing it."

Rose cleared her throat. "I do wish everyone would get off the topic of love. I'm not in love with Viscount Chatham."

Lily nudged her spectacles higher on the bridge of her nose. "You are so obviously enamored with him that even I've taken notice."

Rose groaned, for Lily never noticed anything unless it was written in a book. "Even you, Lily? How did you arrive at your conclusion?"

"Newton's laws of gravitational attraction apply here. I believe Viscount Chatham's gravitational pull is very strong and he's drawn you into his robust orbit. That's why you fidget and turn circles around him whenever he visits." She frowned lightly. "But he hasn't come by at all since your return."

"Perhaps Rose has done something to knock him out of orbit," Dillie teased. "What have you done to him, Rose?"

"Girls," their mother said gently, "Stop teasing your sister. I think he must have used this time to break off his affair with Countess Deschanel. No one's seen her around town in days. Viscount Chatham is being careful not to involve Rose in the nasty rumors that will circulate once the end of his liaison with the countess is confirmed."

Daisy's eyes widened. "This sounds quite juicy. Rose involved in a love triangle."

Their father groaned. "Girls, it is nothing of the sort."

"Indeed, not," their mother assured them. "Viscount Chatham was never in love with the countess. He stared at Rose throughout Lady Winthrop's musicale, and a man doesn't do such a thing if his heart is pledged to another."

"Oh, I see. It's like you and Father." Lily nudged her spectacles up the bridge of her pert nose once more as she addressed their mother. She had such a little nose and little ears that the frames had trouble clinging. "Father has eyes only for you—it matters not who else is in the room. You're the one who brightens his heart."

Their parents chuckled. Rose melted a little at the adorable blush on her mother's cheeks.

Their father smiled at Lily. "That's very well said, child. I'm quite proud of you."

Lily beamed back. "Thank you, Father. I'm glad I settled on that idea, because my first thought was that maybe he just wished to bed Rose."

The men in the room all seemed to choke on their brandy at the same time.

Their mother shot out of her seat. "Ah, Pruitt! Have the carriages been brought around yet? Time for us to head off for Lord Carlisle's ball." Her gaze took in Laurel, Daisy, and the twins. "Girls, do behave while we're gone."

"We always do," Dillie said in earnest. "Well, we always mean to."

Their father rolled his eyes.

Rose checked her reflection in the mirror by the entry hall as she and the family elders made their way out of the house. Agnes, one of the Farthingale maids, had fashioned Rose's hair in an intricately braided chignon and helped Rose to don a gown of white silk trimmed with beaded white lace at the sleeves and square collar and a violet ribbon at the waistline that gathered just below her breasts. "Do I look presentable?"

"You always look lovely," Hortensia said. "Move along or we'll be late."

Within the hour, Rose and her parents, along with the usual horde of Farthingale relations who descended upon them during the season, had made their way through the reception line and were milling about the ballroom chatting with acquaintants while waiting for Lord Carlisle to officially open the ball.

Rose craned her neck to search for Nicola, whom she'd arranged to meet at the gala affair to commiserate in mutual misery about the men they loved who did not appear to love them back. She finally noticed her seated beside Lord and Lady Darnley, who happened to be chatting with her neighbor, Lady Eloise Dayne. "I haven't seen Lady Eloise in an age," she told her mother. "May I go to her?"

"Of course. John, dear, will you escort her? Hortensia and Julia are calling me over to meet Viscountess Glynnemeade, and I know how avidly you Farthingale men have been coveting her woolens."

Her father laughed. "Sophie, you have a charming way with words. We've been coveting her woolen fabrics for our mill. I doubt anyone has coveted her personal woolens in sixty years."

"I'll escort her, Sophie. I've been meaning to ask after Lady Eloise's health anyway," George said.

She took his offered arm as they made their way to Lady Eloise's side. Rose kissed her lightly on the cheek and then greeted Nicola as well as Lord and Lady Darnley. "Did you girls enjoy your time in the countryside?" Eloise asked, smiling affectionately. "You both look lovely. I was just telling Nicola how pretty she looked."

Rose nodded. "We did. It was most interesting."

Lady Eloise arched an eyebrow. "I'm eager to hear all about your time away. Your sisters and I missed you. Good evening, George.

You look quite distinguished, as always."

He kissed her wrinkled cheek. "How are you feeling, Eloise?"

"In the pink, thanks to you. It's most convenient to have my new doctor living next door. Ah, here comes Lady Bainbridge and her nephew. I understand he joined Nicola's brother in escorting you home. Why Nicola, I believe he's noticed you. Is this the young man who made your stay interesting?"

"No, not at all." Her cheeks turned a bright pink, the tell-tale blush completely giving her away.

Rose felt a small tug at her heart, sorry for her friend. Oh dear. She and Nicola had to work on hiding their feelings. It was one thing for trusted friends and family to know, but for the gentleman in question? That would be disastrous.

No wonder Julian was so reluctant to share any bits of war information with them. One had only to look at their faces to know exactly what they were thinking.

John walked straight toward Nicola, sparing not a glance at anyone else. "Rose, help me," she said in an urgent whisper. "I'm going to make a complete idiot of myself."

Rose patted her hand. "You'll be perfect."

"Right, a perfect idiot. Facing him was much easier when I thought him a eunuch. Oh, boils and blisters! Have you ever seen a handsomer gentleman?"

Yes, Nicola's brother.

Where was he?

John wasted no time in introducing Lady Bainbridge and then surprised everyone by inviting Rose to dance. Why her and not poor Nicola, who looked about ready to weep? Was there a reason for the continued ruse?

Rose accepted because she didn't know how to politely decline the invitation. "A waltz, how delightful," he said and began twirling with her in his arms. But they had yet to make a full turn about the floor when he suddenly stopped dancing and led her out of the ballroom.

She stopped when she realized what he was doing and frowned at him. "Lord Randall, I cannot possibly go with you. What are you about? I cannot—"

"Someone's waiting for you in the library," he said with quiet urgency. "You know who I mean. He didn't want the two of you to be seen together just yet."

Her heart skipped a beat. "Julian's here?"

John nodded. "He has a mission for you."

"For me?" Now she was sounding like a parrot, but she was too excited to contain herself. Julian wanted her help. She wouldn't disappoint him.

The ballroom was a crush so it was rather easy for them to slip away and stroll down the hall as though they were walking toward the dining salon. John led her past it down the dimly lit hallway to the quiet end and opened the last door on the left. She stepped in and felt a sudden trepidation, for the air in the library felt thick and tomb-like, and she saw no one else inside. Indeed, there was nothing but shelves from floor to ceiling filled with neatly ordered books. Had John lured her away from the crowd on false pretense? Was he the traitor everyone was searching for?

"Your little package is delivered," John said with a chuckle, seemingly to no one in the room. There was so little light in here, only a small oil lamp standing lit upon Lord Carlisle's imposing carved mahogany desk. Then Julian stepped out of the shadows. Rose wanted to rush to him and throw her arms around his neck in relief, but he appeared tense and not pleased to see her. She hoped it wasn't so, that the play of harsh light and elongated shadows upon his features only made it seem that way.

She hesitated, at a loss for words and uncertain what to do. He made no move toward her, only stood there frowning.

John cleared his throat. "Let's finish with this business so I may return to the far more pleasant chore of dancing with your sister."

Julian's frown deepened. "Remember that you're on duty. You're to protect Nicola and that's it."

"He's now assigned you to Nicola?" Rose curled her hands into fists, wanting to pound sense into both men. She understood their business was important, but did they have to so casually break hearts along the way? "Is that all she is to you? Because if you dare hurt her—"

John raised his hands in surrender. "Wouldn't think of it. I'd rather face Napoleon's armies than your wrath," he teased, then turned serious. "Rose, she's safe with me."

But did that mean he cared for her? Or was she safe because he was assigned to guard her and he took his duty seriously? She didn't want Nicola to be a mere obligation for him.

Why couldn't men fall in love as easily as women did?

She shook out of the thought and concentrated on what Julian had in his hands. "Is that my sketchbook?"

Julian set it down on Lord Carlisle's desk and then held out the large chair behind it and motioned for her to take the seat. "No, it's mine. Rather, it was purchased on behalf of the Crown, but intended for your use. You did a brilliant job of drawing the first villain. You remember those pleasant fellows we encountered while at Darnley Cottage? I hope you can do the same with his accomplice."

"I almost had him," John said, drawing up a chair beside her and sinking into it. "He managed to elude me when a fight broke out at the tavern I'd tracked him to along the London road. I thought I'd picked up his trail again, but it grew cold and I fear I've wasted days on the hunt. I got a good look at him though."

Rose's eyes widened in trepidation. "I'll do my best, but why here and now? You could have called on me earlier at my home."

Julian's shoulder grazed hers as he leaned over her to open the sketchbook, but she had only a moment to enjoy the warmth of his body against hers before he stepped back and withdrew a small tin of pencils from his breast pocket. "We were busy until now."

Of course, how stupid of her. She was responding to him like a besotted ninny, her heart pounding and skin tingling, while he was saving the civilized world... and he smelled divine while doing it, his enticing mix of musk and maleness now causing every pulse in her body to throb. Who knew there were so many? *Eep!*

"Valentina narrowly escaped," he continued, mistaking her silence for concentration on the vital purpose at hand, "but we managed to catch everyone else on our list... all, that is, except for the elusive accomplice and the even more elusive inner circle traitor." He knelt beside her and she couldn't help but notice the lines of fatigue etched into his handsome face. "I know you'll do a wonderful job for us, Rose. If it weren't for the danger to you, I'd eagerly enlist you as the newest weapon in our arsenal."

He thought enough of her to want her in his organization? The man certainly knew how to breach the walls of her heart, not that they were ever very high or insurmountable when it came to Julian. No, they simply crumbled whenever he was near, so that he had merely to stroll in and claim her heart. His rugged good looks and the smoldering heat of his stare had nothing to do with it. Well, only partly to do with it. Most important, he valued her for her mind and talent as well.

How could she not love him?

"Shall we begin?" She winced at the sound of her voice, so tight and squeaky.

Julian mistook it as his cue to move away, although she supposed it was for the best. She'd never be able to concentrate while he remained close, his warm breath tickling the curls at the nape of her neck. Oh, she was getting distracted again.

She withdrew one of the pencils from the tin.

John began to describe the man. "Dark hair… prominent brow… a little jowly… yes, that's it. Heavy eyelids… nose seems to have been broken."

She made several sketches, trying her best to set the man's description down on paper. In one, his eyes were a little narrower and nose broader. In another, his chin was slightly more prominent and earlobes a little longer. She drew as fast as she could, for both men seemed to have their eyes on the clock, wanting her to finish before the music stopped to mark the end of the set. John would have to return her to the ballroom and have her back under the watchful eye of Lady Eloise before the gossips took notice of her absence.

"Are any of these drawings accurate?" Julian asked, now beginning to pace.

John nodded. "This one is it. Excellent job, Rose."

As he pointed to the last one she'd completed, the door latch gave a little click and the door groaned open. Rose held her breath, simply gaping open-mouthed toward it, for her body was too frozen in surprise to move.

John and Julian responded in quite the opposite manner, silently leaping into action so that John now stood beside the door, ready to disarm the unknown intruder, while Julian positioned himself between her and said intruder, pistol trained at the man's heart. Or was this person a female? "Dr. Farthingale," Julian said with obvious relief, lowering his arm and relaxing his stance upon recognizing her uncle.

John stepped out of the shadows and made himself known, giving her usually unflappable uncle a start. "Sorry, didn't mean to alarm you," John muttered, closing the door and leaving the four of them to stare at each other, her uncle obviously eager for an explanation.

Rose jumped to her feet. "Uncle George, this isn't at all what it appears. Although I can't tell you what I'm doing in here, for it might be construed as treason. Not that I'm doing anything treasonous. Quite the opposite. But I dare say no more. My lips are sealed."

He rolled his eyes. "I can't even begin to make sense of what you just said, Rose. What's going on? Why are you in here with these two gentlemen? And I use the term loosely, for they ought to know better than to allow you to remain with them without a proper chaperone, no matter how honorable their intentions. Had someone other than me walked in and seen you, you'd be ruined."

She knew he was right, but still couldn't muster any contrition. She loved that Julian had thought enough of her ability to trust her with this important task. "But no one did."

He scowled at all of them. "That's beside the point."

Julian stepped forward. "I can explain."

Her uncle folded his arms across his chest and scowled. "You had better. Pray, do a better job of it than my niece just did."

Julian quickly brought him up to the present without revealing anything about the earlier attempt on her life or their night in the hunting lodge. In truth, he disclosed as little as he could about his royal assignment. Rose was surprised that he'd revealed any of his mission, but she supposed there was no harm in doing so now. The operation was nearing its end and everyone knew her uncle could be trusted. Julian probably saw no harm in providing general bits of information. "That's why I need more drawings of this man before I leave."

Her uncle was one of the smartest men alive, so Rose wasn't surprised when, to Julian's obvious dismay, he began to put the rest of it together. "Of course, it all makes sense now. You were courting Countess Deschanel because she was the only connection to this well-heeled, inner circle traitor. Bloody hell, you had us all convinced you were besotted with her."

"No need to keep up the pretense now." He held up the sketch Rose had completed moments ago. "I need your niece to copy this exact sketch another six times and quickly."

"I'll do it right now." She resumed drawing while the men continued to talk.

George unfolded his arms and eased his stance, but remained standing in the center of the room. "So the man in the sketch is quite significant."

"Unlike his dead companion, I think he took his orders straight from the traitor and will lead us to him." Julian sighed. "At least, I hope so. We have no more leads now that the countess has fled. We've rounded up all her known contacts, none of whom have ever dealt with anyone but the countess. We've searched her London townhouse and the small manor house left to her by her unfortunate husband. We have nothing left to go on."

John sank into the chair beside Rose once again and spoke to her uncle while he watched her at work. "We've had all the lords in Prinny's inner circle followed, but to no avail. Their contact with the countess was at all times purely social, as far as we could detect. Some had no contact with her whatsoever, not even when at the same social function."

Rose glanced up as she was about to start on her third copy. "Don't you find that telling?"

All three gentleman regarded her quizzically. "How so?" Julian asked.

She resumed sketching. "Well, when a young lady likes a particular gentleman, she's so afraid to let on—at least, until she knows his own thoughts about her—that she responds with the opposite of what she wishes to do. She'll be delightful and cheerful with everyone else, but won't look at the gentleman or ever engage him."

"How is this relevant to Countess Deschanel and the traitor in Prinny's circle?" John asked. "This isn't about coy debutantes and matchmaking."

"Well, it's a question of hiding one's feelings... or in this situation, whatever nefarious deed they're up to. If the scoundrels fear they're being watched, then wouldn't they be safest never approaching each other? Then their looks could never betray them." She turned to Julian. "You said so yourself when refusing for the longest time to tell me what was going on. You were worried what might happen if I knew, that a mere glance or slipped word would betray your entire operation. So why wouldn't it be the same for the countess and her inner circle traitor? If it were up to me, I'd start with those who've had *no* contact with the countess."

Julian stared at her for the longest time. "Rose, that's an excellent suggestion. I could kiss you."

George cleared his throat and stepped between them. "But you're not going to," he warned.

Julian glanced at Rose, grinning when he noticed her disappointment. "Guess not."

He turned to John and motioned to the drawings Rose was still copying, apparently not nearly as disappointed as she was that there would be no kiss. Not that it would have been much of a kiss with everyone watching. Still, she would have liked to feel the warmth of his lips against her cheek.

"John, we'll start with the two ministers who've had no contact with the countess," Julian said, his manner serious and his thoughts clearly not on her, "but he isn't to be arrested once discovered. Come back to me when you have your proof. If one of them is the man we've been seeking, we may have better use for him if he believes he's gotten away with his crimes."

Rose glanced up. "Why would you allow him to remain free? Isn't the point of all this to capture him?"

Julian nodded. "We'll take him in due course, but we can do a lot more damage to Napoleon's cause by feeding him bits of false information through his most trusted source. We may not be able to keep it up for very long, but it's worth a try."

Julian took her sketches as soon as they were completed and started for the double doors that led into Lord Carlisle's garden. Rose stood up and called out to him. "Where are you going? Must you leave the party immediately?" She then shook her head and groaned lightly, realizing she was acting like a ninny, for he had more important matters to attend to than remaining here to dance with her. Why would he remember that he'd promised to do so once her ankle had healed? "Of course, you must go. I'm sorry I stopped you."

His features softened as he regarded her. "Rose, I owe you a dance. I haven't forgotten. I look forward to it."

CHAPTER 17

THE AFTERNOON SUN shone a perfect yellow against the deep blue sky, and a gentle breeze wafted in through the open windows of the Farthingale parlor. Rose sat with Laurel, Daisy, and assorted family members awaiting the guests that would soon arrive for her mother's tea party.

Where were the twins?

Oh, never mind.

They'd turn up eventually.

Rose took a deep breath to calm herself, but she couldn't manage it. She fidgeted with her gown, a simple but elegant muted bronze that brought out the dark honey tones of her hair. Would Julian notice? Would he care? She hadn't seen or heard from him since Lord Carlisle's ball three days ago.

Laurel and Daisy approached and sat beside her. Daisy reached out and patted her hand. "Rose, you'll make yourself ill. He'll be here. Didn't he tell you that he looked forward to claiming a dance?"

She nodded. "But this is an afternoon tea. There's no music. And if he's so besotted with me, then shouldn't he be more ardent? Anyone can look forward to a dance, for it's the polite thing to say." She let out a shaky breath. "What if he only means to let me down gently? Oh, dear! What if he plans to do it today?"

Pruitt, ever poised and perfectly attired, announced the arrival of the Earl and Countess of Darnley. Laurel grabbed her hand. "Come on, Nicola and her family have arrived."

As though in confirmation, Pruitt announced Nicola next.

Rose and her sisters ran to the entry hall to greet her, showing none of the refined grace and restraint they'd been taught in preparation for their debuts.

Where was Julian? Pruitt had yet to announce him.

Rose quickly scanned the entry hall in search of him, but he was nowhere to be seen.

"Have John and Lady Bainbridge arrived yet?" Nicola was obviously eager to see John again, but her expression was a mix of excitement and fear that she tried to hide with an overly bright smile.

Rose gave her a hug of encouragement. "No. Where's your brother?"

"I don't know. He hasn't been around at all these past few days. Has he sent you any word?"

"Nothing."

"Oh dear." Nicola began to nibble her lip. "I really hate this marriage mart business, Rolf. Everything's so much harder when one's heart is at risk. How can one make pleasant conversation when merely crossing a room feels like walking across a bed of hot coals? Oh, look! There's John. He's just arrived with Lady Bainbridge. Do you think he'll acknowledge me?"

"Why wouldn't he?" Laurel asked, eager to speak to him as well.

"Because he thinks I'm a sharp-tongued shrew and he would have nothing to do with me if not for the fact that I'm his best friend's sister and it would be unpardonably rude of him to avoid me," she said with a groan. "I don't think he likes me at all."

Daisy cast her a pitying look. "I'm sure things aren't quite as bad between you as you seem to think."

More guests arrived. Tea and cakes were brought out. After greeting John and learning nothing other than that Julian was busy and probably wouldn't attend her tea, Rose spent most of the afternoon chatting with Lady Bainbridge and showing her the items of pottery and decorative glassware she had made which were on display throughout the house. "And did you draw these? They're charming," the kindly dowager remarked, pointing to the drawings she'd made of herself and her sisters that hung on the walls of the entry hall. "Rose, you are truly talented."

She blushed. "Thank you."

"Well, my girl. You've won yourself a commission. John wasn't exaggerating when he said you were extraordinary."

The tea ended several hours later. The twins, who were missing much of the time, were finally discovered in the garden, hiding amid the branches of the large oak that stood beside their bedroom window. They'd stolen an entire ginger cake and a bowl of strawberries and were eating them as they spied on their guests. To amuse themselves, they'd pretended to be squirrels and dropped acorns on the heads of friends and family, which earned them the punishment of a week's confinement in their room.

Rose snorted to contain her laughter. Those clever fiends! They'd gotten out of having to visit their mother's aunt, Lady Palmhurst, whose entire house reeked of the lilac cologne she doused on herself by the bucketful. The scent of lilac was quite lovely in small doses, almost as delightful as the scent of lavender or rose hips, but there was nothing pleasant about an aroma that struck you hard in the face like a brick thrown at you.

Truly, it snatched one's breath away. There was no escaping it, for Lady Palmhurst would not allow her windows to be opened.

And the woman loved sardines.

Dillie never responded well to sardines.

Lilac water and sardines.

Rose wanted to cheer the twins for so cleverly maneuvering their way out of the visit. If only they could help her as well as they'd helped themselves. She walked down the hall and knocked at their bedroom door. "Open up, I need to talk to you. Sisters meeting." Laurel and Daisy were close behind her. Usually they met in Rose's room, but it was nothing to switch location while the twins were under house arrest, so to speak.

"Rose needs your counsel," Laurel said, giving another impatient knock.

Dillie opened the door and stepped aside to allow them in. "We'll do what we can to help. We noticed Julian's absence and wondered at the reason. He means a lot to you, doesn't he, Rose?"

She shook her head. "I don't have much time before the Earl of Devon's ball. Oh, bother. Less than half an hour to get ready, so we really must talk fast. I care for him very much. I love him, but I don't think Julian feels the same about me. Lord Randall explained to me that Julian was busy. That's it. He refused to tell me anything more."

Dillie nodded. "And now you're worried that Julian wishes to avoid you."

"Yes." It felt odd to confide in the twins, who were barely out of the nursery, yet they had such agile minds, and Lily in particular always had a unique manner of looking at things that could be very helpful. "How do I make him fall in love with me?"

Lily looked pained. "You know what Father always says. You can't make someone love you. They either do or they don't. But I've heard it said at the Royal Society that the Duke of Lotheil has just acquired the statue of a rare African fertility god. It hasn't arrived in London yet, but if I could get my hands on it and figure out how to cast a fertility spell—"

Laurel burst into laughter. "Don't you dare! Besides, Rose needs our help now. Finding herself carrying his child will not help matters. We're speaking of love, not reproduction."

Dillie's eyes grew wide. "Rose, you're blushing! What haven't you told us? Nicola let something slip this afternoon about an abduction. Never say you abducted him and held him prisoner! At Darnley Cottage? That's brilliant! A perfect way to separate him from the herd."

"Not quite. We captured him and locked him away in Lord Darnley's old hunting lodge, and... somehow, I got locked away with him."

Daisy gasped. "Why didn't you tell us sooner? Then what happened? Did he kiss you?"

She gave a reluctant nod.

"Before or after you locked him away?" Laurel asked, soon followed an artillery barrage of questions posed by her curious sisters. They were tossing the questions at her so fast she couldn't answer them all.

Rose didn't think her face could grow any hotter. "The appalling scheme did work to some small extent, but mostly it was a disaster. He kissed me before *and* after, if you little snoops must know. But his family completely botched the attempt and he was furious."

"Before *and* after?" Lily crossed to her desk, picked up a rather large tome, skimmed through the pages until she found the section she was looking for, and began to read. After a moment she set down the book and turned to face them all. "The Emory men have been described as wolves, much like the men in our family, so I wanted to refresh my recollection on the topic."

Daisy sank onto her bed, sitting on the edge of it with marked impatience. "And?"

"Wolves mate for life. They select the desirable female and mark her with their scent. That Julian kissed you before *and* after is quite telling. It means he has selected you, or at the very least, seriously considered you for his mate." Lily sighed. "But I know nothing about matters of the heart, Rose. I only know what's written in these books. He may exhibit the traits of a wolf, but I can't say for certain that he loves you, only that you were under consideration at one time."

Laurel frowned. "But he kissed her afterward."

"Which is promising," Lily admitted. "I have no answer for you. If he attends the ball this evening, look for subtle clues in his behavior and be guided by those."

"Rose! Are you ready yet?" their mother called from downstairs. "We're leaving in twenty minutes. Where are your gloves? Where's the pearl necklace?"

"Drat, I'm nowhere near ready." She gave each of the twins a quick hug. "I'll report back to you in the morning. Thank you, Lily. I know there's no easy answer. I'll look for those small clues and I'll try hard not to get my hopes up."

Within the hour, Rose and the family elders were entering the Earl of Devon's glittering ballroom. The play of candlelight against the crystal chandeliers seemed to give the large room an enchanted glow. Rose touched the string of pearls at her throat, feeling a little shabby in these elegant surroundings, even though this was the Farthingale heirloom necklace that was supposed to bring good fortune to each girl in the family who wore it during her debut season.

She needed all the good fortune she could muster. There were so many young ladies in attendance, many of them pretty and most of them of rank, while she was merely a Farthingale. She was proud of her family, to be sure, but how could she compete with the daughters of dukes or earls or barons? Julian was a viscount, heir to an earldom.

Why would he want her?

She glanced around and saw that the older women in attendance wore diamonds and some of the younger women did so as well, along with sapphires and emeralds that sparkled against their bodies. Wealth, elegance, rank. She suddenly felt quite out of place. She noticed Lady Eloise seated beside the long windows and hurried over to greet her, in dire need of a friend. "Rose, you poor dear. Why the worried look? Does this concern Viscount Chatham?"

She sat down beside her. "Am I that obvious?" She glanced around as the orchestra struck a chord to mark the opening of the ball. The crowd began to collect around the dance floor, leaving her and Eloise mostly to themselves. "I don't think I shall dance at all tonight, Eloise. My heart isn't in it. I wish to remain by your side."

"Nonsense, child. You're no wilted wallflower."

"Perhaps not, but I'm no diamond either." She held up her dance card. "See, it's quite empty."

"You haven't given the gentlemen a chance to find you."

"It won't matter. I'm not going to dance tonight."

"That would be a pity," a deep, rumbling voice said from behind her, "because I'd hoped to keep my word to you."

Rose turned sharply. "Julian... er, that is, Lord Chatham... how lovely to see you, I think." Her face began to heat. Did he have to look so magnificent? The black of his elegant jacket stretched perfectly across his broad shoulders.

He arched an eyebrow and grinned. "You think?"

"How are you?" Was it polite to ask this of a gentleman? "So sorry you missed our tea party. It was quite lovely. Cakes! We had cakes and cucumber sandwiches, too. And the twins were in hiding. No one knew where they'd gone until they began firing acorns from the oak tree in our garden."

He smiled.

"A hot evening, isn't it?" Where was her fan? "Goodness, quite steamy." Or was it the look in his eyes that was steaming up her insides?

Julian held out his arm to her. "There's a nice breeze in the garden. Care to take a turn on the terrace with me before we dance?"

As politeness demanded, he extended his other arm to Lady Eloise. "No, my boy! The last thing you want is an old bat like me intruding. No, indeed. I think I'll stay right where I am." She patted Rose's hand. "Do stop talking and let Chatham get a word in. I think you might like what he has to say."

Rose turned to Julian in expectation, her stomach tied in a thousand knots. "Will I?"

He grimaced. "Come, let's talk outdoors."

Did men in love grimace? Was his intention to let her down gently and allow her to cry her heart out in the relative privacy of Lord Devon's garden?

Julian led her down the terrace steps and along the pebble path decorated with lanterns that gleamed so that the flower beds appeared magical under the moonlight. "Rose," he said with an ache to his voice, drawing her behind a massive tree to hide them from view of prying eyes.

She meant to wait for him to start the conversation, but she was a mass of tangled and frayed feelings and the words insisted on bubbling out of her. "Julian, I missed you so much. I'm so glad you're here now. You look wonderful. You always do. I think you know it." She shook her head. "No, I didn't mean that you're arrogant about it. I mean that you know how I feel about you. But I don't know how you feel about me now that you're safe from the clutches of the horrid countess."

"You haven't figured it out?" He seemed surprised.

"I can be awfully dense when it comes to men. You, actually. I don't know any other men in a romantic way. No one but you has ever kissed me. So if you wish to let me down gently, then do get on about it. I'll cry, but I'll… well, it will take me quite a while to get over you. If ever. In truth, I don't know if it's possible. But it's best to just tell me what's on your mind and get it over with."

"Indeed, let's get it over with." He placed his hands on either side of her and pinned her gently against the tree. She felt the slight scratch of bark against her skin even though he was careful not to hurt her. "Rose, I love you."

She blinked her eyes, suddenly feeling nothing but wonderful. Had she heard him right? She'd wanted to hear those words so badly that she might have imagined them. "What?"

"I've loved you from the moment I set eyes on you, although mine were stinging from all the smoke in the air after your kiln exploded and it took a while for them to stop watering long enough for me to see you clearly." He pressed his body lightly against hers, sending hot thrills coursing through her. "I fell *hopelessly* in love with you when you drew that portrait of Emily as a bright red poppy."

He placed a hot kiss upon the base of her neck. "I knew I would love you forever when you convinced my idiot brothers to stand still for you so that you could draw them as pirates." He placed an even hotter kiss at her throat. "I loved you when I saw you in the library at Darnley Cottage. I'm amazed I survived the encounter, for my entire body exploded in flames at the sight of you in that sheer nightgown. It hid nothing. *Not a single blessed curve.* And did I mention that you have the most blessedly perfect curves in Creation?"

She tried to breath, but her heart had shot into her throat and the butterflies in her stomach were insanely flailing their wings, out of control with joy. *Oh dear!*

She managed a breathy moan as his lips moved lower on her body to the swell of her breasts, and then he kissed his way upward once more. His eyes held the promise of much more to come so she wasn't quite so disappointed that he was moving upward instead of downward on her body. "Rose, I loved you at the hunting lodge, even after I knew you were part of that lunatic scheme. I'm taking you back there. I'm going to finish what I started."

She smiled. "I loved that kitchen table."

"Me, too. I'm going to have it embossed and preserved for all time." She felt the rise and fall of his chest with each rumble of his soft laughter. "I loved the way you responded to me while on it. I love you, Rose." He lowered his mouth to hers and possessively claimed what she'd been eager to give him all along. Her love. Forever.

The orchestra struck up a waltz at that moment, the melodic notes dancing like butterflies on the light breeze, ever so sweet as he continued to kiss her to the rhythm of his own powerful need. "Dance with me, Rose," he whispered against her ear and eased her away from the tree.

The silver moon and stars gleamed brighter as he took her into his arms. The heady scent of roses and lavender filled the air. He twirled her upon the grass and evening dew, and it felt right and magical, for this was their first dance and she was nestled in his arms where she belonged. As the music came to an end, Julian kissed her lightly on the lips and then drew back to smile at her. He withdrew a small box from his pocket and opened it for her to view. "A ring?" she mumbled numbly, gazing at the exquisite sapphire surrounded by a circle of small, glistening diamonds.

His smile broadened. "Yours, if you'll have me. Rose Olivia Lorelei Farthingale, will you marry me?"

She ought to have counted to ten and then given a dignified acceptance. Instead, she threw her arms about his neck, loving the heat and power of his body against hers and the gentle strength of his arms as he enfolded her protectively in them. "Of course I will. You know I will. My heart is yours and always has been."

"Good, because I'll accept no one but you as my viscountess."

She laughed and shook her head, her eyes tearing with joy as he slipped the ring on her finger. "I never imagined myself in that role. It feels right with you."

"Of course it is. You're my Rose. No one else's."

"The viscount's rose." She smiled up at him. "I rather like it."

"So do I," he said and gave her a scorching kiss to prove it.

CHAPTER 18

ROSE PUT HER arms around Julian as he carried her into his bedroom, arrogantly grinning as he noticed the pink flames on her cheeks. They were alone for the evening in his London townhouse, the servants having all been given the day off in honor of their wedding. Not even Prinny had dared disturb him, even though he was still investigating the matter of the inner circle spy. She sensed Julian had an inkling about the identity of this elusive agent of Napoleon, for he'd taken a moment from their wedding day to talk privately to the Duke of Edgeware, and then the duke and John had hurried off.

She didn't press Julian on the matter, for he'd reveal the villain's name once it was safe to do so. He meant to feed this lord false bits of information, so the fewer people who knew his identity, the better.

Julian planted a gentle kiss on her lips, regaining her attention. "We're married, Rose. You needn't feel guilty or ashamed."

"By special license," she said with a wince, but her smile must have given away that she wasn't terribly appalled or overset. "The gossip must be rampant, but I'm glad we didn't wait. I don't think I could have behaved myself with you much longer."

"It took a Herculean effort on my part to keep my hands off you." She loved the way his eyes shone with the promise of passion. "The wedding breakfast felt as though it would never end."

She nodded. "It did go on well into the evening, but I enjoyed celebrating the day with our families. Didn't Emily look adorable with the basket of rose petals as she marched down the church aisle?"

"True to form, my idiot brothers almost set fire to the altar, but the minister survived with hardly an eyebrow singed. I don't think he was too pleased that I used his holy water to douse the flames."

She nestled in the cradle of his arms. "Fortunately, this evening will be much quieter."

"*Hell*, no. I certainly hope not," he said with a choked laugh. "But before I make a sex-starved fool of myself, I have something important to show you." He carried her over to the window and set her down beside him. She leaned her back against his chest and sighed when he wrapped her in his embrace as they gazed out onto his small garden, which was aglow with light from the fading rays of the setting sun.

She turned slightly in his arms to gaze at him. "What am I supposed to be looking at? The magnificent sunset?"

He pointed to the far corner of his garden. "It is beautiful, almost as beautiful as you." He planted a chaste kiss on her nose. "But no, that isn't it. See that stake planted in the ground?"

She followed to where he was pointing and nodded. "It's a stick in the ground. What is it for?"

"It marks the spot for your new kiln. Rose, this house has been a bachelor's quarters for a long time, but I want to make it our home. I want to fill it with the things you love most. Hopefully, you'll include me in that list."

She thought her heart might burst with happiness. "You'd build it for me?"

He nodded.

"Oh, Julian, you'll always be first in my heart. My very own kiln," she said, still amazed by the thoughtful gesture. "Thank you."

"I meant it when I said you're a rare talent. I'll do all in power to support you. I know the letter you received from old Runyon broke your heart. His son was quite angry about it as well. He approached me when he heard that we were to marry."

"Ben Runyon spoke to you?" Her eyes widened in surprise. She didn't dare hope that something could be salvaged with the Runyons.

"We'll discuss the business details tomorrow, but he admires you and wants to work with you. I ought to be jealous, for the man is obviously besotted with you. He has excellent taste."

She laughed. "No, he admires my vases. That's all. My sisters and I scare the wits out of him."

Julian turned her away from the window and led her to bed, but she hesitated as they drew near it.

"Rose?" He was obviously surprised by her hesitancy because she was fearless in most things. "Does this scare you?" He nodded toward the bed they would share.

She sighed. "Mostly I'm afraid I'll disappoint you."

He caressed her cheek. "Sweetheart, you never will. We're in this marriage together, for the rest of our days. Yes, I want to get my hands on your outrageously beautiful body and turn you into an utter wanton in my bed. But I also want to protect you. Cherish you. Keep you safe from harm. I'll never hurt you, Rose."

She put her hand to his lips, now feeling foolish about her doubts. He'd guide her, be gentle and patient as she learned whatever it was that he meant to teach her. "I know. I trust you. Undress me, Julian."

So he did.

She held her breath as his hands covered her body, warm and gentle as he slid the gown off her shoulders and let it pool at her feet. He did the same with her camisole, then began to remove his clothes, his attention fixed on her as he slowly stripped out of his garments and tossed each aside.

"You're blushing," he teased.

"I'm naked and so are you, but you don't seem in the least embarrassed. You're purposely putting yourself on arrogant display." She licked her lips, suddenly feeling quite warm and tingly, for he had a magnificent, muscled body and she couldn't wait to wantonly explore it.

He lifted her in his arms and set her down in the center of the bed, settling his body over hers. Her lips parted in a smile.

She emitted a soft breath as his hand cupped her breast. "I love you, Rose." And then he dipped his head and took the pink tip in his mouth, swirling his tongue across it until she moaned and arched her back and clung to his shoulders. Until all thought melted away, leaving only hot sensations... the damp heat of his skin against hers, the warmth of his mouth on her breast, the tug of his fingers sliding between her slick thighs. Then he was inside her, thrusting slowly at first to give her time to adjust to him, and taking her with him as their bodies began to move together in an eternal dance, no music, just throbbing, fiery desire. Mindless. Beautiful. Hot.

His muscled body straining and aching to hold back, he took her cries of ecstasy into his mouth in a long, deep kiss. He matched her frenzied thrusts with his own until he reached his own release and spilled his seed inside of her to claim her as his own, their connection now complete.

She ran her hands up and down his body, feeling him shudder in powerful surges of pleasure until he was spent and sweating and sapped of all strength. He rolled her atop him as he collapsed against the sheets, their bodies entangled and their hearts even more so.

"I love your colors, Julian," Rose whispered as she lay entwined in his arms, her soft body pressed against his and the scent of sex and lavender on her skin.

He arched an eyebrow and grinned. "Colors?"

She kissed his shoulder, the slight movement causing her breast to graze along his chest and instantly revive his desire. She noticed his response and laughed softly. "The brilliant green of your eyes, the dark blond of your hair. The rippling tan of your muscles. Oh! I thought you were done."

"You're the Lorelei, remember? No man can resist you. I certainly can't." He ran his hands through the wild mane of her hair and began to slowly kiss his way down her body. His lips felt so good against her skin. His arms were gentle as they held her.

The night was dark and silent.

All she heard were Julian's even breaths and the husky timbre of his voice as he said, "I love you, Rose."

THE END

SNEAK PEEK OF THE NEXT BOOK

IF YOU LOVED ME

By MEARA PLATT

CHAPTER 1

Yorkshire, England
December 1819

DESMOND CAMERON, MARQUIS of Blackfell, made three mistakes on this cold and blustery winter afternoon while traveling in his spacious carriage from the thriving market town of Durham to the bustling city of York.

His first mistake was asking his driver to divert from the main road onto a lesser-known path that cut across a desolate stretch of moor in order to shorten his journey.

His second mistake was ordering his driver to chase the careening carriage that had blown past them a few moments ago and now lay tipped on its side just beyond the ruins of Rievaulx Abbey. The abbey was only a short distance from the village of Helmsley, known for the excellent inn that was to be his destination for this evening. The weak sun had already faded into a pale pink horizon so he couldn't very well leave these travelers, some of whom might be injured, stranded on the frigid road as darkness fell.

His third mistake was stopping to help.

"Is anyone hurt?" he asked, his heart pounding as he flung open the door of his carriage and jumped down the moment his driver brought his team of matched bays to a halt. He meant to assess the damage and then invite these travelers to ride along with him, for it was a short distance to the Dragon Sail Inn. There they would all find rooms for the evening and obtain a nourishing hot meal, perhaps a compress and some bandages for the aches and bruises suffered.

He hoped there was nothing more serious.

"Blackfell! You're a sight for sore eyes." Rupert Farthingale struggled out from the broken carriage, flashing a toothy grin beneath his thick black moustache. But he winced as his feet hit firm ground and he began to rub his shoulder. No doubt he'd been slammed hard against the sturdy carriage frame as it began to tip over. The conveyance was now leaning precariously to the right, needing no more than a gust of wind to knock it completely over on its side. "Help me, won't you?"

"Of course, Rupert," he said with concern, for the man was fortunate to be in one piece. "What happened? And what brings you to this part of England?"

"Carrying precious cargo back to London," he said, turning back to his carriage and attempting to reach into it. *"Bloody blazes."* He winced again, drawing back in obvious pain from the shoulder he'd just been rubbing. "You'll have to help her out. I can't manage it."

"Her?" Desmond hopped onto the carriage wheel to raise himself sufficiently to peer inside.

"In here," a delicate, female voice called out. "I'm unharmed, just a little shaken. One of the carriage wheels must have struck a rut and twisted off. I don't know what we would have done if you hadn't come along to rescue us, sir."

Desmond reached inside to assist her. "Grab hold of me and I'll pull you out."

He ignored the pleasurable heat that shot up his arm the moment the young woman took hold of his hand, for he had yet to manage a good look at her in the dim light. But he was already intrigued, for her voice was sweet as honey and gently melodic as it reached his ears. "Wrap your arms around my neck while I help you down."

He silently chided himself for his eagerness to take her into his arms, not liking the effect this young woman was having on his composure.

No, not liking it one bit.

She circled her arms around his neck, then suddenly gasped and clung tightly to him as the carriage groaned and began to teeter.

"I have you," he assured her, securely wrapping his arms around her slender body and speaking into her silky hair. How he managed to speak at all was a mystery, for his heart was pounding a hole through his chest and his breaths were coming in fits and starts. "You needn't fear."

Though she said nothing, he felt her shudders as she continued to cling to him like a barnacle to a ship while he carefully made his way off the wheel.

Hell's bells. Who is she?

Despite his trepidation, he was in no particular hurry to release her. She felt surprisingly good in his arms. He blamed the racing of his heart on the tottering carriage and not on the graze of her lips against his throat or the exquisite feel of her body as she shifted against him.

Hell's bells again.

What was wrong with him? Once his feet were on firm ground, he made certain she was steady on her feet and then released her, eager to have a good look at this girl who was rousing sensations within him that she had no business rousing.

He stifled a groan. She must have been an angel in an earlier life, for Desmond had never met a girl prettier than the one standing before him right now. She wasn't traditionally beautiful, but there was something soft and appealing about her that made his breath catch. "Are you certain you're not hurt?"

She was of average height and nicely shaped from what he could tell when he'd held her and now whenever the wind gusted and whipped her cloak against her slender curves. Perhaps she was a little on the thin side, but it was hard to tell amid the angled shadows of the fading light. She'd felt perfect when pressed up against him.

Her hair was a fiery mix of chestnut and gold, and her eyes were an exquisite sapphire blue. Her mouth was a touch too broad and had a slight downward tilt at the corners that gave it a sensual quality.

She nodded. "I think Uncle Rupert took the worst of it."

"Just a few bruises. Nothing more," Rupert assured her when her expression turned fretful and she began to nibble her fleshy lower lip.

Desmond cleared his throat. "Well, hop in. I'm sure the local farrier will have that wheel fixed by tomorrow and then you can be on your way again. Are you certain you're all right, Rupert?" He swung open his door and motioned for both of them to climb in.

Rupert shook his head and frowned. "I'm in the pink, but I must have the wheel fixed this evening. Tomorrow won't do. My coachman and I will tend to it as soon as we reach Helmsley. You see, I have a meeting in Coventry on Wednesday that I can't miss. Then it's on to London for us."

Desmond nodded. "I'm bound for York, then on to London as well. My grandfather and Evie will have me drawn and quartered if I miss any of the Yuletide celebrations they have planned."

"Same here. But I must make that stop in Coventry first." He climbed in slowly and eased back against the squabs with a lengthy moan and a heavy exhale of air.

Desmond assisted the young woman Rupert had earlier referred to as his precious cargo into his sleek carriage. Inexplicably, his heart began to pound like storm waves against a rocky shore, for her hesitant smile stirred a tempest within him, evoking a physical response that could only be described as lust.

He climbed in after her and settled opposite the pair. "Who are you?" he asked more roughly than intended, not at all liking the effect she was having on him. She'd referred to Rupert as her uncle, but it was not at all uncommon for a sweet young thing traveling alone with an unrelated older man to refer to him as such in order to lend respectability to an arrangement that was anything but respectable.

Rupert made hasty apologies. "I must be more dazed than I realize. Unpardonably rude of me to neglect introductions. Lord Blackfell, may I present Miss Adelaide Farthingale? She's the daughter of my cousin, Hugh. His only child."

Of course, Rupert was all business and not the sort to bring along a "companion" on his travels. In any event, Desmond ought to have realized she was a Farthingale from the first, for she had those beautiful Farthingale blue eyes as well as a refreshing innocence about her. That his body's response was base and primal was of no moment. He was entirely to blame for that.

Adelaide cast him another hesitant smile.

His body turned molten.

No! I'm not about to turn three mistakes into four!

His response was a momentary lapse, that's all. He'd been too busy dashing from one end of England to the other on business these past few months, too preoccupied to think of the more pleasurable comforts. Adelaide was merely a reminder of the needs he'd neglected lately.

Desmond recovered a thread of control and nodded in response, his expression revealing none of the turmoil brewing within. "A pleasure, Miss Farthingale."

She sat upright on the padded, black leather bench across from him, dimples forming in her cheeks as her lovely smile broadened. "Indeed, my lord. I've heard so much about you from my cousins."

"None of it good, I assume." He tried not to fix his gaze on her beautifully shaped lips. Of course, he failed miserably, for they were perfect lips that were meant to be kissed often and thoroughly.

But not by him!

She shook her head and laughed gently. "Perhaps they did not think highly of you at first, but for the longest time now they've written only nice things about you. The impression I have from their letters is that you're awfully serious for a man in your position. Too serious, truth be told… and a bit of a curmudgeon."

Rupert shifted uncomfortably against the squabs and cleared his throat. "Adelaide, I believe it is a little more information than the marquis desires."

Her eyes widened in dismay. "My sincere apologies, my lord. I'm sure they've described me as completely lacking in social polish or sense. Assuming they spoke of me at all, which I doubt. Although we correspond, I haven't seen my cousins in years." She glanced at Rupert, and although she managed another smile, Desmond couldn't help but notice the glint of pain that sprang into her eyes.

Rupert gave her hand a gentle squeeze. "You'll be surrounded by dozens of family members in a few days... and your father has promised to join us this year too."

She tucked a wayward gold curl behind her ear and began to fidget with it, for the mention of her father had obviously ruffled her very pretty feathers. She spared him a glance. "My father and his wife are to meet us in London after they visit his wife's family."

Desmond wasn't going to touch that conversation. Obviously the second wife did not want Adelaide in the household. She turned away, pretending to stare out the window, but he'd seen that same glint of hurt in his own sister's eyes after their parents had died and they'd been forced to live under their grandfather's domineering care.

Adelaide's fragile glance had revealed all of her desire to please and her constant failing at it. What she did not yet seem to understand is that she would never succeed in pleasing her father's wife because the woman wanted to be rid of her. He didn't need to meet the harridan to know that she viewed Adelaide as competition.

To her credit, Adelaide did not appear to be sullen or resentful.

"You're shivering, Miss Farthingale. Here, tuck this blanket around you." He handed her the Scottish tartan he'd received as a gift from his cousin Ewan. It had been folded on the seat beside him, unused.

She looked to her uncle, as though afraid to accept it without his approval. Rupert arched an eyebrow and frowned. "Take it, Adelaide. You're obviously cold." He then turned to Desmond. "Thank you, Blackfell. Seems the sisters at the abbey have taught Adelaide the virtues of deference and obedience a little too well."

Desmond grinned. "She's a Farthingale. Never fear, Rupert. She'll lose those virtues within a week of arriving in London." He turned to Adelaide, his tone gentling when her eyes widened in horror. "I meant it as a compliment," he assured her, realizing that his guess had been accurate. The second wife had wasted no time in expelling the unwanted stepdaughter from her home. The girl had been banished to some northern abbey and been living there for years, no doubt.

"Oh." She blushed, but there was a sparkle to her eyes that hadn't been there a moment ago, and he felt foolishly proud to be the one to elicit that gentle glow.

Hell's bells, yet again.

He refused to be drawn in by the girl. He crossed his arms over his chest and closed his eyes, pretending to nap for the short distance. It didn't work. He felt her soft presence and suddenly caught the fresh scent of lavender on her skin when his carriage passed too fast over a particularly rough patch of road and the girl came flying onto his lap. "Forgive me, Lord Blackfell!"

He might have tossed a jest in response had the girl not appeared genuinely aghast. Any other young woman would have been gloating or scheming to make something more of tumbling onto him. Not Adelaide. He folded his arms around her before she could scramble off his lap. "Not your fault, Miss Farthingale. My driver's a little too determined to get us to the inn before nightfall. Are you all right?"

She nodded as she wriggled out of his loose grasp and hastily settled once more in her seat.

Too bad. She'd felt good in his arms. That was bad too. He refused to feel anything for the girl other than polite interest, but his body was not cooperating. No indeed. His response was anything but polite.

She was responding to him as well. There was no mistaking the confusion in her expression, for she was as easy to read as an open book and had yet to learn to hide her feelings. He liked that innocence about her.

Liked it, but had no intention of doing anything about it.

No, he wasn't going to pursue the girl and intended to ignore her as much as possible without being overtly rude. He understood the danger in befriending Adelaide. There already existed a compelling bond between the Camerons and the Farthingales. His sister, Evangeline, had fallen in love with and married George Farthingale. And his cousin Ewan, a stubborn Scot who detested all things English, fell in love with and married English bluestocking Lily Farthingale.

Of course, it signified nothing. Desmond was his own man and competent to make his own decisions. He was a marquis and heir to a dukedom, so he understood that he would have to marry eventually in order to carry on the Cameron bloodline. He wasn't ready yet. In any event, he wasn't going to choose a Farthingale.

His wealth and title allowed him to aim far higher.

Why am I thinking of marriage anyway?

He shook his head to rid himself of those wayward thoughts and silently rejoiced when Adelaide broke the silence, further distracting him from the dangerous path his mind appeared to be taking.

"What a lovely view," she said, still gazing out the window and studying the hills surrounding them as they rolled along the moors. "There's so much life hidden beneath the browns and ochers and pale purple shrubs along the countryside. I was told the moors were desolate, but it doesn't seem so at all. You can sense vitality across this rugged terrain."

"It's beautiful," he admitted. "A man can hear himself think out here."

She nodded. "The abbey where I was raised overlooks the sea and is also beautiful and isolated. But I spent too much time listening to myself think and am now eager to be swept into the din and bustle of London."

"Where is the abbey?" Desmond asked, feeling a little tug at his heart as he filled in the facts. The girl must have been sent away shortly after her father's remarriage.

"At St. Brigid's near Berwick. I've been there almost ten years. At first, the sisters hoped I'd join their order." She shook her head and grimaced. "But I talk too much and ask too many questions. I don't take instruction well either, so they've long since given up and left me on my own to wander about the abbey lands with their sheep and chickens for company."

Desmond chuckled. "I'm sure your animal friends are better

companions than most of the elegant ladies and gentlemen you'll meet in London."

She graced him with that vulnerable smile again. "I don't think I'm fit yet to go about in society. I haven't learned the art of witty conversation and don't know the latest dances."

Rupert patted her hand again. "Your cousins will take care of you. They'll treat you as their little doll, dressing you up and teaching you all that a gently bred young lady ought to know. In short, they'll hound you with attention morning, noon, and night."

"I think I'll love that," she said in a breathy whisper.

Desmond stifled another groan. The girl seemed to know just how to pierce his heart. "My sister will join in. She's become just as meddlesome as any Farthingale since marrying Rupert's brother."

Adelaide's eyes brightened. "I can't wait to meet Evangeline. I've heard all about how Uncle George fell in love with her. She must be someone quite special."

"She is." Over the years, Desmond had learned to shield his heart and those thick barriers remained securely in place to this day. But Evie had never learned to guard herself from disappointment. Quite the opposite, she wore her heart on her sleeve, just as Adelaide obviously did. Desmond had done his best to protect his sister, but it was George who had truly saved Evie. She was happier now than she'd ever been.

And now that she was so well settled, Evie intended the same fate for him.

Lord help him!

"Adelaide will be staying with us for Christmas and hopefully through the winter unless... well, she'll always be welcome whatever happens."

Desmond frowned. "Are you to be sent back to St. Brigid's?"

She blushed. "No... well, I don't think so... not yet. You see, Mr. Postings is—Ack!" Adelaide tumbled onto his lap again, her soft body hopelessly pressed atop him as the carriage drew to a sharp halt.

Once again, he wrapped her in his arms to steady her, the instinctive response feeling too exquisitely natural for comfort. "We've arrived at the inn. I'll help you down."

She splayed her hands across his chest as though to push herself away but made no move to ease off him. Instead, she seemed frozen in place, her fingers curling on his cloak as she edged closer. *Mercy!* He could feel the rampant beat of her heart despite the thick layers of wool between them… lots of layers… his vest, jacket, and cloak… her gown, pelisse, and cloak.

How is it still not enough?

Their mouths were almost upon each other, separated only by the wisps of vapor that escaped their lips as they breathed—so close he even felt the shiver of delight that coursed through her body. He had to put distance between them before he did something extremely foolish, something that involved his mouth locking upon her tempting lips. That would be his monumentally foolish mistake number four. "Still cold?"

"Not at all." She tipped her head upward to meet his gaze, her expression dewy-eyed. In the next moment, she gasped and drew herself up. "I mean, *yes*. Quite chilled to the bone. Goodness what a bumpy ride!"

She mentioned Mr. Postings again and scrambled out of the carriage before the coachman had fully opened the door, practically knocking the portly man to the ground as she barreled over him to run inside the inn.

He stared at Rupert.

Rupert merely shrugged his shoulders and grinned. "After you, Blackfell."

He nodded. "Who the hell is Mr. Postings?"

Dear Reader,

Thank you for reading *The Viscount's Rose*. If you thought the course of Rose and Julian's courtship would run smoothly, you were mistaken. Their first meeting is explosive, literally, and when the two of them are abducted Julian blames himself for putting Rose in danger and vows to do all in his power to keep her safe until they are rescued or can escape. But Rose isn't as innocent in this abduction scheme as he believes and can't risk Julian finding out. I hope you enjoyed meeting Rose and Julian as they followed their bumpy path to love.

Read on for a sneak peek at Adelaide Farthingale's story, *If You Loved Me*, book 6 in the Farthingale Series. She's a Farthingale cousin you have yet to meet, but you have met bad boy Desmond Cameron, who was not quite so likeable in *My Fair Lily*. He understands Adelaide better than anyone else and can't help wanting to protect her from certain heartbreak, for she's determined to marry the man her parents have selected for her, a man who is completely wrong for her.

Or try another of the Farthingale stories, such as *A Midsummer's Kiss*, which is Laurel Farthingale's story. Sometimes love happens at the most unexpected times and in the most unexpected places. Sometimes it quietly sneaks up on you and sometimes it knocks you over on a London street, just as it happened to Graelem Dayne when meeting Laurel Farthingale in a most unusual way. Laurel's horse ran him over and broke his leg. Add the pressure of Graelem having to find the perfect wife in a mere thirty days or lose a large inheritance, and you have Laurel and Graelem's story. To Graelem, finding the right bride seems an impossible task until he sets his fuzzy gaze on Laurel. But Laurel has other plans and isn't so eager to give her heart to this handsome stranger. Farthingales marry for love and Laurel will settle for no less. Only by treasuring Laurel's heart above a baronial fortune will Graelem stand any chance of gaining it all.

The Viscount's Rose and *A Midsummer's Kiss* are prequels to *Rules For Reforming a Rake*, *The Duke I'm Going To Marry*, and *My Fair Lily*. Yes, I'm finding that I think best backwards, especially with this Farthingale Series. The sisters have decided the order of these books and I am helpless to do anything but obey. However, each book is a stand-alone love story, so don't hesitate to start with any one of them!

Interested in learning more about the Farthingale sisters? Join me on Facebook at Author Meara Platt! Additionally, we'll be giving away lots of Farthingale swag and prizes during the launches. If you would like to join the fun, you can subscribe to my newsletter and also connect with me on Twitter. You can find links to do all of this at my website: mearaplatt.com.

If you enjoyed this book, I would really appreciate it if you could post a review on the site where you purchased it or other sites where you subscribe. Even a few sentences on what you thought about the book would be most helpful! If you do leave a review, send me a message on Facebook because I would love to thank you personally. Please also consider telling your friends about the Farthingale Series and recommending it to your book clubs.

—Meara

ACKNOWLEDGMENTS

To Neal, Brigitte (my fair Gigi), and Adam, the best husband and kids ever. I'm so lucky to have you as my family. To my own boisterous and meddlesome family, who enrich my life beyond measure with your love and general brilliance. To all my readers for your generosity and support of these stories. I wish you all the beauty in your lives that you've given to me. As always, to my intrepid first readers, Barbara Hassid, Lauren Cox, Megan Westfall, Rebecca Heller, and Maria Barlea, and to my longtime friends and terrific authors in their own right, Pamela Burford, Patricia Ryan, and Stevi Mittman. To my talented photographer, Jeff Loeser. To my wonderful web designer, Willa Cline. Heartfelt gratitude to the best support team that any author can have: Laurel Busch, Samantha Williams, Melody Barber, Jennifer Gracen, and Greg Simanson.

ABOUT THE AUTHOR

Meara Platt is happily married to her Russell Crowe look-alike husband, and they have two terrific children. She lives in one of the many great towns on Long Island, New York, and loves it, except for the traffic. She has traveled the world, occasionally lectures, and always finds time to write. Her favorite place in all the world is England's Lake District, which may not come as a surprise since many of her stories are set in that idyllic landscape, including her Romance Writers of America Golden Heart award winning story to be released as Book 3 in her paranormal romance Garden Series, which is set to debut in 2016. Learn more about Meara Platt by visiting her website at mearaplatt.com.

78266307R00147

Made in the USA
Lexington, KY
06 January 2018